ANDREW VACHSS

DRAWING DEAD

Andrew Vachss is a lawyer who represents children and youths exclusively. His many books include the Burke series, the Aftershock trilogy, the Cross series, numerous stand-alone novels, and three collections of short stories. His novels have been translated into twenty languages, his shorter works have been adapted to graphic novel format and stage plays, and his articles have appeared in *Parade*, *Antaeus*, *Esquire*, *Playboy*, and *The New York Times*, among other publications. He divides his time between his native New York City and the Pacific Northwest.

www.vachss.com

BOOKS BY ANDREW VACHSS

THE BURKE SERIES

Flood

Strega

Blue Belle

Hard Candy

Blossom

Sacrifice

Down in the Zero

Footsteps of the Hawk

False Allegations

Safe House

Choice of Evil

Dead and Gone

Pain Management

Only Child

Down Here

Mask Market

Terminal

Another Life

THE AFTERSHOCK TRILOGY

Aftershock

Shockwave

SignWave

THE CROSS SERIES

Blackjack

Urban Renewal

Drawing Dead

OTHER NOVELS

Shella

The Getaway Man

Two Trains Running

Haiku

The Weight

That's How I Roll

A Bomb Built in Hell

SHORT STORY COLLECTIONS

Born Bad

Everybody Pays

Mortal Lock

ANDREW VACHSS

DRAWING DEAD

A Cross Novel

VINTAGE CRIME/BLACK LIZARD

Vintage Books
A Division of Penguin Random House LLC
New York

The Library of Congress Cataloging-in-Publication Data
Vachss, Andrew H.
Drawing dead / by Andrew Vachss.
pages ; cm
I. Title.
PS3572.A33D73 2016   813'.54—dc23   2015030355

Vintage Books Trade Paperback ISBN: 978-1-101-97029-4
eBook ISBN: 978-1-101-97030-0

Book design by Joy O'Meara

www.weeklylizard.com

Printed in the United States of America
10 9 8 7 6 5 4 3 2 1

for . . .

T.T.
who beat the odds to death

DRAWING DEAD

IF THE MEN known as Cross, Ace, and Rhino had other names, no one in Gangland had heard them. So no informant ever spoke them.

Buddha, by contrast, routinely used enough names to fill a small hard drive.

Tiger was infamous for a number of things—her outrageous figure and thick mane of gold and black stripes only a small portion of that list. Tracker presumably had a name, but the only one he answered to was tribal, and that appeared on no birth certificate.

Both were freelancers who had worked with the Cross crew many times, including a "down south" job that cost Rhino the tip of one finger and added a teenage death-match veteran who came to be called Princess.

All this preceded an off-the-books government unit tasked with capturing a "specimen" of some entity that could apparently kill without leaving a trace of its own presence . . . although the skull and spine torn from the bodies of the victims had become its terrifying signature.

• • •

If being imperiously questioned by the slender, ice-eyed blond man seated in a captain's chair at the front of a rolling motor home made him nervous, the unremarkable man wearing a grayish urban duster gave no sign. Cross was good at waiting.

To the blond man's left was a large console controlled by a young Asian woman, displaying various screen inserts as she manipulated a joystick. To his right sat a slab-faced man whose oversized chest easily accommodated a pair of shoulder holsters. Behind Cross, the two operatives who had brought him in: an expressionless Indian and a voluptuous Amazon with a long tiger-striped mane.

"You've seen this kind of thing before?" the blond demanded as the console popped up images of stylized slaughter. "Where?"

"Africa. We came back from patrol, found the whole sweeper team hung up, exactly like that."

"What did you think it was?"

"By then, we all knew what it was. A message from the Simbas. That's the way they did things over there: kill your enemy, then heads on stakes. Discourages anyone else from coming around."

"Did it work on you?"

"Sure," Cross replied, surprising the blond man.

"Then look at these. . . ."

More images. All same-signature corpses, but the settings were vastly different. A penthouse apartment, a hunting lodge, an abandoned warehouse. No individual bodies, all multiple kills.

"They look alike," Cross said, neglecting to mention that he had viewed an exactly similar scene only a short while ago. In Chicago.

"Those scenes are not—"

"Not the scenes—the bodies of the losers."

"Don't you mean 'victims'?"

"Fighters aren't victims. These are all some kind of battle sites. And a C-note to a dime says it wasn't civilians who got taken out."

"By . . . ?"

"I told you. The Simbas."

"Wanda . . . ?" The blond man turned to the Asian woman. She was already busily tapping away at the computer keyboard with one hand, clicking a silver pen against her teeth with the other.

"Simbas . . . Got it. None ever captured alive. Some of the intel says they're a myth. Not really a tribe at all. There's no—"

"A myth?" the Indian interrupted, surprising everyone else on the team. "Like those so-called Seminoles in Florida? They set up base in the Everglades, down where Stonewall Jackson wouldn't go after them. Bad propaganda—so the government started calling Cherokees who refused to walk the Trail of Tears by something other than their true name. It was Jackson who named them Seminoles— that way, he could tell the government that all the Cherokees were accounted for. Same as those Vietnam body counts."

Ignoring a sharp glance from the blond man, the Indian continued, his tone making it clear that he was not inviting a response. "We were here before

Columbus," he said coldly. "Maybe the Cherokee word for 'blanket' should be 'smallpox,' too."

"That does fit the Simbas," the woman at the console said, gently breaking into the silence that followed.

"Yeah?" the heavyset man with the shoulder holsters rasped. "How's that make any sense, Wanda?"

"Start from here, Percy," the Asian recited, tapping her scrolling screen. "Allegedly, the Simbas are the only known tribe of mixed Africans. . . ."

"Black and white?" he asked, now genuinely curious.

"No, tribal-mixed. That almost never happens. And, when it does, it's usually a war-rape. But with Simbas, they eventually accumulated enough people to form their own tribe. Ample reports of this phenomenon from the Congo over the past sixty years. Yoruba with Hausa, Watusi with Pygmy, Kikuyu with Bantu. And so on. Some of them were allegedly part of the Mau Mau, but that wasn't so much a tribe as a movement. All the database shows is a thematic legend."

"A what?" the blond man spat out, annoyed at the lecture.

"Thematic legend," Wanda snapped back, more annoyed at the interruption. "One that retains its characteristics regardless of jurisdiction. Essentially, this one was that, originally, the Simbas were freedom-fighters who had to flee to the bush when the invaders had them outgunned." A quick glance at the Indian. "Tracker would know this: that term probably originally meant 'colonialists,' but its usage has changed over time—perhaps because of mercenary raids on specific targets." She turned in her chair, looked meaningfully at the man being questioned, then returned to her narrative: "The Simbas were classic hit-and-run guerrillas. They can be distinguished from the modern version easily enough. Unlike, say, the FARC in Colombia or the Shining Path in Peru, or the Maoists in Tibet, they—"

"We don't need to know what they're not," the blond man said, now fussily impatient.

Wanda continued as if no one had spoken. "They do not recruit, they permit no looting, rape is punishable by death, and there is no enforced membership. Their minimal requirement—and this is only a rough translation—is that a prospective member must bring a 'hard' part of their enemy as an offering."

She ran her right hand over her hair, as if to smooth it down. "Even the deranged creatures created by that witch doctor Joseph Kony—the Lord's Resistance Army—even those kidnapped and drug-crazed children fear the Simbas." She turned to look at the man they had brought in for questioning: "Their trademark never varies. It . . . Well, you've seen the pictures."

"I wonder . . ." the blond mused. "Could that be the link?"

"Africa?" the Amazon asked.

"Why not? They had to start somewhere. Maybe they started killing for what they thought was a good enough reason and just got to like it. That does happen."

"Yes. I have seen it myself," the Indian said, coldly eyeing the blond.

"Come on," Cross said, in a tone somewhere between tired and bored. "Started in Africa, huh? Wasn't that what you government clowns were saying about AIDS? I mean, before everyone found out it was a lab experiment gone wrong in Haiti?"

"We have confirmed signature kills all over the globe," Wanda answered, looking straight at the mercenary. "I don't see how it would be possible for unacclimated Africans to strike in the Arctic Circle. Do you?"

"Maybe they evolved," Cross said. "Same way we all did, right? Humans, I mean. Some seeds grew in the sun, some in the ice. Or we all started in the Cradle, like a lot of scientists think. Places get too crowded, people move on. Especially when they get a lot of encouragement. When's the first confirmed kill?"

"That is difficult to determine with any degree of accuracy," Wanda acknowledged. "We have references to similar multiple slaughters throughout history. Cave paintings of Neanderthals staring up at hanging corpses, looking puzzled, as if the killings weren't their work. Egyptian pharaohs left what could be records of something similar, unearthed by tomb robbers. Hannibal kept a journal on his way over the Alps. And there are a number of references in futhark—"

"What?"

"Scandinavian runes—probably dating back to early Viking times," she said to the blond man, now seriously irritated at still another interruption of her report. "The references go as far back as we can reach. But, with so many other myths and legends disproven, it's impossible to tell for sure. No way to come up with authenticated facts."

"So those 'Seminoles' . . . they could be from the same root?" the Amazon wondered aloud.

"Of course," Wanda replied.

The motor home went silent.

"Junkyard dogs," Cross finally said. "By now, they've probably formed into their own species."

"THIS IS the place. You sure?"

"You askin' what I'm sure of? *Me?* You looking at a professional here, youngblood. I been putting in this kinda work before you stole your first candy bar, and I'm still doing it. Not to prove I got the heart for it, that part's been done. Now I get paid.

"A pro, he can't make but one mistake. This business, you make a mistake, you *out* of business. And on that paper is the address the boss said. I wrote it down. See for yourself—it's right here on this little paper . . . the one you gonna be putting a match to while I'm inside."

"It don't look right to me."

"What's that supposed to mean?"

"It looks just like a regular house. You'd think—"

"What? That a hit man don't have to live someplace? He'd just float around in the air, waiting to pounce? Live in a different place every night? You watch too many of those movies."

"Listen! Can't you hear it?"

"You really making me tired, boy. I don't hear nothing but—"

"Kids! Playing in the yard, right behind that same house there."

"So?"

"It just don't seem . . . I don't know . . . I mean, kids?"

"You a *long* way from being a pro, boy. That's why it's you driving the car. That's why it's you gonna be *waiting* in the car while I go up, knock on the front door, or push the bell, or whatever. You watch me 'stead of those stupid movies, you might learn something.

"I'm dressed for the part. Got my sample case and everything. One of Hemp's specials. . . . See his mark, right on the flap? Bitch opens the door, sees a man selling . . . whatever—it don't matter what. I push her inside. Not with my hands, just keep stepping forward until she steps back. I kick the door closed behind me, put a couple in her head before she can make a sound. And what I got in this here case, it won't make a sound, either.

"See how it works? In and out, less than a minute. I ease on back to the car—no running, moving slow—and you drive *away*. Some nosy bitch, got nothing else to do all day but look out her window, she writes down the plate—so what? This ride, it's gone inside an hour. The crusher don't just swallow the plates, it takes *everything*. So we don't gotta worry about fingerprints, or fibers, or DNA . . . any of that *CSI* crap."

"What if one of those kids comes in? Like, to get a soda or something?"

"What I got in this sample case is what I'm selling, okay? It's got a ten-round clip, plus one in the chamber. The boss said no witnesses. Anyone inside, it's a blackout call. You got a problem with that?"

"Me? No. I got no problem. But . . . you see the way that house is set up? There's no way for kids to get to the backyard without trampling all those flowers out front. So there's got to be a *back* door, right?"

"All them kinda houses got back doors. So what?"

"So see that driveway? You could just walk up the driveway, and that back door, it'll be *open*. So the kids can come in and out. You know, like kids do?"

"Yeah, I know. Thing is, you *don't*. They'd see me and—"

"They wouldn't see *you*. See a man in a suit, wearing a hat. They remember the man had dreads showing, even better—that wig you're wearing goes into the crusher same as everything else we got on, right?

"The way they're carrying on back there, probably wouldn't even see *that* much. You walk in the back door, like you was expected, see? Then you do the work, walk out the *front* door, and it plays the same way."

"So *you're* the expert now? Ain't done even a single one of these yet, but you gonna give *me* tips?"

"I don't gotta be no expert to know that people, they got peepholes and things like that in their front door. The bitch in there sees you, maybe asks what you want through one of those speaker things. There ain't no guarantee she's even gonna *open* that door."

"You know a lot about all this, huh?"

"The boss said, 'Watch Antoine.' Watch and learn, is what he said. I'm gonna be where you is, cuz. Not today, not tomorrow, I got that. I'm just saying—"

"You said enough, rookie. We *already* been sitting out here too long."

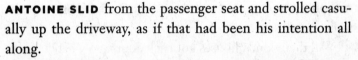

ANTOINE SLID from the passenger seat and strolled casually up the driveway, as if that had been his intention all along.

The sound of raucous children reached his ears just as he turned left, looking for the back door.

A huge Akita, all white except for its black head, lay on its belly, watching the children. It sensed Antoine: whirled, snarled, and launched in the same motion.

Antoine froze. The 9mm in his sample case was miles away—death was much closer.

A mass of chartreuse and tangerine flew across Antoine's vision, snatched the dog, and wrestled it to the ground.

"Sweetie, no!" some cartoon-muscled monster shouted, holding the dog squirming against his chest. "He's probably a friend of Sharyn's."

Antoine blinked, twice. When his eyes focused, he saw that the monster was human . . . sort of. It wasn't just the insanely overdeveloped physique, or the anaconda arms embracing the dog. It wasn't just the shaved head, or the veined muscles covering his upper body like a coat of armor. No, it was the slathered lipstick, the outrageous eyeliner, and the rouged cheeks that riveted the hired killer in place.

"Hi!" the monster said, grinning.

Antoine took off. He reached the car and flung himself into the opened door, screaming, "Go!"

The silverfish Infiniti sedan pulled smoothly away.

"YOU NOT gonna believe what was back there, man!"

The driver was silent, calmly waiting for Antoine to finish his story.

"First this dog—some monfucious thing with a black head—it shoots right at me like a damn missile! Then this . . . Man, I don't know *what* to call that thing—all muscled up like those iron freaks in the joint, but he's a stone sissy! Makeup and all, I'm telling you. He *flies* over the dog, picks him up like he's a little puppy. Saved my life, no doubt!"

"Yeah?"

"*Yeah!* I don't know what was inside that house, and I don't ever wanna know. The boss . . . I don't know how this could be, but he must've got the address wrong."

"Hemp don't make mistakes, you said. And you had it written down, too, remember?"

"Hey! I'm saying this to *you*, bro; it ain't for broadcast."

The driver slashed his right index finger across his lips.

"You got it," Antoine said, sealing their pact.

A FEW minutes passed before the failed assassin looked up, suddenly realizing they were headed in the wrong direction.

The *wrongest* direction. Instead of the crusher safely nestled deep into the West Side, they were within eyesight of the Badlands.

"You stupid—"

"It ain't me who's stupid, cuz. Ain't even you. It's Hemp that's the sucker in this game. He thinks he's gonna put himself on top behind taking out Ace's woman? He's got to be the stupidest—"

"*You* gonna be the one to tell him that?"

The supposedly stolen Infiniti slowed to a stop as the driver's left hand came up. Before Antoine's eyes could register the image of a dull-black pistol, the third hollow-point was already ripping through his upper body. He slumped forward, hitting his head on the dash. The airbag failed to deploy.

The driver shot twice more. Fully jacketed rounds penetrated Antoine's skull, each slug slamming into a flat-lined brain.

Leaving the body untouched, the driver opened his door and climbed out, holding the pistol by the barrel in his upraised hand. *Three to the body, two to the head, just like they told me.*

Within seconds, he was surrounded by a mixed-race mob of teens his own age. Their leader, a gaunt young man with a severely curved spine and a blue Mohawk coxcomb, waved his hand in a "Come here!" gesture.

A pale-green Kia Soul pulled up.

"That's your ride to O'Hare," the blue-Mohawked leader said, pointing. "And here's your ticket. One-way to Phoenix. You land, you take a cab from the airport to the bus station.

From there, you go wherever you want. Here's your new ID. And here's your money."

"I . . ."

"Don't waste time. You did your job, just like you was supposed to. So . . . here . . . you just got paid, too. Now all you got to do is to get *gone*."

"WHAT'S NEXT, Condor?"

The young man with the blue Mohawk looked steadily at a powerfully built youth whose face was a mixture of Asian and African. "Next? What'd I tell you, A.B.? This job, we do it *exactly* like we was told to, the 'next' is that we move up. We get to take care of more business."

"You mean, this was for . . . ?"

"Never say names," Condor warned. "That's a bad habit."

"You say Buddha's name all the time," a slender Latino spoke up, keeping his tone reasonable—a question from someone who wanted to learn.

"Buddha don't care, 'Zeus," Condor answered. "You've seen him do the card trick, right? And you've seen the Shark Car, too. No reason not to say his name, understand? Nobody shoots like him. And nobody else drives that car, neither."

"Look, I'm just . . . I mean, what's going on?"

"Again?" Condor sighed wearily. "Look: all we needed to know was, that guy who drove in here, he was the one who tipped what Hemp was gonna do. He got paid to make sure that *didn't* get done. A man sets up his own boss, you think he gets to just walk away after? No. And here's why: you do one thing for money, you'll do another thing for *more* money. Everybody knows that."

INSIDE A stone-walled room, as dimly lit as an underground bunker. "That two-bit mope actually thought he was gonna just roll up and take out Ace's woman, boss?"

"I guess so, brother," was the laconic response. The speaker was as unremarkable-looking as Condor had been distinctive. Only the bull's-eye tattoo on the back of his right hand distinguished him from a human generic.

"Hemp is as good as dead."

"Already is. Part of the deal was the second sample case. Hemp keeps a lot of them around, thinks they make good cover. The guy we paid, he dropped a package into one of them."

"There's nothing more for us to do?"

"Buddha, what's your problem? All those rubber checks we wrote are *canceled* checks now. You're just—what—professionally insulted that anyone would even think about hitting one of us?"

"I don't see how that wet-brain could've even known there *was* any 'us,' boss."

"What difference?"

"Next thing you know, maybe some fool tries to muscle in on the Double-X. Or maybe even—"

"From what? A spaceship? We've got trip wires three layers deep."

"How about if we—?"

"No pre-emptives, brother. You know that."

"Buddha's always looking for an excuse," said a man occupying the far corner of the Red 71 poolroom's back office. His quarter-ton formless body was covered in a dull-gray jumpsuit, making him nearly invisible in the darkness. Despite his bulk, his voice was a falsetto squeak.

"Cross . . ." Buddha appealed to the man with the bull's-eye tattoo.

"You know Rhino's right," the answer came. "Not that I blame you: I was married to So Long, I'd probably want to go around blowing stuff up, too."

"That was a cheap shot, boss."

"The cost of the ammo doesn't change the result."

"I can't win, huh?"

The back door opened, and the man who had terrified Antoine burst in, the black-masked Akita bounding at his side.

"You wouldn't believe how good Sweetie was!" the outrageously overmuscled man thundered. "We were playing in the—"

"We know," Rhino said. "You've really got him trained, Princess."

"No, I mean he—"

"We know about all of it," Cross assured him.

"Well, I bet Tiger doesn't. And when she comes over, I'm gonna . . ." the huge child said, sulking at the disinterest everyone seemed to be displaying in this latest proof of his homicidal dog's excellent manners.

THE WOMAN who entered by the same back door had once been described as "an Amazon on steroids" by a man too dense to understand the inherent contradiction in his words.

He didn't live long enough to learn.

"Tiger!" Princess boomed out. The woman whose striped hair matched her one-piece spandex outfit flowed forward, moving in five-inch spike heels—tiger-gold with black soles—as naturally as a jogger in running shoes.

"Calm down, honey," she said, as softly as the throwing daggers she wore strapped around one massive thigh could enter flesh. "Just give me a minute to find out what's going on."

Princess instantly transformed from full boil to docile.

"What was so . . . ? Oh, I see," she said, turning to glare at the man with the bull's-eye tattoo.

"You don't see anything," he replied, tonelessly.

"Sure, baby. Whatever you say," Tiger purred. She perched one perfectly curved haunch on the heavy wood slab positioned above a pair of iron sawhorses that Cross used as a desk, keeping her eyes pinned to just below the man's right eye . . . where a tiny blue hieroglyph seemed to be burning without flame. The mark was unreadable even at close range, but the man who bore it had felt its dry-ice burn days ago.

"Wait for Tracker," Cross said. "No point saying the same thing over and over."

"And Ace," Buddha added.

"No," Cross said. "This isn't something Ace can be in on."

"Why is that?" A voice from behind Rhino.

"Damn! When did *you* get here, Tracker?" Buddha asked. "That ghost-walking stuff you do is just plain spooky."

"I move as myself," said Tracker, an Indian whose facial features were somewhere between Cherokee and Apache. "Just as you do, Buddha."

Cross swept his eyes around the room, as if drawing all the others under the same outcropping in an enemy-occupied mountain range.

"Somebody wants a seat at our table," he said.

"One seat, or the whole table?" Rhino squeaked.

"What's the difference?" Buddha sneered. "He sits in on *our* game, he's already drawing dead."

"HEMP WASN'T the takeover man," Cross said. "He was just a tool."

"Whose tool?" Tiger asked softly, her tone as sweet as sufuric acid.

"Don't know," Cross told the whole room. "But, whoever he is, he's not local."

"That's got to be right," Buddha said. "Nobody from around here would even—"

"That's not the puzzle," the gang's leader interrupted. "What have we got that's worth a war? The club? This joint?"

"That's the truth," Tiger agreed. "Who'd want a cement-block building standing inside a junkyard? For that luxurious poolroom of yours?"

"We've been here a long time," Rhino spoke, slowly and deliberately. "Plenty of mobs in Chicago know where to find Red 71. And Tiger's right—there's no 'operation' anyone could cut into here."

"The club?"

"Come on, Buddha. Sure, the Double-X makes some money, but what's it take to open a strip joint? There's empty buildings all over this town, and never a shortage of girls who want to work. Add any lawyer who knows how to grease his way to a liquor license, and you're all set."

"Yeah, but—"

"There's no 'but' in this," the man behind the sawhorse desk said. "Plenty of joints way more upscale than ours. Plenty of others down the other side, too. And we're not exactly taking in a fortune."

"The overhead," Rhino squeaked his agreement.

"Hey, we could cut *that* way, way down, if the boss didn't want to turn a moneymaker into a . . ."

"Domestic-violence shelter?" Tiger picked up the thread. "Anyway, I thought everything was voted on."

"Sure," Buddha said, bitterly. "But there's only five votes—you and Tracker, you started out freelance, so you don't qualify. Cross and Ace, they did time together. That's when they first put together a crew. Not big, but they went all-in on every hand until nobody wanted to play no more, see? Rhino was locked in there, too. And Cross got close to him—he was the only one who ever did.

"Ace had a parole date, but Cross was never gonna get one. And Rhino was gonna do life in that wheelchair. The plan was, they were both supposed to hit the fence and go. But that dental-floss ladder they used wouldn't hold the weight—Cross made it over the wall, but they put Rhino back in those chemical handcuffs.

"Cross came back for him. All legal-like. Rhino'd never even committed a crime; they were just . . . holding him because there was no place to put him. And that made the first three OGs, see?"

Buddha paused, making sure his audience was still attentive. Or, at least, not getting restless enough to cut him off.

"Cross found me working a contract in Laos. He was coming over from Cambodia. So by the time we did that job down south, I was on the team, too. Why Rhino brought Princess back with us, I'll never know. But he answered the crew's prove-in, same as I did."

"Do you hate them?" Cross said, just above a whisper.

"Yes," Rhino answered. Exactly as Ace had, when Cross first asked that core question, back when they were both still incarcerated children.

"Do you hate them *all*?"

"Yes!" Rhino, Princess, and Buddha spoke as one.

"See?" said the pudgy man with nerveless hands and eyes a falcon would envy. "If Ace was here, it'd be the same answer. So any damn vote is gonna be five–zip. Only way it *can* be. It don't matter what any one of us might think is a better way to travel, we're all going down the same road. Don't matter who walks point, who walks drag—we're one unit."

"So you all took a vote to make the Double-X into a DV shelter?" Tiger was not an easily deterred woman.

"That does not matter," Tracker addressed her. "What you see here, what you have seen before—what Buddha says now—that will never change."

"WHO'S GONNA tell Ace?"

"Depends on what Sharyn actually registered," Cross

answered Buddha. "If all she saw was Princess and that beast of his scaring off a stranger, that wouldn't be any big deal."

"Sweetie was just—"

"Poor choice of words," the gang boss said quickly. "He was just doing his job, Princess. We all understand that."

"And the kids *love* him!" Princess half-shouted, still not fully mollified.

"We know," Rhino agreed, his squeaky voice somehow making soothing sounds.

"So if Ace doesn't know . . . ?"

"He *doesn't*." Cross finished Buddha's thought. "If he knew, we'd already have heard."

"Even a sawed-off blasting both barrels don't make noise enough to carry this far, boss."

"We wouldn't need noise," Cross said, pointing at a thin strip of LEDs flickering against the wall to his left. "Police scanner. Rhino's got it wired direct, all color-coded. If Ace had started taking out what's left of Hemp's crew, the whole strip would be flashing red. 'All Units.' Ace knows we have to work calm, but anyone going after Sharyn? No way he'd wait to start canceling tickets."

"Nobody would hurt Sharyn," Princess said. "That's crazy."

"That *would* be crazy," Buddha agreed.

"And suicide is crazy," Tiger added.

"Hemp was dead as soon as we got that first phone call," Cross said, acknowledging the Amazon's deductive powers. "We couldn't be sure he'd be using one of his little sample cases anytime soon, but we know he keeps them on the top floor. That was part of the deal. By now, anything under fifty yards of Tracker's scope is as good as gone."

"I NEED to talk to Tiger alone, okay?"

"Just in time," the Amazon said, as the others crossed through the hanging strands of black ball bearings that made up the "door" between the back office and the poolroom. "How come I'm the only one who didn't know about this thing with Hemp?"

"You know what a rolling bounty is?"

"No, I don't. And I don't see what that has to do with—"

"A rolling bounty is like a river, only it runs below ground. Everybody in Gangland knows, you got something that's worth something—something to *us*, I mean—we'll give you a fair price for whatever it is. And we'll make sure nobody will ever find you, too."

"You got a call Hemp was going to have Sharyn *killed*?"

"Yeah."

"So you—"

"Took care of it," Cross interrupted, deliberately avoiding any details. Tracker had reported to him, and it wasn't a report he wanted to share with the others.

"It was a head shot. Only way to make sure. At that distance, it's easier to stop a high-speed round from being a kill-shot. Only time for one try—I wasn't going to use a suppressor, not from that far away. If I couldn't be sure, it would have to rain .50-cals, and that would be like calling 911 ourselves.

"Only thing is, I put the one shot on the 'X' spot—he was dead before he dropped. But then his chest kind of . . . exploded. I couldn't see that well through the scope, but the whole cavity opened, like it burst open from the inside."

"What's with this secret-society stuff all of a sudden? If I'd known about it, I would've—"

"You just answered your own question. The last thing we need is for one of us to step on a land mine."

"Killing Sharyn, that was just a play? To lure Ace out into the open?"

"Ace? Sure. Him, and anyone else who couldn't . . . control themselves. The hit didn't even have to be successful. If Princess thought anyone had so much as *tried* to hurt Sharyn, he'd just stroll over to Hemp's building, climb the stairs to the top floor where that punk has that famous 'terrace' of his, and start throwing pieces of him over the rail. And Rhino'd have to go with him."

"*Hera!*" Tiger chuckled, picturing a cartoon-muscled man in full war paint casually walking across town with a giant black-headed Akita on a chain that would take two strong men to lift, followed by a formless shape that dwarfed them both. A formless shape carrying an Uzi in each hand, with four more on straps around his telephone pole of a neck. "The only thing you'd shoot at *any* of them would be a cell-phone camera."

"Don't leave out Ace. And he wouldn't be walking."

"So it was just you and Buddha who could get cold enough to TCB?"

"And Tracker."

"But not me?"

"No, not you. Even if you could control your temper—which is *always* a guess—you'd draw a crowd."

"And Rhino and Princess, never mind Sweetie, *they* wouldn't?"

"Even a canned-heat-drinking schizophrenic off his meds would know enough to give them a wide berth. But every man you passed would just *have* to get a closer look."

"Huh!" Tiger half-growled, but her heart wasn't in it.

"THAT PLAY didn't work. But it won't be the last one."

"Who?"

"Hit the light switch."

"I thought you'd never ask."

"Tiger . . ."

The room plunged into darkness.

"I see it!" the Amazon whispered. "That's their way of . . . warning you?"

"I don't know. All I know is, whatever they are, they're not from here. And I don't mean Chicago."

"You still think it's this . . . tribal thing?"

"Only way I could reason it out, girl. I'm not saying I *did* reason it out, just that I couldn't come up with anything that made more sense. Ever since I got out of that basement in the MCC, it's been there. Like a brand, only it's . . . alive, somehow. I can feel it when it burns. And when I look, I can see it, too. But I'm the only one who can."

"Except for me."

"Except for you," the urban mercenary agreed. "And I

have a guess about that, too." He touched one of a series of buttons on the underside of his desk. "Just wait a minute. . . ."

⊕

TRACKER ENTERED the squid-inked back room as sure-footed as if it was a patch of sunny daylight.

"Yes," he said, answering an unspoken question.

"But you can't . . . I don't know . . . read it?" Tiger asked.

"A tribal symbol, maybe," the Indian answered. "But no tribe known to me."

"Tracker saw it first. That's how I know it has to mean *something*. Remember Buddha's speech about OGs? He wasn't wrong. There's a five-man core—you and Tracker have your own work, and that comes first for each of you. So you don't get a vote on what we do, but you're not bound by any vote we take, either. You sign on or you don't, job by job, always your choice."

"Just because you're late to a party, that doesn't mean—"

"It is not the timing," Tracker interrupted, managing to do so with an ingrained courtesy that stopped Tiger from being offended. Stepping closer, the Indian said, "You and I, we each have our own tribe. Our loyalty is first to our tribe, always. Is that not so?"

Tiger flipped her striped mane in silent agreement.

"Perhaps this is why only the two of us can see that strange blue brand. It *must* be tribal, but not from this earth."

Cross surprised them both by slowly nodding his agreement. "I don't know exactly when it was . . . put on me, but I know it had to be when we were down in that prison basement, trying to trap that . . . thing, whatever it was."

• • •

"Goon squad," Banner side-spoke to Cross, while looking in the direction the guards were running. "Must be some weird stuff going on over there again."

"What's 'over there' mean?"

"That whole block," Banner answered, nodding his head in that direction.

"Upstairs, it's PC. Middle is for the psychos. Down is the Death House. Two rows of twenty cells each . . . with the Green Room in the middle."

"Green Room?"

"Used to be the gas chamber, long time ago. Now it's just an empty room. No executions here. For that, they have to move you to a Level Seven."

At the words "Death House," a concrete-colored blotch semi-materialized high up on the wall behind the two men. As the goon squad moved in, "Death House" was repeated at below-human-threshold. Then . . .

"Hit!"

The guards began to club a prisoner repeatedly on his unprotected head, continuing even after the man slumped to the ground, blood running out of both ears.

A mural flashed on the overlooking wall. The ace and jack of clubs appeared, then immediately vanished, leaving some convicts blinking. And the TV monitors blank.

• • •

Cross sat next to Banner at the mess table. His mouth barely moved, but his body posture was so intense and urgent that other convicts moved as far away as possible.

Finally, Cross stood up. Slowly and deliberately, he walked into the traditional No Man's Land of cleared space between whites and blacks. A guard started to step forward but stopped in his tracks as Nyati arose from the black table and moved toward Cross.

The entire mess hall was silent. Dead silent. The guards froze, knowing that if a full-scale race war jumped off in that enclosed space, they weren't going to make it out alive.

When Cross and Nyati were close enough to bump noses, Cross started to speak, his words inaudible to all but the leader of the United Black Guerrillas. When he finished, he stepped back an inch. Then he said, still under his breath:

"If you buy it, there's nothing else for me to say. I just told you all I know. For this one, it's us against them. You believe that, then it's the Death House. Bring whatever you want, bring whoever you want. But it's only going to be the five of us doing the actual work. That means we all lose some men."

"All?"

"All," Cross confirmed. "No kind of body armor is going to keep them off for long. If they get to us before we're ready, we're done, too."

"Five? You and me, that leaves three short."

"Ortega and Banner."

"Banner? That Nazi's already been breathing longer than he should. What do we need with two white men?"

"Who's the boss of the Hmongs?"

"Recognized them right away, huh? They a seriously bad bunch. But they ain't all same tribe, man. His crew, it's also got Vietnamese, Chinese, Japanese . . . probably others I don't even know about. And, listen now, in here, they forget all that. They play it like an all-for-one mob. They got no choice. But you can see they really don't like each other any more than they do us."

"It's only the Hmong I want."

"Why him?"

"I speak a few words of the language."

Nyati stared hard at Cross. And took the same in return.

"Okay, man. It's your show. What time?"

"Midnight."

"Done."

"For the race!" Cross shouted. Before anyone on either color-side could react, Nyati echoed, "For the race!"

Then, to the stunned surprise of the watching convicts, they stood in the middle of No Man's Land and clasped hands.

Midnight. The Death House area was clogged with convicts, still divided along racial lines, but not openly antagonistic toward one another. "Frightened" would be a better description of their mood; fear was the single unifying factor among them.

Whites, blacks, and Latinos were all there, with a sprinkling of Asians. Everyone was armed with whatever they were able to procure from the broad spectrum of prison-available weapons.

Soldiers just before combat act the same way in prison as they do on any battlefield: some smoke, some pace, some pray. Every man was anxious to get it on, and even more anxious for it to be over.

Cross was standing with Nyati and Ortega, their backs against the gas chamber wall. One of the Asians approached, a short, thin man holding what looked like a strip of razor blades on a string. His face was unlined, but his eyes were not those of a young man.

Banner detached himself from his crew and moved over to where the others were standing. "Deal me in," he said.

"Just you?" Cross asked.

"Look around, brother. We're all here. But it's got to be me up front. I'm the shot-caller, so this is my place. Like you said, this is for the race. So, whatever goes down, I'm down with it. But I have to go standing up, see?"

Cross nodded. He turned to Ortega. "Your man knows what to do?"

"For this, I am my man, *hermano*. After you first talked with me, I reached out. What you say, it is true. It has always been true. All the way back to the

Aztecs. The Mayans and the Incas. So it is just as you and Nyati called it out. For La Raza!"

"For the race," Banner echoed, but very quietly.

Each man held up a fist, waist-high. And then they slammed them together in an unmistakable gesture of final unity.

"You sure it's coming, man?" Nyati asked.

"Look around," Cross answered. "If it wants to hunt the real life-takers inside these walls, we're the best game in town."

The Hmong nodded but said nothing. Then he vanished.

A shadowy blotch materialized within the densely packed men. It thickened and lengthened, gathering mass. Then it began moving like an anaconda through a swamp.

Blood spurted wildly as individual men were torn into random pieces. Their body parts flew through the darkness until they hit the nearest wall, where a stack of ripped-out spines began to pile up.

Some of the men tried to run; others stood their ground, desperately striking blindly at whatever was attacking them. This had no effect on the presence, which continued to work its way over to where four men stood against the gas chamber wall, two on each side of its door.

The darkness was filled with screams as body parts continued to fly. A red haze formed, so intense it seemed to attack the darkness itself.

Ortega slipped off to one side of the death chamber, Banner to the other. The Hmong was nowhere to be seen.

Cross and Nyati remained, now standing alone. At a "Go!" from Cross, they both stepped back through the opened door of the gas chamber, still watching the inexorable progress of . . . something as it moved through the wall of human flesh.

"Sweet Jesus!" Nyati muttered under his breath.

"This is too soon," Cross hissed. "I was sure they'd—"

Cross cut himself off. The presence he felt to his right wasn't the one gutting and discarding individual prisoners; it was the Hmong, joining them.

The three men backed all the way into the chamber. Cross seated himself in the chair where condemned convicts were once strapped down. He lit a cigarette.

Nyati took the other chair—dual executions were far from uncommon in Chicago's past.

The Hmong crouched in a far corner, covered entirely in a dark mesh blanket.

A black mist approached the threshold of the death chamber. The men instantly realized the presence had been divided into small pieces by the slashing attacks of the mass of convicts it had oozed its way through. But then they all saw it begin to regroup into a unified mass. Slowly, it struggled to form a single entity. The black blob had been deeply wounded—chunks of its border were missing, and gaping holes were visible within its remaining mass.

And yet it kept moving forward, as if the human flesh it sought would be the replenishment it needed.

As the misty black mass entered the death chamber, Ortega and Banner slipped behind it and slammed the door closed. They dropped the heavy outside crossbar into place and took off, running.

They didn't run far. As soon as they reached the control room, both men threw a series of heavy switches, releasing cyanide pellets into a shallow pool of acid under the death chairs. A greenish gas immediately began to billow up, filling the chamber.

"Now!" Cross yelled, reaching behind his neck and pulling into place a flat-faced mask with a dark filter over the front. Nyati and the Hmong did the same.

Cross jumped to his feet, drawing a heavy bear-claw knife from behind his back. Nyati unsheathed a thick length of pipe and waved his wrist; a razor-edged arrow popped free at each end. The Hmong cradled a beautifully crafted blowgun.

Without warning, Nyati and Cross attacked, slashing at the encroaching blackness . . . and finally penetrating the shadow-blob, which became more visible every time it took another hit.

The Hmong was the last to act. Holding the blowgun as a brain surgeon would a tumor-seeking scalpel, he emptied his lungs to blast off a single shot.

The shadow collapsed, breaking into patches of black on the floor of the chamber. But the patches immediately began to pool once again.

Nyati crawled over to the mass, tentatively extending his hand.

"It's still alive. I can feel . . . something. Like a pulse, maybe. If we're gonna finish it—"

Cross pounded his palm hard against the door to the death chamber. Banner and Ortega threw off the crossbar and left it just long enough for two of the men inside to dive out.

Cross pulled off his mask, opened his mouth wide, reached in, and wrenched the phony molar free. He pressed the top of the tooth, which immediately began to hum.

"It's down. In the chamber," he barked into the mini-mike, his voice calm, precise . . . and urgent.

The blond man was in the War Room, Wanda at his side. He was shouting into a fiber-stalk microphone. "All units. Go! Go! Go!"

Percy was behind the wheel of the unit's war wagon, cruising the highway closest to the prison. The human war-machine had picked up the blond man's message and stomped the gas pedal, simultaneously hitting the red button on the dash that kicked in the twin turbochargers.

Tiger and Tracker were already in the shadow cast by the prison wall. They moved in from different directions.

Tiny black splotches began to reassemble inside the gas chamber. If the poison gas had any effect on this process, it was not apparent. Adapting its shape to circumstances, the blackness flattened itself to micro-thinness. Then it slowly began to probe the seals of the death chamber's door, seeking an opening.

Nyati, near death, was trying to stand, using a wooden spear as a crutch. Banner stood with him, still slashing with a prison-built sword. But he, too, was fading.

Cross wasn't doing much better. He opened his eyes just as the chamber door began to crack at one of the top seals, pushed open by something blacker than darkness. That blackness told him the Evac Team was going to be too late. He sensed the shadow calling to whatever pieces outside the chamber were still unattached.

Calling them home.

Ortega and the Hmong attacked the thickening blackness from either side of the door, but their knife thrusts no longer had any effect.

Suddenly the shadow-mass stopped writhing. A tiny blue symbol glowed briefly on Cross's right cheekbone, just below the eye. As the blue mark crystallized into what would be a permanent brand, Cross plunged into unconsciousness.

The online edition of the *Chicago Tribune* screamed:

RACE WAR AT FEDERAL PRISON!
277 CONVICTS KILLED IN PRISON RIOT!
"WORST IN HISTORY" SAYS BUREAU OF PRISONS

"Tell me again, goddamn it!" the blond man said, almost incoherent with rage.

"By the time we got there, they were gone," Tiger repeated. "Maybe back to wherever they came from. The only trace they left behind was the body count."

"I'm done with this," Percy said. "Taking one alive, yeah, that was a brilliant idea. Look what it cost! And all for nothing."

"As long as I'm the head of this outfit, I don't give a damn what you think," the blond man responded, back to his bloodless self-control. "Get out of my sight, all of you. I've got to work up another capture scenario."

Except for Wanda, all the others walked away.

"WE COULDN'T pull it off—even that sealed gas chamber couldn't hold it. A lot of men died. I didn't. But that wasn't some random thing, wasn't just luck.

"Luck, that's like when a plane drops a bomb. It's not aimed at any one man—it kills some, cripples others, and some just walk away. This . . . This was a choice. So that means there had to be a *reason* for it."

"You have any ideas?" Tiger asked.

"Not a damn one. It wasn't race—there were plenty of other white men down there."

"I mean this not as offense," Tracker added. "But it could not have been some kind of moral judgment, either. You were not guilty of the crime that allowed you to enter that prison to hunt that . . . thing. That was a ruse. But you are not an innocent man, Cross. By law, none of us are."

"Princess is," Tiger snapped. "He hasn't got one evil molecule anywhere in that scary body of his. He's like a huge child—"

"I said 'by law,'" Tracker interrupted. "Princess has no bad *motives*, but many things he has done would be crimes if judged by a jury. Rhino is no different. Had Cross not protected him when they were both very young, I don't know what would have happened in his life, but if he'd had a choice, *any* choice, his would not be the life of an outlaw.

"Ace kills for money. Buddha has no moral compass. Still, I feel that, somewhere back in their early lives, each was sent down a path from which no retreat was possible."

"Ace stabbed a man who was beating his mother," Cross said. "If he'd had a *real* lawyer, the jury would've given him a medal instead of a jolt Inside. And Rhino should never have been *near* a prison. Buddha, all I can say is, the second I met him, I knew he was one of us."

Tracker nodded. "Only you are different, Cross."

"Me? What's that mean?"

"Of all of us, including myself and Tiger, you are the only one who is a true criminal."

The room went silent.

A long minute passed.

Tiger's hard-edged, sultry voice broke the quiet. "You can't be born a criminal."

"This is true," Tracker agreed, speaking as if only he and Tiger were in the room. "But Cross is . . . an enigma. He could have done many things with his life. He is extraordinarily intelligent, a master tactician, the finest strategist I have ever met. But all of these gifts are in the realm of crime. I don't know why he was first imprisoned, but—"

"It doesn't matter," Cross interrupted. "It was a long time ago."

THE MAN with the bull's-eye tattoo on the back of his right hand ground out his cigarette after the third drag.

"This whole thing smells bad to me," he said. "Hemp *had* to know what would happen if he took out Ace's woman. That means he was trying to draw Ace out into the open. And there's no upside to that move."

"Ace does not have your . . . coldness inside himself," Tracker spoke. "He is an assassin, so not a man ruled by emotion. But if his woman, the mother of his children . . ."

"I still can't see it," Cross said quietly. "There's no way it makes sense. And nobody to ask about it."

Tiger slid off the desk and pointed a long fingernail at her wristwatch. The large digital display was flickering. "We may have somebody we hadn't thought of," she said. "We need a big monitor and some cords with heavyweight USBs on one end."

"Get Rhino," Cross said to Tracker.

As the Indian walked through the curtain of black ball bearings without seeming to disturb them, Cross turned to Tiger.

"What?"

"Mural Girl was working yesterday," she said, again

tapping her heavy wristwatch. "The camera's still in place. Maybe the footage . . ."

The wall had once been whitewashed, but time had faded it to a shade of ecru that seemed to blanket certain parts of Chicago . . . parts known to be don't-go-there dangerous. The DVD that Tiger was playing showed all kinds of ghetto artistry. Not tagging, more like murals. Mostly portraits and scenes.

"Martin Luther King on the same wall as H. Rap Brown—haven't seen those two together before. Look to you like the same artist did them both?"

"It was the same artist," Tiger told Cross. "No secret about it. We talked to her ourselves. She said it was a 'spectrum mural.' Nobody bothered her while she was working."

"Who was watching her back?"

"Nobody, is what she said. She's not affiliated, and she wasn't flying colors."

"A mural like that one . . . a lot of work."

"Took her a little more than two months, working every day."

"Neighborhood girl?"

"You could say it like that," the Amazon answered. "Let's add it up. This girl—and she's a pretty girl, mind you—works on that mural every day. Nobody bothers her. Nobody even . . . I don't know, it's like she's got protection everybody knows about, but it can't be that. Rhino ran her through our system. No hits—she's not with anyone.

"Now, here's the thing. Ace said there was a gunfight right across from the mural one night. Not late at night, when it was only just getting dark. None of the bangers got hit, but a little child took one in the back as she was running for cover. Died in the street, waiting for transport to a hospital.

"Just as Ace was coming back, first light, he sees a pair of playing cards on that wall. Huge ones, covering the whole mural. Two cards: ace of clubs, jack of hearts."

"Painted over what that girl was—?"

"No. That's just it. It was kind of like a hologram. Ace said he could see right through it."

"The pretty girl, the painter, she show up later?"

"Yep. And went right back to work. The cards, they were gone. Like they'd never been there at all."

"Ace doesn't see things. He doesn't drink, doesn't smoke, wouldn't touch drugs."

"I know that."

"So that's why you mounted the camera?"

"Right."

"And . . . ?"

"See for yourself," Tiger said, softly. "It's just about to come up."

The screen was still filled with the mural when a pair of playing cards materialized over it, just as Ace had described to Tiger. This time, it was the ace of hearts and the jack of spades.

"Stayed like that for almost ten minutes," Tiger said. "Then it just . . . disappeared."

"Same time?"

"Yeah. Like it was filling in the crack between night and dawn."

"Got a date on that thing?"

"Of course."

"You checked, right? So . . . anything happen that night?"

"Anything . . . ?"

"Come on, Tiger. You know what I mean: violent deaths?"

"Not in that neighborhood."

"But . . . ?"

"You remember that puny little 'Führer'? The one that ended up with a long sentence for plotting to kill the judge who sentenced him?"

"Sure. But that was—"

"Few years ago, I know. Anyway, he put together some 'followers.' He's locked in PC, but that Facebook page his 'storm troopers' put together claimed he was secretly running the AB from Inside. He went from a terrified little twit to shot-caller for the heavy hitters. Magical, huh? Only that was pure Facebook baloney. Still, somebody didn't like it much."

"He got—?"

"Not him. That little group of play-Nazis. The ones that put up that Facebook post. They had a store-front. And I mean 'had' . . . past tense."

"Bomb?"

"Nope. Five people—two female, three male,

none of them over twenty-five—all got shot in the head. What the papers love to call 'execution style.' The shooters sprayed 'AB' over everything in there— walls, computers, posters."

"What happened to the Facebook page?"

"Nothing, Rhino says. But it hasn't been updated since that night."

"So where's the connection?"

"I don't know, okay?"

"Sssshhh, girl. There's nothing to get worked up about."

"Really?" Tiger said, reflexively touching the knives in her holster. "I'll buy that. I'll buy it the minute you explain how Ace's calling card changed color. How did the ace of spades turn into the ace of hearts?"

Cross felt the spot below his eye burn, as if in answer to the warrior-woman's question.

THE MONITOR showed a blended-race woman dressed in a orange jumpsuit with DOC · ILLINOIS black-stenciled across the back. She was standing on an adjustable-length ladder that widened out to form a platform above the top rung.

The woman was facing a freshly whitewashed stucco wall, dipping a variety of paintbrushes into an assortment of small cans, working steadily but unhurriedly. If keeping her back to an empty lot in "claimed" gang territory concerned her, she gave no sign.

The mural was a thick ribbon of varying shades of purple, from pale lavender to a murky violet to a near-black plum, the ribbon itself flowing from ground level toward the top, the reverse of a river's path down a mountainside. Within it were a series of portraits, men and women, all different races represented. Some were instantly recognizable, some not.

"Who's that?" Cross asked, tapping his finger on the monitor's image of a sharp-featured young white man.

"Wesley Everest," Rhino answered immediately. "An icon to the Wobblies. Served in World War I, lynched in Centralia, Washington, in 1919. The IWW still has a Chicago office."

"This one's loaded with faces like that. What's the—?"

"Some are symbolic," Rhino said. "The police officer, see the 'BOSS' on his helmet? That was the old Bureau of Special Services, the Red Squad of the forties reactivated during the sixties to deal with the Weathermen and other anti-Vietnam activists. But see the looping arrow? It circles from that pile of black boulders back around to Fred Hampton. And—"

"Who—?"

"Fred Hampton was the leader of the Black Panthers in Chicago. A very small group, nowhere near the size of the street gangs. But the Panthers were a serious threat to them, anyway."

"How?"

"The gangs always flew under the banner of community service. Some even got federal grants to run literacy programs, things like that. But they used most of the money to buy drugs and guns. The Panthers were actually trying to *do* those things: Breakfast for Children, GED programs . . .

"And guns, sure—that was kind of a trademark with them,

the way they first got started. But not to protect dope-slinging turf. The contrast could not be missed. It didn't matter what the newspapers said; people who actually lived in the places they were writing about, they could see for themselves."

"How did that all play out?" Tiger asked.

"Fred Hampton was killed in a police raid. The police said a tipster told them he was stockpiling bombs. The house he was living in was hit with enough rounds to kill a whole village. The ground-level belief is that it was an assassination. Cold-blooded slaughter. Either way, that was pretty much the end for the Panthers here."

"So those black boulders—"

"Blackstone Rangers. The mural is saying *they* were the so-called tipsters. It was an everybody-wins deal. The Rangers re-invented themselves a number of times. But any claim that BOSS was some kind of patriotic force within the Chicago PD kind of went to hell when some of the Rangers made a deal with Qaddafi to blow up Sears Tower."

"What?"

"It's well documented, Tiger," Rhino said calmly. "And this was *decades* before the World Trade Center. Qaddafi was a madman—Osama Bin Ladin to the tenth degree. It was his vision that he could become the World Leader of All Muslims, the Ultimate Ayatollah. That's why he financed the Lockerbie bombing . . . and who knows what else.

"Whether he was sending troops over the border to 'reclaim' Chad or paying famous people to entertain at his parties, being insane was always in there, somewhere."

"That's him, over in the left-hand corner?" Cross asked, indicating a man dressed in traditional Muslim robes but wearing what looked like a yacht captain's hat.

"Yes. That mural, it's a connect-the-dots piece. Those young white people over to the other side—see the jail bars in front of some of the images? And the others kind of clumped together in some banquet room? Mural Girl, she's saying calling them all 'revolutionaries' doesn't make them comrades. Some came in from being on the run, worked out no-jail deals, wrote their books. But not all of them had those options. Some are dead from gunfire, some still doing their life sentences."

"So the message of that mural is supposed to be . . . what?"

"That's not what's important," Tiger said, confidence back in her voice. "Watch this."

The screen flickered. The image of the mural disappeared. In its place, a fan of five cards: three aces, two eights.

"A full house," Cross said. "Poker. Not those blackjack hands like before."

"Look closer," Rhino said. "All three aces are spades, both eights are hearts."

"Dead man's hand," Cross said softly, "only with an extra ace. It's not hard to read, not now. But how's this help us?"

As he spoke, the cards vanished and the mural reappeared.

"I don't know," Rhino said. "But they . . . whoever they are, they've got their eye on Mural Girl."

"Five cards, Cross," Tiger said, so softly she might have been speaking to herself. "Like Buddha said before, five OGs. So maybe they're making sure you understand who their message is *for*."

FOR THE working outlaw, midnight is morning; darkness is dawn.

"It ain't like last time," Ace said. "Not even close."

"Because last time *we* jumped it off? That whole 'urban renewal' deal So Long cooked up?"

"Hey! That brought in a nice chunk," Buddha said, defending his wife, a beautiful, seemingly ageless woman who wore larceny as another might wear lipstick.

"Okay!" Cross shut down any potential sidetracks. "That doesn't matter. Those cards, sure, that has to be a message from . . . I don't know what to call them . . . 'Simbas' doesn't feel right, but that's the closest I can come."

The room went silent, as if waiting for Cross to finish.

"Look," the gang leader said, very softly, "I know it's all guessing about . . . them. But they're not pulling Mural Girl's strings. I don't know why they're protecting her, but she's not just some channel for their messages—she's got her own story to tell."

"For the bangers, maybe," Ace added. "Something about unity, you think? Even the biggest gangs, they're all broken down into sets now. There's no central leadership, like before. And that spot Mural Girl works in, only time you *don't* hear gunshots is when some fool's using a silencer."

"Mural Girl is telling about the failure of a revolution," Rhino squeaked. "Too many generals, not enough soldiers. No shortage of martyrs, though. Or of informants, either."

"Hemp isn't the key to any of this," Cross said, his voice as flat as ever. "There isn't enough money in Chicago to make him send a hit man after Sharyn. He was a dead man as soon as he gave the word."

"Boss, he *had* to know that," Buddha said. "Kind of like

Mural Girl was saying. Everyone had to . . . I don't know . . . maybe *play* a part to *be* a part, okay? But maybe Hemp wasn't going for that. Maybe he wanted it all. Not enough for the sets to just consolidate, they all had to be slinging for *him*. That was the deal he put out there: anyone who doesn't get the message gets dead."

"Shows that he can take out anyone who doesn't go along? That's what Ace was for? Send *that* message?"

"Send it, yeah, that would do it . . . *if* he pulled it off. But say he did, he'd have to get all of us to make that work, and—come on, who's *that* crazy? What was his plan? Set up a PO box in a graveyard? Turn zombie and open a bank account?"

"Is it possible this Hemp was not actually responsible?" Tracker asked.

"He's sure as hell responsible for the hit ticket," Cross answered. "The one who let *us* know, the guy who thought he was gonna get paid—paid by us—he spelled it out. And it went down just like he said it would."

"Who's 'us'?" Ace said. "Doesn't matter who picked up on the rolling bounty we got out there, me, *I* wasn't told."

"You wouldn't be cold enough," Tiger said. "I know that's your rep, and you earned it. But compared to *this* one"—she nodded her head in Cross's direction—"you're always on full boil."

"It was the tactically correct decision," Rhino said, to defend the only man he had ever dared to trust while in captivity. "Sharyn was never in danger. She was inside, with her children, in the safe room. I was behind the front door, Buddha at the back. The only thing actually in the yard was a speaker system. If the informant was wrong—or lying—it would not have changed the result."

"So what's next?" Ace asked, grimly.

"Whatever it is, we have to wait for it," Cross said. "Whoever put this game together, they're not some ghetto grabbers. For them, Hemp wasn't a player; he was a chip."

THREE DAYS later, the entire crew was assembled in the back room of Red 71.

Cross stood facing the others—a blue marker in his right hand, a blank whiteboard to his left. To a casual observer, he might have been the head of an ad agency, brainstorming with his team.

"It's been quiet," he told the group. "Nobody's made a move. Waiting, that's fine. But it can't be permanent. So let's see what that leaves us."

"Guesses?" Tiger snarled. "That's what we're down to now?"

"No," Tracker said. "We have to start eliminating what we can before we—"

"—start eliminating everything that's left," Ace sliced in.

Cross patted the air in front of him with both hands, in a "Calm down!" gesture.

The black-masked Akita made a sound deep in its throat.

"Ssshh, Sweetie," Princess told the dog, patting its triangular head. "It's gonna be okay."

If any of this made the gang leader impatient, he didn't show it.

"One," he said, writing the number on the whiteboard, "it *was* Ace they wanted. But they'll never try Sharyn's house again."

"And it wouldn't matter if they did," the slender man in his trademark black Zorro hat and matching leather duster said. "I sent them all back down home—*Sharyn's* home, I'm saying. She still owns that little piece of land where she was born. Her daddy has a place there. He's a real old man, but he ain't never lived no place else. Got himself a lot of respect. People down there, they'd take a hard look at *any* stranger. If they didn't like what they saw, he wouldn't be a tourist no more; he'd be there to stay."

"Two," Cross went on, as if Ace hadn't spoken, "the real target was Hemp. He was a dead man from the second he gave that blackout order."

"That would be too elaborate," Rhino squeaked. "Anyone who could hire Hemp to murder someone could hire someone else to murder *him*. Why move in circles? Why involve us at all?"

"So what's 'three'?" Tiger snapped.

"There's more than three," Cross said, calmly. "I don't know how anyone could have wanted Sharyn dead. Who gains from that?"

"Yeah, I was wondering when you'd get to that," Buddha said, bitterly. "We all know how the Trust was set up. Everything's in my name. This dump, the Double-X, the—"

"So?" Tiger cut him off.

"So it's a tontine. The way it works, if we're all gone, everything's supposed to be split between Sharyn and So Long. And you all think she'd—"

"There's a safety net under that," Cross said. "You know it, I know it . . . and So Long, she knows it. Nobody's greedy enough to steal the money to finance their own funeral."

"Ah, he's right," Buddha said. "So Long, she knows how

it would work. I'm not saying she was happy about it when I told her, but she's got nothing to gain from Sharyn being dead. I mean, all of us, we're still alive and—"

"She would not be," Tracker finished the sentence.

"You think Mural Girl knows what this is about?"

"How could she? She's got her own messages to spread. But that . . . that hologram thing or whatever it is, that's tribal. And not on this plane. Something parallel to us, as near as I can figure."

"Yes," Tracker said. "The Simbas. The tribe you described for those government people who hired me and Tiger."

"You back to that voodoo stuff again?" Buddha scoffed.

"Every tribe has a name for what it fears," the Indian answered, as if Buddha was actually seeking information. "Every tribe has a name for what it cannot explain. It has always been so."

"I never met a bulletproof ghost, myself," the pudgy sharpshooter said, holding his position. Unchanging ever since the presence Cross called "Simbas" had entered the gang's world.

"Me, either," Cross said. "But I never met a ghost, so it's not something I ever tested."

"That does not mean what you call a 'ghost' has never met *you*," Tracker said, his tone clearly communicating that he was done with the topic.

THE ROOM went quiet.

Cross opened his left hand. A flame sprouted from his

cupped palm; he lit the cigarette he was holding in his right from it. Nobody reacted. They had all seen this too many times to be impressed. Collectively, they assumed that if Cross wanted them to know how that trick worked he would have told them.

The gang leader took a long, deep drag, as if he was considering what he was about to say. Then:

"You remember the lunatic? The one who never left that . . . attic, or whatever you call what his parents had built for him?"

"They weren't trying to protect him," Rhino said, bitterly, "just make him invisible. But after they were killed by that drunk driver, he had to use what he had, all by himself. And he was a genius, with plenty of money."

"I don't—"

"It was a long time ago," Cross told Tiger, as if that was all the explanation she'd need.

"His head was much too large for his neck to support," Rhino continued. "He only had one complete arm; the other was like something that had been grafted on as an afterthought—the hand was the size of an infant's."

"A thalidomide baby, that was our best guess," Cross said. "There wasn't much we didn't know about him by the time it ended. Except . . . why us?"

"He tried to attack you?"

"Oh, he *did* attack us, Tiger. And he wasn't *just* a genius; he was an all-in, no-limit psychopath."

"THE WHOLE damn thing kept us peeling back layer after layer," Cross told them. "It wasn't that long ago, but now it seems . . . far back, somehow."

"You had this place, right?"

"We owned it," the gang's leader answered the warrior-woman's question. "But all we had was the property, not the . . . not the way it's fixed up now."

"So you were . . . ?"

"Pretty much freelancing," Cross said. "Just the three of us, at first. But once we brought Buddha in, that's when we realized that we couldn't hide. And, after that, Princess. Some of us could blend, but not *all* of us. We weren't going to separate, and we weren't going to link up with outsiders. So we put this place together. Makes us easy to find, but just about impossible to take out."

"Just about?"

"The airspace is full of electronics now," Buddha said. "We don't know if the rumors of the government testing drones in cityscape models are true, but it's a good guess."

"What's a 'cityscape'?"

"Actual cities, small-scaled," he answered Tiger. "Built on desert ground, so no lives would be lost in the experiments."

"What are the odds that we would all be in the same place at the same time?"

Cross plucked the "we" out of Tracker's question, deciding to save it for another time. "Long ones," he said. "This place never closes. If it was some 'storm the castle' scenario, we don't know any gang in Chicago that would risk it."

"And we've got the tunnels!" Princess thundered. "Now we can *always* get out!"

"That's the idea," the gang's leader said. "And"—holding

up a flat palm to stop what he knew what was coming—"your dog could come, too."

ONLY CROSS and Tiger remained in the back room.

"You never did learn why this . . . why this strange man wanted to kill you?" she finally asked.

"We . . . spoke to him once," Cross told her. "But it didn't seem as if he even knew us when we did. So it was nothing personal. Near as we could tell, all he wanted was to prove he could do what other people had failed at."

"Maybe he was just crazy," Tiger said, softly. "Being . . . crippled that bad, never going outside, no friends. And then his parents being killed. If someone told him *you* were responsible for that, well, that would do it, all right. But the way you talk about him, he's way too smart to have been suckered by some rumor."

"He was," Cross agreed. "Maybe he picked up on that 'many tried, many died' thing, and he wanted to be special. Who knows? What we *do* know is, we can't ask him."

"Maybe it was only Ace he—?"

"Look, what kicked this off, that whole Circle of Skulls deal, we thought that *was* about us. We thought we were his targets, and everything else was all a setup for the finale."

"So what did you—?"

"I'll tell you," Cross said. "Paint you a picture, even."

In the front office of what had been a thriving gas station before the economic blight, a boy barely into his teens clicked off the mate to the watcher's communicator and turned to a group of young people. The bright-blue Mohawk standing straight up on his shaved head was his badge of leadership.

"Johnny Eyes says someone's coming. He said it was some big grayish thing, blacked-out windows, couldn't tell the make. Has to be . . . them."

"We don't say their names, G-boy," the leader said. "You're new, so listen: What Johnny Eyes picked up on, that's the Shark Car. Means the Cross crew is rolling. Those guys are very, very bad news. But not for us, you following me? In this country, they're the lions, we're the jackals. We take what they leave, whatever it is. Could be money, could be a body, could be a message. Could be all of those in one bundle. This piece of Chicago, it's not called the Badlands for nothing. And it's ours. That rusted-out semi I showed you when you first came in? That's the toll booth. Anything comes through that way, even their car, that's our business. Comes in any other way, it's not."

Buddha's short, pudgy form slid out, his undefined shape a perfect match for the car's paint. He lounged next to the door for several minutes, listening. Satisfied, he pushed against the wall with his palm, waited for a greenish glow, and descended into a tunnel. Moving confidently in the darkness, he spotted a tiny red light at the end of the hall. Drawing a deep, silent breath, he walked toward it.

A quick climb up an unlighted steel staircase brought him into the back of Red 71. A shadowy man was seated in the corner, his lower jaw illuminated by the light from a single candle.

"Thanks for coming, boss," the pudgy man said.

"You said it was important, Buddha. And you wanted it private."

"It's So Long," the pudgy man said, drawing another deep breath. "Here. Look at this."

He handed over a single sheet of commercial-grade typing paper. The shadow-shrouded man tilted the sheet so he could read by the faint light:

> YELLOW WHORE
> YOU HAVE ONE WEEK TO GET OUT
> THEN WE COME FOR YOU

"What's this at the bottom?" he asked, his finger touching a circle made from skull symbols.

"That's their mark. The name is just what it says: The Circle of Skulls."

"Means . . . what?"

"Rapes. Gang rapes. They've been linked to a half-dozen of them, all over the city. First the warning, then they make their move. One of the women went crazy behind it—she's still in the hospital."

"A race thing?"

"Yeah. I mean, I guess so. None of the victims was white, except for one. And she was Jewish, living with a black guy around Edgewater. So maybe it's one of those. . . ."

"No," Cross said. Not theorizing, stating a fact: "It's some kind of cover."

Buddha did not question the conclusion—he knew the other man had an ability to decode messages others wouldn't even recognize as messages.

"Cross, come on. You know what I want. Same as you'd want if you had . . ."

"I don't have, Buddha. And you know the deal. This thing, it's not crew business. They're not after us."

"They're after my wife!"

"I understand. I understand now, okay? But that doesn't make it crew business. You know the pact: only way we're going in on something is if we get paid, or if we're under fire. This thing you showed me, it doesn't fit."

"Just like that, huh? If it was Ace's—"

"Don't push that button, Buddha. We brought you in on my word, nothing else. The others, they all . . ."

"I know. I'm just . . . Look: all I want, I want to ask the others if anyone wants to volunteer."

"Sure. Who would you ask first, Princess? You tell that maniac they 'started it,' he's in. That pulls Rhino right along; he doesn't trust Princess not to get himself killed. That's half the damn crew right there. Then, the way you figure, I look for Ace to ride shotgun. That way we're all in. All of us, all in. Not gonna happen."

"Cross, you're my brother. Ever since that . . . jungle, right?"

"Yes. But you know the score. We talked it over,

before you came in with us. No more fighting other people's battles."

The pudgy man hung his head, his voice laced with something more powerful than sadness. "Cross . . ."

"Go home," the shadowy man said. "Stay with So Long. Let me get some eyes and ears out there. Who knows? People go to this much trouble, maybe there's some real money in this."

On the roof of Red 71, Cross approached a large box constructed of weathered wood; it appeared to be pieces of wind-deposited scraps.

As Cross neared the box, a distinctive "killy-killy-killy" shrilled, sounding a warning. A kestrel suddenly popped its head out of the box, fixing Cross with an implacably fearless gaze.

Cross pulled a heavy leather gauntlet onto his right hand and held out a strip of still-bloody raw meat with his left. The kestrel glared briefly, then swooped the short distance to the upheld hand. The mini-falcon perched on the gauntlet, tearing at the piece of meat suspended in Cross's fingers, briefly fluttering its blue-gray wings. The male, then—Cross could never tell them apart until he saw their undersides.

The kestrel shrilled again, and his mate raised her head out of the box. As the female swooped toward Cross to take the rest of the dripping meat, the male snapped his wings once and was gone. Cross knew he would be soaring far above the city, riding the vectors, hovering.

Cross held the female high above his head. She flicked her rust-colored wings once, as though she wanted to join her mate, but then she banked and returned to the nesting box. Standing guard while her mate went to bring more food to the hatchlings.

Cross knew the babies were there—he had built the nesting box himself. But despite the many hours he had invested in working with the birds, he never considered approaching their shelter any closer. The kestrels were only inches high but were capable of extreme speed on a dive, hitting prey with fisted talons turned into blunt-tipped crossbow bolts.

Downstairs, the gang boss sat in a tiny corner room on the second floor. The single window was covered with X-braced strips of plywood, allowing only a sliver of daylight to penetrate. Cross removed a brick from the side wall, reached behind it, and used the leverage to take out two more. Then he extracted a flat box of blood-red lacquered wood. Inside was a single sheet of rice paper, hand-pulled.

The box also contained a stylus made of ivory with a fluted tip of gold and a tiny stone jar with an inset top. Cross shook the jar next to his ear, then replaced it, satisfied. He touched the rough surface of the paper with his fingertips, staring at its blankness. Finally, he replaced the calligraphy instruments, closed the box, and took up a thick notebook with a black leather cover.

He opened the notebook and turned the pages

slowly. Each page held only a few lines of writing. The script wasn't elaborate, but it was clear and knife-edged.

Cross lit a cigarette, watched as the smoke rose toward the boarded-up window. He took two more drags before he stubbed it out in an inverted hubcap he used as an ashtray. Then he picked up a black felt-tip marker with a fine point and drew some experimental slashes and intersecting lines on a blank page of the notebook.

He closed his eyes. It was another forty-five minutes before Cross used the felt-tip pen to write.

He stared at the new line for several minutes, breathing so quietly through his nose that the sound was inaudible. If a later inspection proved the new line worthy of the stylus, it would be added.

Finally, he closed the notebook. After replacing everything inside the flat lacquered box, he returned the brick to its home.

"You really think McNamara's going to give up police intel?"

"Why not?" Cross answered. "This gang, no matter what their endgame is, they're still rapists. Nothing Mac hates more than a skinner . . . unless it's a whole pack of them."

"Here he comes, right on time," Rhino said, pointing his finger at a solitary figure just entering the running track on a suburban high-school field. The tip of that finger was missing; the second-knuckle stub looked like the polished aluminum case for an individual cigar.

Past midnight, the field was deserted. The two men waited in the black pool in front of an empty grandstand. As the jogging figure approached, Cross stepped forward, hands at his sides, open.

"Appreciate you coming," he said.

"I was going to put in some laps anyway," the jogger said, slowing to a full stop with the smoothness of a man in sync with his body. He was about six feet, muscular, sandy-haired, his face distinguished only by the often broken nose of a prizefighter.

Without preamble, Cross asked, "You know anything about a gang calls itself the Circle of Skulls?"

"What's your interest?" the detective asked. The honey-Irish lilt—one of the many tools that earned him the title "King of the Confession Coaxers"— notably absent from his voice.

"You don't want to know."

McNamara moved closer to Cross, who opened his left hand, then lit a cigarette from the flame that appeared. "We know there's at least three of them," he said quietly. "Only reason they haven't already gone down is the damn federales. Once they start this 'hate crime' crap, the paperwork gets more important than the investigation. You know how it works—they have to get the press conference set before they make their move."

"And that's soon?"

"Maybe. Maybe not so soon. There's another problem."

"What?"

"This gang, they're a collection of freaks. The three we ID'ed for sure, they met down in Kankakee."

"The loony bin?"

"Yeah. All on violent sex beefs, all from good families . . . families with good money, anyway. All went NGI, best lawyers, expert witnesses. . . . Maybe money changed hands, too. They opted for bench trials, so no jury heard what they did, and the press only got the broad strokes. When they got out—and those kind always get out—they got together and started this Circle of Skulls thing."

"But you know those NGIs were just a slick lawyer's game. So you could drop them anytime you wanted, right? They gotta be on some kind of parole hold. . . ."

"Probably. But once they put on that NGI jacket, it's a Get Out of Jail Free card, you understand? Can't bust them for Association—after all, they have to attend 'group.' Besides, there's something else . . . something that hasn't made the papers. All of the victims told us they were attacked by two men. And they also said there was another man there. A man with a video cam."

"They were taping that?"

"Looks like it," McNamara said, his face set in hard lines, locking eyes with Cross. "That wouldn't be anything special, not today. Punks are always working their cell-phone cameras when they gang-stomp some poor bastard—they have it on their Facebook page before the victim gets to the ER.

Dimwits like them save us a lot of trouble. But this was a real camera, full-size. Like they were shooting a movie. We got a reflected snap from a store camera—my son says it's an old Bolex."

"Your . . . ?"

"NYU Film School," the veteran cop said, half disgusted with himself for saying too much, half full of pride at his boy's achievements.

"They under surveillance?"

"In Cook County? Can you see the department green-lighting a twenty-four/seven on three different guys? Not RICO material, so no 'asset forfeiture'? No cash to snatch, no chance it happens."

"Give me the locates," Cross said, snapping away his cigarette after the third drag. "We always wanted to be Neighborhood Watch. You won't even have to give us those toy badges you guys hand out."

A double-sized man holding a canvas carryall tapped lightly on the inlaid mahogany door of a suburban house.

The door opened. Buddha stood just inside, a shoulder holster prominent against his white T-shirt. His pudgy appearance had been discarded with his trademark field jacket.

"Cross says to meet him at the spot, right away."

"I can't leave my—"

"I'm supposed to stay here," the huge man said, stepping across the threshold as if he had answered any possible objection.

An Asian woman with long black hair and chisel-point makeup entered the living room. "What is—?" she began, then stopped abruptly when she saw the mammoth form of the man talking to her husband.

"It's okay, honey," Buddha assured her. "This is one of my business partners. Rhino, meet So Long."

The huge man bowed deeply. A brief smile creased the woman's face as she clasped her hands and bowed her head in return.

"Welcome to our home," she said, graciously.

"I am honored," Rhino replied, so gently that the usual squeak of his voice was inaudible.

"Baby, I have to go out for a bit. Business, okay? Rhino's gonna stay here . . . here with you . . . until I'm back."

"As you wish," the woman said, bowing again.

Buddha's face flushed. "Don't pull that geisha crap on me, So Long. You know I said I'd take care of this. Just let me do it, all right?"

The woman stepped past Rhino to stand next to Buddha. Her facial expression didn't change: "Be careful, husband," she whispered.

The Shark Car entered a narrow alley and glided to a stop.

It was late afternoon, but the sun had long since given up penetrating the unchanging darkness of buildings built so close to each other they might as well have been attached.

"You stay here," Cross said.

"Look, boss. That's a nasty place—and they're not gonna like strangers just walking in. 'Specially ones that look like you. What's gonna happen if there's trouble? How about if I just—?"

"Stay here," Cross repeated, as if saying it for the first time.

Buddha's face showed nothing, but his fingers twitched at the lapel of his field jacket.

Cross exited the car and walked through the narrow alley. He quickly turned left. A few steps brought him to the entrance of a bar. Above the door was a neon Indian war bonnet flashing red, white, and blue in a warning no one had ever mistaken for a show of patriotism.

He walked in, hands held carefully away from his sides. The noise didn't stop, but its tone shifted as various Indians from all America's tribes watched the newcomer. Cross looked straight ahead, making his way toward the bar. He took a seat at the very end, lit a smoke, and stared at his own reflection in the cracked mirror. After a long five minutes, an Indian with his hair braided in traditional fashion approached from the other side of the bar.

"What'll it be?" he asked.

"I want to leave a message."

"For who?"

"Tracker."

"Don't know nobody by that name, friend."

"I understand," Cross said. "Thank you, anyway."

He slid his hand across the wet surface of the bar,

palm down, the bull's-eye tattoo clearly visible on the back. When he pulled his hand back, a fifty-dollar bill remained.

The two men rolled a series of empty fifty-five-gallon oil drums away from the wall behind Red 71's back office. They walked through the ball-bearing curtain into a poolroom. Cross slid behind a small round table set up against the far wall. Buddha took a stick from one of the wall racks and chalked it as though he was going to play. But his eyes were focused two tables down, where Rhino and an Indian were playing nine-ball.

The Indian was coppery-complected, his hair combed straight back, tied into a ponytail with a strip of rawhide.

Rhino drove the cue ball at the rack, scattering it. Two balls dropped: the one and the seven. He delicately tapped the white cue ball into the green six. It kissed gently, deflected off a short rail, and nudged the yellow-and-white-striped nine ball into the corner pocket.

"Awrrright!" Princess shouted in triumph, leaping from his seat to offer Rhino a high-five. Nobody in the room even looked up, although they had all heard quieter gunshots. The Indian stood motionless, sweeping the room with a trail scout's eyes. Then he turned and walked over to Cross's table. When Cross nodded, he took the vacant seat.

"Thanks for coming," Cross said.

"A job?" the Indian replied.

"Some shadow work."

"There are plenty of very good—"

"For this, 'very good' isn't good enough."

The Indian bowed his head slightly. Enough to acknowledge the respect he was being shown, but not enough to indicate acceptance of the job.

"You know about this Circle of Skulls thing?"

"Only what is public. They have never entered our territory. And none of us would be mistaken for white."

"They're just playing it like a race thing. You know: Get out of the area or we'll make you wish you had. Hard for them to pull that when everyone in the area's the same color.

"That's a deep game," Cross continued. "It scans like camouflage, but—"

"Because . . . ?"

The Indian let his question hover, patiently waiting.

"Because it's two of them that do . . . the actual thing. And they got another man with them. A man with a movie camera."

"They are making rape movies?"

"Not Hollywood movies—this is the real thing. Nobody's acting. So it's either freakishness or business. Maybe both. If they're just making slimy home movies, like the way some of those freaks take trophies . . . But if they're making them for the hardcore market, or even customized to order . . ."

"I will do this."

• • •

Herman Holtstraf—a.k.a. Leonard Lippe, according
to the stack of papers Cross had studied for hours—
stepped out of his two-bedroom apartment on the
ninth floor of a near-Loop condo conversion.

He carefully double-locked the door, then tugged
on the knob, making sure the dead bolt was firmly
in place. His footsteps were soundless in the deep-
carpeted hallway. He took the elevator downstairs,
exited the buildings, and strolled casually away.

Two blocks later, Holtstraf quickened his pace. He
spotted a black Jeep Cherokee, used another key
to open the driver's door, and slid behind the wheel.

He started the engine, hit the power window
switch, and reclined against the seatback; it was
over eighty degrees outside, but Holtstraf knew
it was better for the engine to wait a minute or so
before putting a vehicle in gear. He was a man who
took good care of his possessions.

The phone in Cross's jacket pocket buzzed softly.
"Go," he answered.

"Four, one, X-Ray, Charlie, eight, Bravo."

Cross quickly checked several sheets of paper
spread out before him. "Doesn't match. Which one
you on?"

"Number two."

"He's on the move?"

"Yes."

"Need a box?"

"Negative."

• • •

"He's not checking for tags," Buddha said to the Indian as the pudgy man gently coiled the Shark Car around a tight corner.

"Or he's got some cover."

"I hope so," Buddha grunted, half under his breath, his hand flicking at his lapel again.

"Remember what Cross said," the Indian warned.

"Yeah, I heard him," Buddha assented. "But it wasn't your wife they threatened to rape."

"Chain of command," Tracker replied.

"There's always a chain of command. That's why a lot of those college boy LTs got themselves fragged."

"You volunteered for this one, Buddha."

"I know," the pudgy man said grimly, continuing to maintain visual contact with the black Jeep.

The target drove sedately, not risking a ticket, courteously slowing to permit a jaywalking pedestrian to cross. Finally, the Jeep circled a block twice, then pulled into a parking garage. The Shark Car followed, moving at a crawl around the sharply ascending curves.

"You want me to . . ." Buddha turned to Tracker. It was only then that he noticed the Indian had vanished.

Cross was drawing a series of intersecting lines on a blank sheet of paper when his phone rang again.

"Go."

"He switched rides. Try Alpha, seven, Foxtrot, Bravo, six, four."

Cross quickly scanned the papers in front of him. "Chevy Volt? Dark red?"

"Yes."

"That's his. Registered. The Jeep connects to a—"

"Out of the Loop now," Tracker interrupted. "Heading for the border, east."

"You need what?"

"Backup. With legit plates. I'm in a borrowed car."

"Say why switch."

"Last driver unstable. You know how fast he is. If I made a locate with him along . . ."

"Roger that. I'll get something over the border. One around Cal City, another East Chicago. When you land, call."

An hour later, the cellular phone buzzed. Cross picked it up, glancing across to Rhino as he did.

"Go."

"I'm on the ground. Cal City. In a bar called Mary's Show Place. You know it?"

"I know where it is."

"I made a locate. Need transport out."

"Fifteen minutes, max."

Tracker sat alone at a far corner of a long bar, head in his hands. To the bartender, just another redskin laid off from the steel mills, drowning his prospects in booze. *Funny, never heard of one of them drinking straight vodka with water on the side. Hell, the way this one kept asking for refills, you couldn't even tell how much firewater he was putting away.*

Princess walked in the front door, wearing a sleeveless leather vest over his bare upper body. A long chain dangled from his right ear, a small steel ball swinging gently at its end. A red handkerchief was half out of his back pocket. He reeked of cheap perfume. The bodybuilder went out of his way to make eye contact with everyone he passed. Nobody held his gaze. He spotted Tracker in the corner, went over, and sat down.

"I have the house spotted," the Indian greeted him.

"You think they're all in there?"

"Forget it, Princess. Cross said no physical contact. We're here for info only."

"I know. But if they start something . . ."

"Me, they won't see. And you, you're staying right here. I'll be back soon as I can."

"Okay," Princess replied, handing over an ignition key. "It's out by the curb. I'll be over by the pinball machine."

Tracker straddled the big Harley, shocking pink with matching saddlebags. As the engine roared to life, he cursed Princess under his breath.

The house was green, with freshly painted white shutters; a matching trellis thinly laced with struggling ivy shielded the front porch. Tracker made one swoop on the garish motorcycle, marking the

Chevy Volt in the driveway, the closed door to the two-car garage, the white picket fence surrounding the property. Maybe two, three hours to sundown, he calculated.

He rolled the bike into a 7-Eleven parking lot, pulled his phone, hit a button.

"Go."

"Too much daylight."

"You got a place to lay up?"

"No," the Indian said, underscoring the single word. "And I'm not hanging out with Princess in that bar. You know what's bound to happen, he stays there too long."

"Yeah, I know. We're on our way. Can you hold out there for another forty-five?"

"Your ETA seven-fifty, right? I'll find someplace to stow this damn scooter, get back to the bar just before then, yes?"

"Yes."

At seven-forty-five, Tracker entered the back parking lot of Mary's Show Place on foot.

He noted how full it was but drew no conclusions—"maybe" was for generals, not combat soldiers.

As he walked in the front door, he glanced toward the pinball machine, but Princess was nowhere in sight. One eye-sweep picked up the bodybuilder, his bulk mostly obscured by a crowd of men who had arranged themselves in a semicircle. The Indian walked carefully around the group, saw an opening, and seated himself on the bench next to Princess.

"Hey, what's happening, partner?"

"They will be here in a few minutes," Tracker said quietly, his lips close to Princess's ear. "Cross said to wait for him, understand?"

"I'm just having some fun," the hyper-muscled child said, defensively. "We're all having fun."

"What kind of fun?" the Indian asked warily, scanning the bar for signs of destruction.

"Arm wrestling! For beers. I already won over a hundred."

"You drank a hundred beers?"

"Nah. You know I'm not supposed to drink. I've been buying for the house. They all like me. I beat everybody so far. That's why I'm waiting around— they got some hotshot they're gonna bring in for me to try."

The Indian grunted.

"It's just fun. But no more playing for beers. When this guy they're bringing in shows up, I'm gonna make myself a couple of thousand. Any minute. You watch."

"Princess," the Indian said, keeping his voice level and reasonable, "you're betting two, three thousand dollars and you don't know anything about this guy they're bringing?"

"Sure!"

"He's probably a professional. There's a whole circuit where they—"

"I could be one, too. A professional. A couple of the guys here already said so."

"Do you have that much money?"

"Well . . . Not on me, but . . ."

"Geronimo save us," the Indian muttered to himself, his eyes threat-scanning the room.

Cross and Rhino walked into the bar and took a table in a deep corner. The gang leader caught Tracker's eye across the room, jerked his head in a "Let's go!" signal. The Indian shrugged his shoulders helplessly. Cross got up and moved toward where Princess was seated.

Before he could get within earshot, Princess piped up: "All right! Here's the money. My backer," he proudly announced to the watching crowd.

A slender man with a mop of dirty-blond curls, wearing a red varsity jacket with white sleeves, spoke to Cross: "You? Okay, how deep you want to go?"

"Hold up a minute," Cross told him. "I need to speak with my boy first."

He walked around the table until he was behind Tracker and Princess, leaned his head down, whispered, "What the hell is going on?" to Princess.

"Arm wrestling! It's really fun. I beat everybody in the place. So they're sending this guy over for me to go against. That guy in the fancy jacket? He's the one who said I needed a backer."

"We're here on business," Cross whispered to the bodybuilder.

"Sure, but . . . come on, it'll be fun!"

The crowd parted as a leviathan slogged his way forward. A wide bench was ceremoniously moved into place across from Princess. The leviathan lacked the bodybuilder's vascular-defined muscles, but his sheer mass was overwhelming.

"This is The King," the manager said to Cross, patting his champion on the back. "I suppose you want to up the bet now?"

Several men in the crowd sniggered on cue.

Cross stood up, catching Rhino's eye over the shoulders of the seated men. He tapped his right temple twice. Rhino got up and exited the bar. Cross turned to the manager. "You cover five?"

"You look like a flaming faggot to me," The King sneered at Princess. "Smell like one, too."

Princess smacked his lips in an air-kiss.

The King started to rise from his bench, but his manager restrained him with a hand on his shoulder.

Cross pulled a sheaf of folded-over bills wrapped in a rubber band from his shirt pocket and tossed it on the table. The manager reached for it.

"You want to count it, let me count yours," Cross said quietly.

"Ante up," the manager called out to the semi-circle of men. Bills started flying onto the tabletop. He gathered them together, moistened his thumb. "I got thirty-three hundred here."

He put the bills in a neat stack, opened his own

wallet, and elaborately counted out seventeen hundred-dollar bills. "Satisfied?" he said to Cross, reaching for the rubber-band-wrapped stack.

For about five seconds, the place went quiet.

"Let's get it on!" the manager called in a fight announcer's voice.

Princess and The King reached out their left hands to grab the wooden pegs set into the table. Each placed his right elbow on a tabletop pad. They felt for a good grip of each other's hands for a long minute, then locked in.

"I'm gonna break your arm, homo," The King promised.

Princess giggled.

"Ready?" the manager asked, pointing at The King, then at Princess. Both men nodded: The King glowering, Princess grinning broadly.

"Go!" the manager screamed.

The King rammed his arm to his left, bouncing off his seat to get more power into the thrust.

Princess's arm didn't move, containing The King's hand as gently as a curious scientist might hold a butterfly. The bodybuilder stared deep into the face of his adversary. Princess's eyes, usually a deep blue, took on a purplish tint.

"This was supposed to be fun," the disappointed-again child said in a sad voice. "I was having fun. Making friends. Why did you have to go and call me names?"

The King grunted, redoubling his effort—it felt like isometric impossibility.

"You started it," Princess said. "I didn't do anything. I was nice to everyone. They liked me. You started it."

Cross exchanged glances with Tracker. The Indian twisted his head to the right slightly. Cross followed his lead, saw Rhino back inside the bar, standing near the door. All other eyes in the room were on the two contestants.

Veins bulged in The King's face, blue lines on a red background. He didn't hear the cheering support of the crowd, didn't feel the pulse of their feet rhythmically pounding on the floor.

"Let it go, pal," Cross said to The King. "Just relax. There's no way you're gonna budge my boy, believe me. He's all worked up now. You don't let go, he's gonna snap your arm like a dry twig."

The King was bathed in sweat. The whites of his eyes dominated their sockets. "Aaaargh!" he roared, throwing every remaining ounce of his strength into a final attempt at a slam.

"You started it," Princess said, sorrowfully. Then he quickly shoved The King's hand all the way back to the tabletop. The snap-crack was audible ten feet away.

The King opened his mouth to scream, but he fainted before any sound could come out. The manager knew what he'd just witnessed: "Call the paramedics! Hurry!"

Princess got to his feet, his eyes glazed, a thin stream of drool coming out of the corner of his mouth. Cross reached out, swept the money off the table and into his jacket pocket.

"Don't anyone be stupid," he said to the crowd.

He and Tracker bracketed Princess, herding him toward the door. All three men had their backs to the crowd when a tall, slender man with a dark crew cut reached into his red-and-black-checkered jacket. Rhino stepped forward, pulling the Uzi out as though it was a derringer.

"Don't!" he squeaked at the slender man.

The room froze.

The Shark Car was at the curb, engine idling, Buddha at the wheel, the back doors standing open. Cross jumped in first, pulling Princess after him, Tracker right behind. Rhino slid into the front seat, next to Buddha, and the Shark Car took off.

"He started it," Princess mumbled.

"It's done now," Cross told him, patting the bodybuilder's huge biceps the way you would gentle a horse. "All over now. Take it easy. Breathe through your nose. Come on. . . ."

"He gonna be all right?" Cross asked Rhino.

"Yes. You know how he gets after he . . . does something. He'll be okay. It's a poison his own body makes . . . has to work its way through his system before it finds an exit."

"He's dangerous, brother."

"We're all dangerous," Rhino said, locking eyes with Cross.

Cross ran a hand through his hair. When he

brought his head up, his eyes were clear and calm. "Okay, brother. But watch him close, all right?"

The huge man solemnly and sadly nodded his agreement.

Three nights later, Tracker descended the stone steps and entered the Red 71 poolroom.

He stood at the counter, waiting patiently, until the old man turned away from his small black-and-white TV. Tracker handed over a ten-dollar bill. The old man gave him a set of balls in a plastic tray, saying, "Take number nineteen."

The Indian was halfway through the first rack when Rhino appeared.

"Come for a rematch?"

"Cross," the Indian answered.

"Follow me."

Tracker took a seat facing Cross in the back room. They sat in silence for a few minutes. Finally, he said, "You are the most patient white man I ever met."

"What tribe are you?" Cross replied.

"Chickasaw," Tracker replied, his chest swelling with pride. "You know anything about our people?"

"I know you didn't farm and you didn't hunt."

"Which makes us what?"

"Makes you just like us," Cross said.

Tracker nodded his agreement. "Those three in that house? They're not in charge. Somebody with money is behind this. That place doesn't look like much, but it's plush inside. Expensive. High-tech equipment. Audio, video, everything. High-end editing gear, a duping machine . . . a complete studio."

"So they're in business." If Cross felt any surprise at Tracker's ability to get inside the house, his face didn't show it.

"They kept talking about another man. No name, though."

"Motion sensors? Dogs?"

"Nothing. It's a cheese box. It doesn't look like anything special—that's their security."

"If they're making product, they'll have to deliver it to get paid."

"I followed the first one to leave that house for a full forty-eight," Tracker answered. "He went out when it was heavy-dark, but I could see there's some kind of compartment in the trunk of that Chevy. He went all the way back across the border. Not talking just geography—the place he drove to was in Winnetka."

"You think the money's there?"

"Can't say for sure." The Indian shrugged. "But why else would that Chevy go into such a ritzy suburb? He wasn't scouting, knew exactly where he had to go, and he's got the clicker for one door of the garage. And that house where they've got the equipment, it feels . . . temporary. Like I said, it's got nice stuff in there, but there's no real furniture, nothing much except the equipment."

"Keep watching," Cross told the Indian. "We're close now."

• • •

"What it comes down to is this," Cross said to Rhino. "Is the guy in that Winnetka house bent like the others, or is he just a businessman? He's got to be either a dealer or a collector."

"Could be both," Rhino replied. "We've seen that before."

"If he's a merchant . . . if that's all he is . . . no way he takes those freaks back to his place if they're on the run. But if he's with them . . .

"We need to spook them. Spook them bad. Then they'll run, no doubt. What we need to see is where they run to."

Herman Holtstraf pushed the button to summon the elevator, his face twisted into a grimace of impatience.

It was only the ninth floor—what the hell was taking so long? Finally, the DOWN button lost illumination and a faint *ping!* announced the car's arrival. The doors slid open.

He was already striding forward when he noticed the elevator car was filled with . . . something. Holtstraf opened his mouth, but he was too late— something clapped a hand across the front of his throat, cutting off the air supply.

Rhino walked off the elevator, holding Holtstraf by the throat at arm's length in one hand as if he were a bag of especially bad-smelling garbage. A man in a dark business suit was waiting by the door to Holt-straf's apartment. He dipped into Holtstraf's pocket and expertly extracted his keys.

The three men entered the apartment, Cross in the lead. Rhino continued his throat-lock on the target, effortlessly maintaining the grip as Cross checked the place for anything that might be a problem.

Cross re-entered the front room, came up behind Holtstraf, and kicked the back of his right knee, knocking the man's legs out from under him. As Holtstraf collapsed to the floor, Rhino rode him down, maintaining his grip.

Cross snapped a set of anesthetic nose plugs onto the target, blocking his mouth with a steel-mesh-gloved hand in the same motion.

In less than a minute, Holtstraf was out, breathing deeply through his nose.

Cross pulled out a cheap cell phone, tapped a number, hit SEND. He heard a receiver picked up at the other end, said "Yes," and hit END.

Leaving Rhino to watch the captive, Cross pulled a roll of heavy construction paper from his coat. He spooled the paper and quickly taped it to the empty white wall along one side of the front room. On the paper was a neat circle of cutouts—some kind of stencil.

Cross took out a small can of spray paint, shook it a few times, and sprayed a tiny test pattern on an edge of the white paper. Satisfied, he sprayed the cutouts in a careful circular motion. He replaced the paint can and gently lifted off the stencil. On the wall

was a circle of skulls in bright red. A broken circle—
three of the skulls were missing from the right arc.

Four sharp raps on the apartment door. Rhino
got up and unslung his Uzi as he moved. When
he opened the door, Princess stepped inside. The
bodybuilder was dressed in a bulky set of dull-gray
sweats, his head covered by a Navy watch cap. Over
his shoulder was a blue leather golf bag.

Cross and Rhino each took one arm of the unconscious Holtstraf and dragged him toward the wall,
until his back was flat against it. They took a firm grip
on Holtstraf's wrists and pulled upward.

"He's too tall for me," Cross said. "Wait."

He came back with a wooden milk carton that
Holtstraf had used to store his collection of LP vinyl
records. Cross dumped out the records, turned the
box on its side, and used it as a step-stool. This
time, when the two men pulled, Holtstraf was suspended between them, arms outstretched.

Princess unzipped the golf bag and carefully
removed a harpoon. He tested the tip with one
gloved thumb, nodded.

"He started it," Cross whispered to the bodybuilder. "He's the leader of that rape-tape gang. If
he walks away, he's going right back to them. We
have to leave a message so the rest of them come
out from where they're hiding."

Princess nodded, looking more sad than angry.
Then he took up his position about four feet from the
suspended target, torqued his hips, and launched
with all his strength. The razor-tipped harpoon took

Holtstraf in the sternum, piercing him as easily as an ice pick through cardboard.

When Cross and Rhino dropped their grips, Holtstraf stayed in place—pinned to the wall like an insect on a spreading board.

The Web tabloids competed for "Most Lurid Headline," their entries all some form of . . .

BIZARRE CULT MURDER!
GORE-SOAKED SCENE IN LUX CONDO!

Expert speculations ranged from a Midwestern version of a resurrected Manson Family to the Zodiac Killer finally emerging from hiding. But Chicago had the edge in local connections, from William Heirens to Richard Speck to John Wayne Gacy.

And since the Second City was still number one on the hit parade, the NRA gifted it with an Op-Ed pointing out that even a total ban on firearms wouldn't have stopped this hideously violent homicide.

How anyone had managed to snap a photo of the pinned-to-the-wall body stayed a mystery, but word that one of the ultra-sleaze national papers had paid a million in cash for that prize became a "verified rumor" within hours.

Sales of the red T-shirts with . . .

CHICAGO POLICE ✸ HOMICIDE SQUAD
OUR DAY BEGINS WHEN YOURS ENDS

... in white lettering emblazoned across the front forced continual reprinting to satisfy the orders ceaselessly pouring in. The stress of filling the orders caused three consecutive price increases in two days. How else was the city going to pay those working round-the-clock shifts just to keep up with fulfillment demands?

Cross idly shifted through a stack of newsprint in Red 71's back room, an ashtray next to the cellular phone by his elbow.

For all the tension in his posture, he could have been a Miami pensioner scanning the Early Bird Specials.

In diametric contrast, Buddha sat across the small table as rigid as an I-beam, barely containing the neurons and synapses blasting off inside his body. Both men were smoking: Cross in his usual way, three drags per cigarette; Buddha taking each down to the filter—and he was already on his second pack.

The phone buzzed. Cross opened the line, said, "Go," softly.

"Running." Tracker's voice.

Cross put down the phone. "They're spooked, brother. Got to be heading for home base. And our money."

"What about the . . . ?"

"Relax, now. There's only two of them left."

"Three," said the pudgy man with unblinking agate eyes. "There's still someone in that place in Winnetka."

"You could be right," Cross conceded. "They have to go to ground somewhere, and whoever lives in that house, he could be the bankroller. They ran that racist crap as an excuse, but they *did* run it. No telling how many crews are after them right now."

"Yeah. And whoever hits them gets a pass. But, boss . . . they're all partners, right?"

"Not if the guy in that fancy house is buying those rape tapes. He never went along on any of their attacks. Like a general, okay? He could care less what happens to the grunts. You remember how that plays. . . ."

"Yeah. But if this guy was a buyer or a collector, he'd be a user, one way or another. The only way he could be sure the others wouldn't roll on him would be to get them out to where he is. They might need escape cash, sure. But this guy in the mansion, he needs them dead. We've got to make sure—"

"Buddha, look: we can't spare the manpower to watch his house. Not in that neighborhood. We'd have no cover, so we'd have to keep switching off. Soon as we know they're moving, *then* we take them. Not before, understand?"

"Yeah . . ." the pudgy man said grudgingly.

"What?" Cross snapped at him.

"Look, boss. You got us all deployed, right? I mean, like you said, everyone's in the field. I'm here, wheelman, in case we need to jump. Okay, I got that. But that means So Long's alone now."

"You think—what?—they're going to stop and

pull off another gang rape now? Anyway, she's not alone," Cross said quietly.

"Who's on it, then? I know it can't be Ace. You're not using a contract man, are you? Not for guarding my wife?"

"Tiger's there," Cross told him. "I just told her it was a job. But when she heard what it was about . . ."

The pudgy man visibly relaxed. A faint smile flickered across his lips. "Tiger in the same room as a couple of gang rapists. Put that bout on pay-for-view, you'd get a few million buys."

"It's illegal to sell snuff films," Cross replied, at peace somewhere inside himself.

Four hours later; just shy of eleven at night.

The two men were in the same position. Only the overflowing ashtray gave any indication of the passage of time.

"Boss?"

"What?"

"You sure that phone's batteries are working?"

Cross pointed a finger at the glowing green LED on the cellular, then at the wire leading to the charger. He closed his eyes again.

It was another half-hour before the phone buzzed. Cross picked it up, held it to his ear without a greeting.

"He landed," came Tracker's voice. "He was running a loop. A long loop. Back to that spot in Winnetka. Fancy joint, big fence all around. Could be a hot LZ."

"You okay there?" Cross asked.

"Negative. I stick out worse than a white man on a reservation. One with no casino."

"Mark the spot and take off. We'll meet you at your bar. An hour, hour and a half tops."

"I'm gone."

The Shark Car cut through the night, Buddha at the wheel. "Rhino and Princess—how they gonna get there?" he asked.

"Probably take the CTA," Cross replied.

"Jesus," Buddha muttered, the picture of Rhino and Princess riding the elevated train at that hour of the night too much for his sensors. "I hope nobody says something stupid to Princess. . . ."

They found the two men just past the corner of Wilson and Broadway. Princess was watching a three-card-monte operator, enthralled at the slickness of the man's pitch.

"Find the Lady," the monte man crooned. "Find the beautiful Lady. Where is she hiding? Oh, she's right in front of you, men. But she's such a clever little thing. Who wants to try?"

The Shark Car pulled to the curb. Cross was out before it came to a complete stop. Rhino whirled, saw who it was, and dragged a reluctant Princess behind him. They piled into the backseat—Cross sat next to Buddha.

It was only a couple of blocks to the Indian bar. Buddha left the engine running while Cross stepped inside. He was back in seconds, Tracker at his side. Cross again took the shotgun seat as the Shark Car blended into the night.

"It's just around the next corner," Tracker said, leaning forward to speak to Cross.

The Shark Car slowed as though attuned to the Indian's voice and gently cruised to a stop between two palatial homes.

"You see anything?" Cross asked him.

"Just the fence. Could be any damn thing behind it."

"Yeah. We can't stay here. Neighborhood like this, a prowl car would spook at anything strange."

"Can't we just Rambo it?" Princess pleaded. "It'd only take a minute."

"Neighborhood like this, houses probably all running Central Station alarms. Pass."

"How about burning him out?" Rhino suggested in his squeaky voice.

"And burn the cash, too? Tracker, you up for a whistle job?"

"Yes."

"Okay. You guys split. Stay close. Keep moving. Soon as we're ready to roll, I'll buzz you."

"Boss?"

"What?"

"Let me go, too. Rhino can drive the—"

"Be yourself, brother," Cross said, quietly rejecting the offer.

Cross and Tracker, both dressed totally in black, hooded sweatshirts down to silk gloves, skirted the target's property. The fence was wrought iron, with spikes at the top of each stake. Tracker knelt, made a low whistling sound guaranteed to bring out any dog that might be nearby.

Silence followed.

Cross knife-edged his hand, moved it parallel to the ground. Tracker shook his head—no motion sensors as far as he could see.

Several lights were on in the big house, glowing faintly yellow from behind drawn curtains. Cross made a steering motion with two hands. Tracker nodded agreement—the garage was their best approach. The two men walked the perimeter of the grounds until they were next to the garage, which was set up in an unusual configuration: a double door in between two singles.

Cross spread his legs and cupped his hands, interlocking the fingers. Tracker put one foot into the cup and drove up as Cross heaved with both hands. He caught the top of the fence and jackknifed over in one motion. Cross stayed where he was, a silenced semi-auto in his hand.

They waited a full two minutes. Nothing stirred.

Cross handed his pistol to Tracker through the fence. Then he climbed over the fence himself, not as smoothly as the Indian, or as quickly. Tracker led the way across the grounds, moving behind the big garage toward the house. He spotted a fieldstone patio, clean, bare of any furniture. Only a screen door stood between the two prowlers and the inside of the house.

Tracker looked a question at Cross, who shrugged in response. Then he hooked a finger through the door handle and tugged lightly. The door held. A pair of wire cutters materialized in Cross's hands. The screen door yielded without further resistance.

The men entered the house: Tracker first, then Cross, the silenced pistol back in his hand. The first floor was empty, unfurnished. On the second floor, they passed a staircase with a special elevator to carry a wheelchair. Whoever lived in that house wasn't some mere collector, or even a merchant—he was something more than that. Worse than that.

At the top of the next floor, Tracker signaled "Stop!" He held up his hand, cupped an ear, motioned Cross to step closer.

"I want protection," a deep, metallic voice said. "Exactly as I was promised. Protection. Which means I can't stay here. I don't have mobility, but I have to move. Do you understand me? Out of the country. And it has to be now. Right now!"

Silence. Broken only by the sound of constricted breathing as the speaker listened to the other end of a phone call. Then:

"Perhaps I haven't made myself clear. You have the keys to the Audi—it's already rigged to transport me. Remember, it's only you two little worms on those tapes, not me. Whoever killed Holtstraf, they know. It feels like there's a Santería priestess somewhere in this. And those people, they're all insane.

"So I'm getting out. And you're coming with me—I've got enough cash so we can all get out of the country and live like kings. But it has to be now! Either you both show up here ready to go in ninety minutes . . . That's right, ninety minutes, no longer!

"Listen very closely: if you don't show, I've got other options. You don't, neither one of you. And if I have to use any of my other options, I'm going to be sending a little present to the FBI."

The sound of a connection being severed. Harsh whistle-breathing. Wheels rolling. Refrigerator opening. Closing. Something poured into a glass.

Cross and Tracker exchanged nods, then slipped their stocking masks off before they stepped into the room where the voice had come from.

"Urghh . . . ?" The speaker looked like a random assembly of body parts, with a mouth no bigger than most nostrils. But there was no mistaking the vertically linear–iris eyes of a born predator.

"Shut up," Cross told him, his voice as calm and detached as a 911 operator's. "You got something we want. Here's the equation: You give it to us and we're gone. You don't, then you are."

The creature pointed to a console with his one complete arm, a handless appendage that ended in a pointed, bony stub. When Cross nodded his understanding, the creature tapped some buttons:

"I don't . . ." came out of a muted speaker, in a human voice.

"One more time," Cross said. "You got money stashed here. We want it. Now."

More taps: "You must be . . ."

"Mistaken? We heard you call those two over here—you weren't lying about cash on hand. You didn't give them much time, so we don't have much time, either, understand? You remember what happened to your pal? Holtstraf, or whatever the hell he called himself? He didn't tell us what we wanted to know, so we pinned him to the wallpaper. We never waste time with torture. And you, you can always get more money—probably with just a couple of key-strokes. But you'd have to be alive to do it."

A series of rapid key-taps. "How do I know you won't kill me anyway?" came out of the speaker, now in an eerily calm tone, two registers deeper than before. Tracker's eyes picked up a large knob on the console—*Voice adjuster, some form of harmonizer,* he thought.

"We were here to kill you, you'd already be dead. We're professionals. Just like you. You know there's always a cost of doing business, and we're only after hard cash. So . . . what's it gonna be?"

Rapid key-taps: "I'll show—"

"No. You'll tell us," Cross interrupted, nodding at Tracker, who now held the silenced semi-auto leveled at the creature's protruding forehead, which bulged like a shelf over his eyes. "This is all about time now. You tell us, you live. You don't, you die. Your pals are on the way over right now. If you make us kill you, we get more time to look for the cash, see?"

The creature's pointed arm tapped rapidly: "In a suitcase. An alligator suitcase. In the master bedroom. On the next floor up. In the closet. Once you see I'm not lying, then maybe we could . . ."

"Take a look," Cross said. The Indian handed the pistol back to him and vanished.

The creature reached toward the console.

Cross held a finger to his lips, keeping the pistol carefully trained on its target.

The Indian came down the stairs, the suitcase in his hand. He placed it across the creature's lap.

"You open it," Cross said, standing back a few feet.

The creature popped the hinges with the protruding bony stub of his arm. Inside was cash. Carefully banded and shrink-wrapped. The bills showing were all hundreds. Cross thumbed open a box cutter and slit one package. Bills tumbled out. He held one up to the light, rubbed it hard between thumb and forefinger. Satisfied, he turned to the creature.

"Where's the rest of it?"

"There's three-quarters of a million dollars there!" the man in the wheelchair tapped out on the console. "That's all I have in—"

Cross aimed the silenced pistol and shot . . . whatever it was . . . between its unblinking eyes. Watched the huge head loll on the useless body. The shot made a soft, wet splatting sound.

"Ready?"

By way of response, Tracker hefted the suitcase. Cross hit the cellular phone. "Now" was all he said.

• • •

The two men went out the way they had entered.

This time, Cross was first over the fence. The suitcase wouldn't fit between the bars—Tracker needed both hands to swing it back and forth until he built up sufficient momentum, then heaved it over the top. By the time they reached the street, they could hear the heavily muffled tremors of a rapidly approaching vehicle.

The Shark Car pulled in, its trunk open and flapping in the night air.

Tracker threw the suitcase inside, slammed the trunk shut. Rhino jumped out, landing with a lightness that belied his weight. He dropped to his knees, the Uzi up and searching for targets. He was the last man back inside; then the Shark Car took off.

"You think those other two freaks are on their way?" Tracker asked Cross.

"Can't tell. Doesn't matter; they're sure as hell not calling the cops."

Everyone in the car heard it at the same time—the scream of tortured tires. Something was coming. Coming fast.

"Stay smooth," Cross cautioned. "It could be Law, could be a drunk driver, could be rich kids. . . . Everybody easy, now."

As the Shark Car entered a long sweeping left-hand curve, another car charged toward them. A white Audi Q7. Buddha suddenly stomped the gas, wrenching the wheel to the left and jerking the handbrake. The Shark Car fishtailed into a perfect bootlegger's turn as the Audi came past.

Buddha had his night-beaded pistol out, resting the barrel on his forearm over the windowsill. A string of killer bees popped out, stitching a neat row across the other car's windshield.

The Audi almost rolled, then righted itself just before it smashed head-on into a parked car. The impact was magnified by metal-on-metal shrieks into a suburban night long accustomed to silence.

Lights flashed on in houses. The Shark Car skidded to a stop. "Box it out!" Cross yelled.

Rhino and Princess rolled out of their separate back doors. Rhino took up his position with the Uzi, guarding the flank, as Princess rushed to the other car, waving his Nitro Express pistol. Cross wrenched a shotgun from under the dash and charged the wrecked car. He fired both barrels simultaneously, whirled, and ran in the same motion. The gas tank of the Audi exploded into a throbbing fireball.

That explosion was a kid's cap gun compared with the rocket-launch blast taking the top off the house where a dead thing had spent his life. Accounts varied, but the Fire Marshal's office later reported the structure had been ripped by what they called a "staged series" of shocks. Blocks of C-4 had apparently been placed on the top floor and threaded downward. When triggered, the charged substance had worked its way down, only to be met in the middle by an equally powerful force climbing its way up.

As sirens ripped the night, the Shark Car purred smoothly along, putting distance in the bank.

"What was in those shells?" Tracker asked.

"White phosphorus," Cross told him. "Instant fire. The cops'll be along any minute. . . ."

"I'm sorry, boss," Buddha said, no trace of regret in his voice. "I thought of what they were gonna do to So Long and I just . . ."

"You know the rules," Cross said quietly.

For several slug-slow seconds, the car was quiet. Even Princess kept still, as if waiting for something he wasn't sure would actually make an appearance.

"You know what?" Buddha broke the silence. "My share, so what? It was worth every dime. Not like I'd see most of it, anyway—that wife of mine could squeeze a nickel until it spit up quarters."

"ALL THAT was years ago," Cross told Tiger. "And that . . . thing . . . it's not like he could come back from where we sent him."

"Then . . . why this business with Hemp and Ace? And where does Mural Girl come in?"

"I don't know."

"None of it makes any sense."

"It makes sense to someone," Cross said softly. "And one is all it takes."

"IT'S BURNING *bright* now," the Amazon whispered.

"I know. I can feel it. But I'm just . . . sitting here. Not even . . . not even *thinking*. So whatever it is, it's not warning me off. Or pushing me harder. It . . ."

"It . . . what? Doesn't make *sense*?" Tiger filled in the blank end of the gang leader's sentence, her voice still at whisper volume despite the sarcasm.

Cross opened his left hand and lit a cigarette from the flame.

Three drags and out.

"The only person I ever knew who was . . ."

Another cigarette. On the second drag, the tiny blue brand was throbbing. On the third and last, it flickered.

"Tiger, I got a problem. One only you can take care of."

"I already knew *that*."

"Stop playing around. I'm serious."

"And you think I'm *not*—?" The deadly beauty cut her own words in midstream. "What do you need?"

"I need to talk to Rhino. Talk to him *alone*. There's only one way to keep Princess out of the conversation."

"Keep your eye on what you're missing," she said, throwing an exaggerated wiggle at the man behind the sawhorsed desk as she hip-slapped her way through the ball-bearing curtain.

LESS THAN a minute later, she stepped back through the curtain, this time courteously held open by Rhino.

"Anything else?" she asked Cross.

"No."

"Well, I'm not going to sit around looking beautiful when

I could be having fun," she purred. "Princess, want to go shopping? Just you and me?"

"And we can take—?"

"Sweetie? Of *course*," she told the mass of muscle. "We wouldn't leave him behind, would we?"

"No! You hear that, Sweetie? We're going with Tiger! I need some new—"

"What*ever* you need, Cross will pay for it," she said, cutting him off. Turning to the gang leader: "Right?"

Cross nodded expressionlessly.

"Come on, honey. This place is gloomy enough without listening to *him*. I once asked Cross if he knew any jokes. You know what he said?"

"Nothing?" Princess guessed.

"That'd be about right," Tiger said over her shoulder as she walked past the desk, Princess and his homicidal hound following close behind.

"WHY ALL this?" Rhino asked.

"Because I just figured something out. And it was nothing I'd want Princess to hear."

"I already knew that last part."

"Yeah," Cross said, lighting another smoke. "I know you did. But there's something I *don't* know." Another pull on his cigarette briefly lit his shadowy face. "Why did you go back?"

"Back?"

"As soon as you looked over those photos of him we Minoxed, I could see it in your face. You went back to the house where that thing lived. Years ago. Long after the Circle of Skulls was done."

"How could you know that?" Rhino said.

"Because I know you. We go back together as far as you can probably remember. You couldn't leave it where *we* did. What if whoever gave birth to you had treated you the same as him? Would you have . . . I don't know. . . . Would your life have turned out the same?"

"Yes. I had to know," the behemoth admitted. "I don't remember much. About being a little kid. I know I was . . . I was intelligent. I was big, but not anything like I am now, not when I was first locked up. So why would they have just . . . thrown me away? *His* parents didn't. They did everything for him they possibly could, but . . . he still turned out too vicious to leave alive."

"You're saying what? He was born bad?"

"I don't believe that. I never believed that. You don't, either, Cross. None of us do. That's why we've got a right to hate them."

"Hate them *all*."

"Yes," the huge man agreed, again cosigning the prove-in for the Cross crew. "We're criminals, but not like . . . not like *they* are. Even Buddha, he'd never hurt someone just for . . . entertainment."

"You went back to see if you could find anything that would . . . ?"

"Actually, I never went back to that house—not really—just drove by once. How could I search that place? I knew the little bit that was left of it would be wrapped in yellow tape for weeks. And probably watched for months after that. That . . . thing, he wouldn't be there. Even if he had been, somehow . . . even if he had answered any question I asked, how would I know if he was telling the truth?"

"What *did* you do, then?"

"I went back over his life. At least, that was the plan. It wasn't *that* long ago—every public record from that era is databased. So I just walked into them—all that 'security' is a joke. Even for the places where they keep stuff that's supposedly not for public viewing."

"So what did you—?"

"He never existed," Rhino said, his squeaky voice coming out like the rumble of a diesel's exhaust pipes, as it always did when he spoke very quietly. "His parents, there was no child born to their marriage."

"You mean the cops went back in and—"

"No. Not a wipe job. It's a good thing you took those pictures of him—it's the only proof that he was real. I don't know what kind of system he had rigged, but I guess he needed to rearm the safety switches to keep it functioning. Push a button every day, maybe.

"We'll never know. But the whole top of that house blew off. Straight up, like a rocket. It only rose maybe fifty yards, and then it disintegrated. Something like that, Homeland Security would trump every other agency, and they've got the best forensic tools in the world. But none of that would matter. Whatever was still there was as close to atomized as that glass from the Twin Towers."

"That had to be one of those 'options' he was telling the freaks who made the gang-rape tapes he had."

"Probably the only one. He could never survive outside

that one environment, the one that was built for him. No way, no matter *what* he was."

"So how did you find out anything?"

"It was those pictures of him. Something like that, how could you hide it? But no matter where I searched, there were no deletions, no gaps. No place to start, so I couldn't move forward.

"I found the records of his parents easy enough, and with those I could go back as far as I wanted. Married a little late, but nowhere near late enough to explain . . . him. The father was just turning thirty, his wife was a couple of years younger. If they'd tried to have a child, some fertility treatments, maybe . . . But there was nothing like that. And nothing to show anything went wrong with a birth, either."

"But how could you make something—whatever he was— how could you make him disappear? What about the hospital admission record?"

"*That* was what got wiped. All I could learn was just that. Whatever he was, he *never* was. Never born, never lived, never died."

"You're saying . . ."

"The father was a whiz kid. Scholarships right through his M.B.A. All the best schools. Not a blue-blood: he had to earn his way. The mother, now, she was born to the manor. The one her father had inherited from *his* father. All the way back—DAR throughout the maternal line. At first I thought, okay, his father had the brains, his mother had the contacts, how could you mix a better formula for success?"

"He was a stockbroker?"

"Better. Capital management. He was good at it. Fast-tracked to upper echelons, other investment banks always looking to poach him. By the time he died, he was probably worth a few hundred *million*. Money like that, it can buy . . .".

"Anything that's for sale. And everything is."

"Yes. The parents, they had a will. If they 'perished in a common disaster,' the money would be split among the only two children anyone thought they had. But they still left plenty to . . . him. That piece went into some kind of blind trust. Multilayered, all offshore. Plus the house. So all that . . . all that thing they left behind had to do when he wanted something . . . or someone . . . paid, was to press a button."

"That doesn't sound like they were . . . I don't know, cruel to him."

"You mean, like, beat him, or starved him, or . . . ?"

"Yeah."

"There's worse things than that," said the mammoth who had been chained to a wheelchair when the mega-tranquilizers started to lose their hold over a monster who seemed to feed on them. "They never *acknowledged* him. I don't know what kind of pre-birth screenings they had back then—they weren't fashionable, the way they are now. So they probably didn't really have any way of knowing. Not until they saw him. But then they'd know. Right at that moment, they'd know."

"They wouldn't be the only ones," Cross said. "The doctor, the hospital, the—"

"All for sale. And they *had* the money. I learned something else. Even stillborn births are recorded."

"Just another record they could make disappear?"

"Yes. But the mother, after that pregnancy, she was too delicate to take another risk. Or maybe they made up some other story—we'll never know. What we know is that they adopted two children. Newborns. A boy and a girl, less than two years apart. They grew up and slipped into that same river their parents rafted on. I doubt they even knew who . . . what was living just above their heads. That house, it was big enough to keep him isolated. All they had to do was seal off the top floors."

"Why didn't his parents just—?"

"Kill him? *Way* too much risk. People like that, they know, if they reach out to our world for a job, they're setting themselves up for permanent blackmail. In their world, they were safe. Any of the doctors, they'd be risking their own licenses if the truth came out. The hospital? It was a small, private place. Funded by a foundation. I don't have to say more, do I?"

"No. And what would they get out of it, anyway? Remember, those kind of people, they need children for more than just their image—the line has to continue, too. Probably how that . . . thing was created in the first place."

"Fertility drugs?" Rhino speculated.

"My money would be on inbreeding, brother. That maternal line, I'd put serious money on some of those girls' fathers being their grandfathers, too. Plenty of ancient dynasties were— *Damn!*"

"What?"

"My . . . face. That thing they put there, that little blue symbol, it's gotten hot before, but this time it felt like a damn plasma cutter."

"Do you think . . . ?"

"I don't know what to think. It'd all be guesses, anyway."

"I WONDER if they knew."

"Knew what, brother?" Cross asked Rhino. The searing pain below his right eye was gone, but the tiny blue symbol still throbbed as if alive.

"Knew how much it . . . how much it hurts, to be just . . . erased. To have a child and not admit he even exists. I used to think about that. They hurt me. In the institutions, I mean. You know about a lot of that, Cross. But what you couldn't know was how the people who gave birth to me, how *they* could hurt me. More than any torture. And they *had* to know."

"But if—"

"I don't mean they had to actually *witness* anything. But . . . you know how everyone's talking about 'emotional abuse' now, like it's some new discovery? How many boys did you meet when you were first locked up who thought their middle name was 'Stupid'?

"Sure," the behemoth answered his own question. "But this was even worse. To know that the same people who . . . created you, they wouldn't even admit you existed? That's this 'emotional abuse' thing, all right. Weaponized emotional abuse."

"You're talking about . . . what? *Your* parents?"

"I guess I am. I must be. To them, I must have been like some form of . . . him. I mean, I never knew what *they* knew. I never knew if I had brothers and sisters. If I had—"

"You *found* family, Rhino. Maybe I'm nothing to be all that proud of, but I've been your brother ever since—"

"I know," the mammoth said. "And I couldn't have a better one, Cross. You think I don't know what everyone thought? That you'd played me into helping you escape from that prison? But when you said, 'I'll be back for you, brother,' those words, they kept me alive.

"You're nothing to be proud of? That's not true. You did something nobody else ever did in my whole life. It wasn't just that you kept your word, or even that you rescued me. You showed me how to . . ."

Cross felt the tiny brand below his eye burning again, but now it was intermittent, not steady. Slow-pulsing. Suddenly his mind made a connection. Back to his first "interview" in the government capture-van.

"*That's* why you took Princess," the urban mercenary said. "He was—"

"Yes," Rhino said, quietly. "He was *me*. He didn't want to be in that combat cage any more than I wanted to be in that wheelchair. We were both strapped in. I couldn't leave him. . . ."

"I get it," the gang boss said. Thinking: *That's the way it really works. You pay your debts when they come due. You keep your promises. A promise, it's the same as a threat—a rep that you always keep your word, that's the only way anyone ever takes your threats seriously.*

"Buddha said there were five votes before. But it's really just the three of us, isn't it?" Rhino said, very softly. "We're family, all of us. I know that. But . . . Ace, he's got Sharyn and his children; Buddha, he's got So Long.

"Sure, I know. And they're always fighting. But imagine if those two *weren't* together. Now it's like they . . . mesh. If it wasn't for that, if they were operating on their own . . ."

The man with the bull's-eye tattoo on the back of his hand went quiet for a long moment. Then he said, "You're right. They don't have limits—there's nothing either of them wouldn't do. So Long's *got* money—but she's a grafter in her heart, so she keeps on scheming and stealing. The same way Buddha's a shooter. He wasn't with us, he'd still be working merc jobs, somewhere. They each . . . I don't know how to put it, exactly. It's like they found a reason to live besides themselves."

Rhino made a snorting sound: "To hear Buddha talk, the only reason he's not divorced is that So Long would end up with all his money. But remember when that Circle of Skulls gang had her targeted, how he went crazy?"

"Yeah, he did. But he never thought we wouldn't back his play, not for a second. You and me, anyway. Princess, he'd do whatever you did, so it comes out the same. Tracker, he's the same as we are . . . but he's got his own tribe. Tiger, too."

Cross lit a cigarette. Took a drag. Closed his eyes. Realized the pulsating brand had gone quiet. "There's just one difference, Rhino. Just one, between us and those two. One difference, but it's too far apart for either side to bridge."

Rhino said nothing, waiting.

"That difference . . . it's . . . it's the tribes. *Their* tribes. Their tribes were there before they were—they were born into them. But not us. There was nothing for us to be born into. We had to make our own.

"They call us a gang, and we know who the OGs are, like Buddha is always saying. But what if we're not a gang? What if we're the first members of a tribe?"

"Tribes were created by geography," the huge man responded. "Climate, actually. Africans are a different race from Scandinavians. That's all evolution is: successful adaptation to climate."

"But weren't *we* all born into the same climate, too, Rhino? Ace killed the man who was beating his mother. I don't know if she was some low-rent whore or a woman who did what she had to do to get food on the table . . . but Ace, he loved her. You don't know who your mother even *was*. Or your father. Or anything else, really. So maybe we weren't *born* in the same place, but we grew up in the same place. Forget that Tigris-Euphrates stuff: for the three of us, for me, you, and Ace, the Cradle of Civilization was behind bars.

"You know where I ran across Buddha. So Long, she was, I don't know exactly, more like a girl than a grown woman. But a *hard* girl. She'd've had to be to survive in that hell.

"I don't know how it happened, but by the time I ran across Buddha, she and him, they were already together. He didn't tell me right away—she was back in one of those foul caves, and Buddha was . . . watching out for her. She was safe in there, but she couldn't have *stayed* there, not without food and water.

"See, brother? Different cages, but the same bars. Down south, where you grabbed Princess? Just as we were pulling out, one of the guards called out to me. He was really torn up, pieces of him leaking out. So much pain he could hardly speak. He asked me to put him down. The thing that really stuck with me was that he spoke English—not even an accent.

"I saw you already had Princess over your shoulder, so we made a deal, real quick. The guard, he tells me what I want to know; I give him what he wants. I picked up his pistol—it was only a couple of feet away from his hand, but he couldn't reach it—and said I'd hand it back to him, told him he could make his own decision. Treated him like a *man*, showed respect.

"So he spit out answers. He said Princess was captured when he was just a kid. He was a *little* kid, but he was in the jungle by himself. And he almost tore his way out of the nets before they could get him chained."

"I think that must be true," Rhino said, soberly. "He doesn't remember much, just being snatched up by some army. They started training him for cage fighting as far back as he can go in his head. I never really asked him . . . what difference would it make now?—but . . ."

"What?"

"What about you? Do you know who your—?"

"Yeah," the icy man said, closing the subject forever.

TIGER SUDDENLY slid into the back of the office.

The best Cross could manage was "Really?"

"Princess, you know how he—"

"Aren't they *amazing*?" the massively muscled child half-shouted. "Tiger didn't want them. I mean, she *did* want them,

I know she did. Maybe they don't go right with her outfit *now*, but they're so beautiful. . . ."

Even Rhino was transfixed by the thigh-high boots the Amazon was wearing in place of her usual spike heels.

"Are those real alligator?"

"*Albino* alligator!" Princess boomed, excitedly pointing to the red, blue, green, and colorless glittering stones covering the boots. "And those're all real, too."

"You didn't find anything like that on Michigan Avenue."

"Don't be silly!" the Amazon admonished Cross. "Princess took me to this little shop. In the back of some graystone building in Andersonville. The guys there—"

"It was a *surprise*!"

"It was to *me*, no doubt."

"Oh, they've been ready for months," Princess said proudly. "I got your shoe size from—"

"Oh, honey, you can't tell a woman's size from her shoes. The more expensive they are, the more the people who make them will lie about them."

"But you'd never lie, Tiger."

"Not to *you*, sweetheart. But I'm not talking about some salesgirl lying; I'm talking about the shoes."

"What?" Rhino interjected. The absurdity of shoe leather's participating in fraud was causing an overload inside his logic-driven mind.

"Ah, don't any of you know *anything* about women?" the Amazon said, parking herself on a corner of Cross's desk. "Look, girls don't want to admit they have big feet, ever. So, the best places, they'll call a size eight a six and a half when they're putting the shoes together."

"Why would they care?" Princess asked, sincerely.

"It's just . . . vanity. But it's men who *make* them that way. You think it's easy walking around in high heels all day, like women have to do for business? I don't care if she's an executive or a waitress, flats are out. And the higher the heel, the harder it is on your whole body."

"But you always—"

"Baby, I'm different. My spikes *are* spikes. Watch!" The Amazon grabbed one of the shoes she'd obviously taken off to put on the boots—lipstick-red four-inchers with black soles—and snapped the heel off in one smooth motion. Her hand flashed. A block of wood next to Rhino suddenly sported a new decoration—a deeply driven steel shaft.

"Wow!"

"I practice all the time, honey. I don't want to run out of ammo," she told Princess, patting the two slim throwing-daggers she wore strapped to one muscular thigh. "And I hate guns; they're so noisy."

"Uh-huh," was all Cross said.

Tiger flashed her eyes in response. With the Amazon, every facial expression was an invitation or a threat: you took your guess . . . and proceeded at your own risk.

"You know what those cost?" Princess erupted, clearly not about to be shoved off-topic by practicalities like self-defense or intentional homicide.

Cross shrugged. Not "Who cares?" but "Who could guess?"

"Nothing! They wouldn't take a penny! Ask Tiger."

"True enough," she verified. "They said it took almost three months just to make them. 'Your gift to her; our gift to you,' that guy with the thick glasses said."

Cross nodded. It made sense now. Princess was a legendary figure in the gay community. Once he discovered that wearing makeup would make some nasty humans brave, it became his trademark. Some knew, and always greeted the huge child with a fake-friendly wave. Others . . . well, Ace probably put it best when he said, "Some fools gonna *stay* fools, 'cause they ain't gonna live long enough to be nothing else."

But Tiger wouldn't be put off the scent. "These fit *perfectly*, baby. How could you . . . ? I mean, we've been shopping plenty of times, but you heard what I just said about shoe sizes, right?"

"Oh, pul-leeze," Princess said, in unconscious imitation of the staff at the leather-crafting shop where he'd gone to order the custom boots for the Amazon. "They asked me, how did I know? I told them I wasn't sure . . . and they told me to bring them one of Tiger's shoes. One she *wore*, I mean. I told them I couldn't make the surprise work if I had to ask her for one."

His shaved head rotated slowly on his neck as he turned to Tiger. "So . . . remember when we went to that place where they always have shoes you like? I carried the packages out. When you were paying the parking guy, I copied down *everything* from one of the new pairs. What it said on the box and all. Just like they said."

"You are one smart cookie," Tiger said.

Princess blushed.

RHINO CAUGHT the hand gesture from Cross.

"You're going out, right?" he said to Princess.

"Me and Tiger" was the answer. "But first I got to change clothes. There's this club Tiger said she'd—"

"I guess tonight's as good as any other," the Amazon agreed. "I've got to change first myself. And we are *not* going in that insane truck of yours!"

"But Sweetie could get all cramped in the back of your car. I mean, he was in there for a long time when we picked up your boots. It's not—"

"Oh, Sweetie can come in with us."

"Into a club?"

"Into *this* club."

"Well . . ."

"What, honey? Everyone will love him, I promise."

"Can he wear his party chain?"

"Why not?"

"Hear that, Sweetie? You're gonna *represent*. Isn't that great?"

Whether the black-masked Akita understood he would finally get to wear the heavy rope of 22-karat gold that once adorned the neck of a gangstah drug merchant who had grossly overestimated the loyalty of his personal posse was doubtful . . . but Princess certainly believed he did. After all, Sweetie had been present when that posse leader still *had* a head.

"**I UNDERSTAND** why you waited for an organic opening to call us together," Tracker said. "So now you have Princess away. And, as you said, this creature had never tried to attack

Princess, even when he was alive. Tiger was not . . . known to him."

"He's not back from the dead," Cross said. "Whoever's trying to get us out in the open now, it's not him. But it all *connects* to him, somehow. All we know is that someone tried to get Ace to move on Hemp."

"By spooking him," Rhino said, very softly. "The same way that . . . thing spooked Buddha years ago, even though he didn't mean to. And with Ace, it worked. We just got lucky."

"Lucky? We had Hemp tracked from the—"

"Yes, I know," the mammoth whispered. "But Ace was going off the rails. He doesn't do research—he'd just start shooting until he ran out of targets. And in *that* neighborhood . . ."

"Okay. Let's say that's what would have happened. It *didn't* happen, though. And it doesn't explain why Ace got targeted."

"There is a tribal name for the descendants of those who did not survive a battle," Tracker said. When he added nothing to his words, Cross looked over at him:

"Which is—?"

"Enemy," the Indian said, gravely. "This is why no war ever ends."

"Tell that to the—"

"Who?" Tracker cut off the gang's leader mid-sentence. "It doesn't matter what words you use, the answer will be the same. The Japanese, did we end all their thoughts of vengeance with Hiroshima and Nagasaki? It is true, we do business with them on a colossal scale. But why do they celebrate every time a survivor of that war appears out of a cave in the islands? A hero, such a man. *He* never surrendered. A samurai to his core. Worthy of his nation's greatest respect."

"Not a samurai," Rhino argued. "For a soldier, his master would be the Emperor. And it was Hirohito himself who signed the surrender papers."

"And never stood trial for war crimes," Cross added.

"Ah, you confuse facts with truth," Tracker said, almost sadly. "Did you miss the tone of my voice when I said 'we' had won that war? Do you not understand that your tribe and mine were never one? We . . . all of us who once walked this country before you 'discovered' it . . . we were not brought into a partnership; we barely survived attempted genocide.

"And ours was a culture more accustomed to war than *any* of yours. The Vikings were a warrior culture, but they fought wars of conquest. Genghis Khan, the Crusades—go back as far as you like, they are the same.

"But not us. We call ourselves 'the People' now. Now, when it is too late. Before any man with white skin took a single step onto what is now America, we fought wars . . . wars among *ourselves*. Not for conquest—nomads care nothing for property. We fought as *tribes*.

"Was that better? No, it was not. And look at the price we paid for that embedded insanity! Why should an Apache hate a Comanche? Why would a Hutu hate a Tutsi?"

Tracker paused, as if waiting for an answer. Or a challenge. When neither came, he continued: "In this country, people of color are all ranked below those *without* color. Black people will say this is because they were brought here as slaves. But who *captured* those slaves? No European ever entered the deep jungle and dragged out captives. The human cargo was already imprisoned, awaiting the arrival of the men with . . . with whatever the Africans on their western coast valued.

"This was acceptable. It was acceptable because, in Africa, color meant nothing, but tribe meant *everything*. Is that not the message of your brand, Cross?"

As if in response, the tiny blue symbol under Cross's right eye burned. "But only I can see it. And Tiger, too. It is not visible to you, is it, Rhino? Even in this darkness, you see nothing."

"I don't," the mammoth said. "Even when Cross told me where to look, I saw nothing."

"Tiger and I, we are tribal. You are not. Nor is Buddha. Nor Ace."

"A family is a smaller unit than a tribe. Than *any* tribe."

"You call yourselves family," Tracker said, holding up his hand to cut off any response. "And because you do, you are. I accept this. But there is more to know."

"The Simbas," Cross said. "Like when we were first hired—"

"I was *part* of that team," Tracker reminded the other two men, "although my connection to you was not something those government people needed to know. Tiger felt the same. Neither of us have what the world would call a 'family.' Both of us come from what the world would call a 'tribe.'

"And that is a tribal brand on you, Cross. It was not your birthright—it came to you in that prison basement."

"Then . . ."

"The brand is a message for me. And for Tiger. We both have lineage. Long lineage. An ancestral trail that could be followed back to its original seed. Neither of us have renounced our own . . . but neither of us have ever been put to the choice."

"You would be with us?"

"Am I not?" Tracker answered Rhino. "Have I not been, ever since . . . ?"

"Tiger, too?"

"Surely, you know this, Cross. Whatever your . . . feelings for her, or hers for you, can there be a doubt that she would step between Princess and *any* threat? Even one coming from her own people?"

"You're saying . . . ?"

"I am saying the truth, Cross. You call Ace your brother, and brothers are what you have been to one another. Rhino was your choice. Princess was his. It goes on, does it not? Say I am not your brother."

"I can't do that."

"Tiger is not your sister. She could not be. Your code would never allow this, I understand. Not for the same reason you exclude Buddha's woman, but no less the truth. Whoever . . . *what*ever placed its brand on you, it will come to all of us. From family comes tribe."

"And all tribes—"

"*No!*" The Indian's voice sliced the air. "All tribes are not fated to war with each other. There is no Great Book in which this is written—this is a Law of Nature. The human race is *one* race. We would be gone from this planet had we not mixed our blood. Somewhere, somehow, sometime—it does not change the result. We invented different gods because we could not explain what we knew to be true. Rain, storms, snow. Dryness so pure that there is not enough oxygen for most of us. Thunder, lightning . . . those are weather. And weather is within climate. So the nomads—"

"He couldn't *leave* his climate!" Rhino's voice rose to a high-pitched squeak. "It was as artificial as an aquarium, one even a whale couldn't escape. But he could reach out past it. . . ."

"That Circle of Skulls crew," Cross said. "Whatever that . . . thing was, he wasn't a rapist. He wasn't a dealer. He didn't need money. But he made that whole rape-tape gang. *Created* them."

"I . . . I think I understand him." Rhino's voice dropped back to a whisper. "They made him . . . not exist. But he proved them wrong. All of them. Only one thing drives a person that hard."

"Always the *same* thing, brother," Cross said. "We always knew this. Somehow. But it's just like Tracker said. . . ."

"I've seen it ever since you escaped from that prison basement," the mammoth suddenly admitted. "I didn't want to say anything—I kept thinking it would go away on its own. That blue mark. It's flashing now, like a signal."

"A warning signal," Tracker added, unsurprised. "That creature we destroyed years ago, we should have known. He would never have gone without leaving behind the one thing we must all fear now."

"Descendants of descendants," Cross said. "Whatever evil he created in some—and that's what he must have done with that rape-tape crew—he could create in others."

"He *has*," Rhino said. "That's why I can see your . . . brand. It's *letting* me see it."

Cross opened his left hand. A flame sparked in his palm.

The man with the bull's-eye tattoo on the back of his other hand didn't reach for a cigarette. He watched the flame, feeling Rhino and Tracker move closer to its campfire.

⊕

"TOO MUCH to be coincidence," Cross said, speaking very quietly. "Same method used twice, that wouldn't qualify. But maybe it wasn't."

"I'm not following you," Rhino said.

"I'm not sure I'm following my own damn self," the gang's leader responded sourly. "Years ago, Buddha was lured out because of a threat to So Long, and we're looking at it like the same game was played with Ace. But there's really more differences than similarities, right?"

"I believe that is true," Tracker said. "No matter who was involved in that ugliness with So Long, she would have been a random target. A woman of color living in a white neighborhood . . . what else would they need?"

"Buddha's not the same as Ace," Rhino responded. "No question but that Ace would respond were his wife to be the victim of a rape. But Hemp sent an assassin to *kill* Sharyn. Whoever was responsible had to know . . . something. Not who Ace is—that's well known in Gangland, probably even to the police. But the house, that is *not* known. Ace would never endanger his wife and children. Remember, the authorities have his name from when he was locked up. Supposedly a juvenile record, so it would be sealed . . . but that's a joke. I found it in their database easily enough.

"But Hemp couldn't have gotten information on that house from Sharyn's name on any marriage license. She

bought the house under her maiden name—a cash pur-
chase, so no mortgage. And *she's* not on any public record,
like Section Eight or Welfare. Her birth certificate wouldn't
show in Chicago. She purchases whatever she needs—a car,
furniture—but those are all cash transactions."

"Pays taxes, too," Cross added. "In business for herself.
Professional ghostwriter, and the terms of her contracts
always include keeping her employer's name a secret. Hell,
you know all about that, Rhino—you were the one who set
it up."

"Her 'agent' pays her by check," Rhino's voice rumbled,
as it did when he spoke quietly. "And he takes his fifteen
percent off the top. He couldn't say who the actual writers
are even if he wanted to—he doesn't know. All the contracts
are close-ended: any other money the books make—a movie
deal, foreign rights, all of that—Sharyn's not even entitled to
know, much less take a share."

"It's worked perfectly for a long time," Cross said, opening his left hand—this time to light another cigarette. "And
no one's taken a shot at Sharyn all these years. Her kids,
they've all gone to private schools, sure . . . but they never
walked around with bodyguards."

"So, for this to work, Hemp had to have found out not
just where Sharyn lives, but that she was married to Ace. And
that all her children are his," Tracker said, thoughtfully.

"Yeah," Cross said, slowly. "Buddha and Ace each being
smoked out, those don't *have* to be connected. All that's in
common is a threat designed to flush out a target. But with
Buddha, it could have been no more than it looked like—a
bad accident. That thing we killed, he could have been in the
rape-tape business just to test his ability to pull off something

like that without ever leaving that cage his parents kept him locked up in. We'll never know.

"Anyway, we used the same tactic ourselves, didn't we? On him, I mean. Princess harpooning that dirtbag, that would spook anyone. And it worked. But we never thought to stop and ask him anything. We didn't have much time, and we wanted the money. Remember, all we have is what kicked *us* off . . . that letter So Long got. Not a rape, the *threat* of one."

"So . . ."

"That's right, Rhino. Time for another talk with Mike Mac."

THE RUNNING track circling the football field had been kept in good repair.

The same could not be said about the man slowly churning out lap after lap, not increasing or decreasing speed but doggedly determined to finish whatever number of circuits he believed he should be doing. *What do those doctors know, anyway?* So he had a torn meniscus behind one knee, and they'd have to replace the other hip at some point. The titanium implanted in his forearm hadn't stopped him from competing last year, had it?

"You always look the same," he said, as he slowed to a gradual stop in the grandstand shadows.

"Clean living," Cross replied.

"I wouldn't know about that," the detective said. "What I meant was, you look like you always do."

"Uh-huh." Cross nodded, lighting a cigarette, as if

to acknowledge that the cop's statement hadn't been a compliment.

"Last time I saw you and Rhino here—"

"The same thing."

"Are you serious? That rape gang was put out of business a long time ago. All we found were a couple of charred bodies in the wreckage of a car in Winnetka, of all places. And right across from it was a beautiful limestone mansion. 'Was' is right—a cracked foundation was all there was left. If anyone had been alive inside when that explosion went off, they weren't a half-second later.

"It was a big case. Got checked out every way you can imagine. The owners of that house, they'd been done in by a drunk driver years before. A teenager . . ."

"Sure. No motive there. By the time the place went bang, the former owner's kids were somewhere off the Bahamas, on their yacht. They'd left *their* kids in some boarding school. No live-in staff at the house."

"Yeah," the detective said, drawing out the word. "You seem pretty well informed."

"I read the papers."

"You make some headlines, too, the way I figure it."

"Me? Come on, Mac; you know how much I love publicity."

"I know how much you love C-4. Or whatever new witch's brew you've cooked up lately."

"Not me."

"Actually, that's true enough, I guess. Buddha's always blowing things up, but his style is more RPG than plastique. Likes to admire his work, huh?"

"I'm not following you."

"Yeah, I know. That's just me, talking in riddles again, right?"

"I was just about to—"

"Ah, that's right," McNamara interrupted. "I forgot to tell you. The fire marshals are good at what they do, and they checked every little bit of that house. But in the car, the one that got firebombed in the street, you know what the CSI guys found? Strangest thing. The bodies were all charbroiled, but we recovered a few slugs. Tiny little things. Maybe .177 caliber, could even have been smaller, like whoever put them together turned them into armor-piercing rounds. Must've been close-range, too, that tight a grouping."

"What's that got to do with what I'm asking?"

"You haven't asked anything."

"I would, if you'd take a damn breath."

"That case is closed," the detective said. "The two men in the car, they must have been the ones who blew up the house. Probably took fire on their getaway from . . . who knows, maybe a bodyguard?"

"Then you wouldn't mind telling me if that gang was sending warnings before they hit."

"Warnings? You mean like . . . ?"

"Specific threats. To specific targets. 'Get out of the neighborhood or else,' that kind of thing."

The cop's stare was implacable. Cross dropped out of any impending contest quickly, knowing it was a game he couldn't win—not dropping his eyes wouldn't get him what he wanted.

"No," McNamara said, his voice hardening. "Targets of opportunity. Remember, none of the *rape* victims were killed . . . if that's what you're asking about. The Department is sure that if they'd gotten threats, any of them, they would have reported them. If not to us, to their families."

"But they were always—"

"In mixed neighborhoods, so what? The way this city is shifting its borders, you can't tell who's going to be living next to you when you wake up in the morning."

"Okay."

"What do you want to know something like that for, Cross? Nobody's looking at you for anything."

"Somebody's always looking at us." Rhino's low, rumbling voice joined the conversation. "It doesn't have to always be the police."

"You guys haven't made a lot of friends, that's the truth."

"Legitimate businessmen, they've always been pushed around by organized crime, Mac. Ever since Capone's day, you can't run even a bush-league—"

"If you guys are legitimate businessmen, I'm a liberal. And don't waste your breath on the Double-X, Cross. I admit even I don't know what *that's* all about."

"I know you don't dip your beak, Mac. For all I know, you might be the only cop in Chicago who doesn't."

"Now, that's profiling." McNamara smiled. "You think all blue is—"

"Nah. But tell me you don't know about any shakedowns, never mind getting in bed with . . ."

"I'm not with Internal Affairs," the cop said, the words coming out like he was spitting steel darts.

"Good thing you're not. You'd need twenty-four/seven protection, and even then you'd have to stay off high floors."

"You want anything else?"

"No."

"You got anything for me?"

"No."

"Always a pleasure," the cop said.

"WE'VE BEEN looking at this all wrong," Cross said on the drive back to Red 71.

"Just because we haven't made any connection—"

"No," the gang leader said. "Because we *have*. I just missed it. Looking for a ham-and-cheese sandwich in a kosher restaurant."

"Meaning, what, there's other restaurants?"

"Yeah," Cross said, handing Rhino a burner cell. "We need everyone at the spot as soon as they can get there."

"BUDDHA, YOU remember that time when So Long was threatened by that gang of rapists?"

"I *already* gave up my share of the take on that one, boss. What else do you—?"

"We've been trying to connect it with Hemp's move on Ace."

"It *wasn't*?" Tiger half-sneered. "It was the same move. Lure one of us out into the open and—"

"You just said it," Cross cut her off. "Nobody's *that* patient. It was too long ago. But it doesn't link to that creature in the fancy house."

"Huh? Boss, I thought—"

"So Long wasn't that one's idea, Buddha. The others, the three of them, they must have liked what they were doing. A lot. The person in that fancy house, we don't really know much about him. And we never will. But Rhino has a good read on him. It makes sense that he'd go nuts, being like he . . . was."

"The best we can figure it, the . . . the man in that house, he *discovered* what those three were doing," Rhino said. "And he dealt himself in. Probably by offering them a ton of money. That wouldn't mean anything to him; he had an unlimited supply."

"So those three scumbags, they decided to get some more of their jollies on their own. Who gives a damn?"

"Only one person I can think of," Cross answered.

"The timing's all wrong."

"That's why I'm saying it."

"Saying *what*?" Tiger snapped. "Stop code-talking, 'boss.' The rest of us outsiders can't translate."

"Remember when I was brought in on that government job? Where they tried to capture that . . . whatever it was?"

"We were there," Tracker said, his tone more measured than usual. "Tiger and I both."

"And there it is," Cross told them all. "As far as Blondie and his pals were concerned, they recruited you. But you were on board with us way before they ever contacted you. And when they brought me in, you both played it like you'd never seen me before in your lives."

Tracker nodded. Failure to deliver that "specimen" Cross had never collected may have been more costly than they had first thought. If a nameless blond man and an Asian cyber-expert called Wanda were still alive, it wasn't known to the Cross crew. The whereabouts of Percy—a human war machine who returned to an inert state when not on combat assignment, as though a switch had been thrown in his operating system—were unknown. The government wouldn't have held the rogue nature of the entire operation against him: Percy would always be a high-value asset.

"WHY GIVE them any—?"

"Right. 'Them.' Not 'us.' Like Buddha's always bitching about, neither of you go back to the beginning, Tracker. I was the one who brought Buddha in. I ran across him in the same place I met Rhino—not locked up, but he might as well have been. And he had So Long with him, even that far back.

"You and Tiger, you're freelance, sure—but that just means you might take a job without bringing us in. And we might do likewise. But inside, we're all the same. We hate them all."

"So do the Simbas," Tracker said, deliberately shifting his eyes to Cross's face, seeing the confirmatory flash of the blue brand he expected. "That's more than any prove-in you could come up with, Cross."

"How come you're so sure?"

"I can see their brand on you. Tiger can see it, too."

"The little blue mark under his eye? It's blinking like a damn neon sign now, bro," Ace said to his brother.

"And you, too, now? Princess?"

"Sure," the muscle mass said. "I just thought it was some kind of trick tattoo."

"Buddha?"

"Yeah," the agate-eyed killer said. "I could see it. Before tonight, I mean. Thought you were testing another misdirect, like that bull's-eye on your hand."

"There's only one of us who could have known where Ace's wife and kids lived. In that house, I mean."

Buddha punched his cell phone.

"Go to Location Three. *Now!*"

The pudgy sharpshooter punched his phone again, as if he had a grudge against it. "Let's get this done," he said, dead-voiced. "Me, you, Princess, and Rhino, one car. Either of you two have a ride out back?"

"No," Tracker said. "Just a borrowed cab. Can't keep it long."

"Driver doesn't know it's missing?"

"Not yet."

"Me, either," Tiger added. Then she turned to Cross: "But I've got one at Orchid Blue. You can pick up that stick thing you keep in my safe. And Tracker can leave the cab on the street."

BEHIND RED 71, Cross tugged lightly on Tiger's mane, pulling her close.

"When you get your own car, follow *tight*," he whispered. "I don't know where Buddha's taking us."

"Yes, *sir!*" the warrior-woman said, throwing a mock salute, before launching herself at the backseat of Tracker's cab.

Tracker climbed behind the wheel, turning Tiger into a passenger, in case anyone might question the "Off Duty" sign on the roof.

"Follow that car!" Tiger ordered, in her best gangster-moll voice.

"JUST KILLING time," Buddha said, answering an unasked question. "It's gonna take her a little while to get to where we're meeting, but we're only five minutes away," he continued.

"From Old Greytooth's—?"

"Good guess, boss."

"He's not Lao, so why . . . ?"

"We're not visiting him. There's a side door. Just opens into another room. Three-sided, one door per wall."

"And the door that'll be *behind* us when we step in?"

"Just you and me go inside, boss. Everyone else stays on the street. We're not going in hot. Not coming out that way, either. But there's no reason to—"

"Got it," Cross said.

THE SHARK CAR slid to the curb.

"She's inside," Buddha said. "The dark-green Lexus we passed half a block past, that's her car."

"Let's go," Cross said.

Buddha killed the engine by pushing a keypad sequence. "You remember the—?"

"Yes," Rhino assured him.

THE TWO men walked to the only door visible on the windowless side of a large brick building.

As they stepped inside, they saw So Long, standing with her arms at her sides. Her long, straight black hair had a deep sheen no colorist could duplicate. Everything else was green, from her silk sheath to her reptile-skinned high heels. Even her long nails had a freshly applied coat of emerald gel.

That's her color, all right, flashed in Cross's mind. But he kept his mouth closed and his face expressionless.

"Ace bought one of those houses," Buddha said to his wife. No preamble was necessary: it had been So Long's scheme to buy up five houses on the same block, all in various states of disrepair after their owners had walked away from mortgages. Because the houses stood between two gangs whose claimed territories ended several blocks to either side, police presence was minimal, at best.

Stone takes a long time to decay, but neighborhoods don't. After the gang's urban renewal plan was put into action, the houses were rehabbed and sold, clearing a seven-figure score. So Long had handled all the transactions, washing the money through several LLCs, which disappeared before any capital gain would be declared.

"*Your* idea, your friend buys one of the houses," was So Long's only response. "Your idea; less profit."

"Sure. Whatever. That house wasn't bought in Ace's name—hell, I don't even *know* his name. But someone who wanted to smoke him out sent a hit man over to visit Sharyn."

"To *kill*? And you think . . . ?" So Long's voice hardened as she turned to Cross.

"The plan was to sell five houses," Cross said. "We agreed on everything, who paid what, all that. But Ace wanting one of the houses, that came as a surprise. And, yeah, before you say anything, surprised us, too."

"But when you told me, then *I* knew, yes? This killer, he did not succeed?"

"No," Buddha said. "But we know who put the whole thing in motion. The guy who wanted Ace out in the open."

"And no way to ask *that* one any questions now, yes?"

"Yes."

"Impossible to *guess* information like that."

"That's right."

"So that leaves . . . that leaves *me*, you are saying?"

"Yes," Cross said.

"Pekelo," So Long spat. "The headman said he was . . . not sure of him, but Ace decided to buy that house after Pekelo was already in the paper chain."

"Headman?" Cross said. "You mean Old Greytooth, the man who owns this building? He's not Lao."

"He is Hmong," So Long said. "As am I."

"You were in Laos when I—"

"I was a girl when you found me, husband," So Long said to Buddha. "Just a girl, but a clever girl. Our people— Hmong, I mean—our people are all fighters. There is no choice. The mountains shield us, but they do not always feed us. Sometimes we are forced to venture down to lower ground. When all of Cambodia was nothing but death, a bargain was made with the Americans to fight on their side during that stupid war.

"A bad bargain that turned out to be for us. But at the time, there was no choice. The Vietnamese—or their Russian masters—they would kill us once that war ended. The Americans could not win, but still they made us many promises. The only one they kept was to let us come here—America—to live. All this I was told. All this was over years before I was born. Born here. I returned to find my. . . . It does not matter, not now."

"Hmongs don't exactly blend in *here*, either," Cross said, no emotion in his voice.

"No," she said, coldly. "We are not welcomed, because our skills, our traditional skills, they are of no value here. Only the ginseng harvesting, and that brings death. I tell you this: that name, 'Pekelo,' in Lao it means 'stone.'"

"That's all you know?" Cross asked.

"Oh, no," So Long said. "Much, much more." The room went quiet.

Clearly, So Long was not going to volunteer whatever she meant by "much, much more," yet no one spoke.

Cross was replaying a piece of their past in his mind. "Headman" was the word So Long had used. Cambodian, not Lao. But maybe a Hmong. Maybe the same Hmong whose mortal enemy, a Chinese overlord named Chang, had been destroyed in a complex chain of events years ago.

A master strategist, Chang used his contacts to confirm there was a bounty on Viktor, a Russian boss who was trafficking in bear claws, routed from Kamchatka to Japan.

Chang had hired Cross to put a halt to Viktor's

trade arrangements. The crafty old man envisioned a war by which he would profit regardless of its outcome.

And Chang had paid off, in gold, just after learning that Viktor's entire gang was literally ripped apart by . . . something not yet known. Within minutes of that transaction, Chang's own headquarters had been hit by several RPG rounds.

Cross got word to an ancient Cambodian headman that the destruction of his mortal enemy—Chang—was a gift. A gesture of respect, for which no payment was expected.

Later, a package had been delivered to Red 71. An elaborately carved ebony stick, whose characters Rhino laboriously translated: "We can redeem this for a body. Payable anytime. And it can be any body we want."

"YOU KNOW Old Greytooth?" Cross finally broke the silence.

"Yes" was all So Long said.

"And he would know this Pekelo? And wouldn't trust him?"

"Yes."

"Could you speak to him? And tell him that Pekelo is the body we want?"

"I don't understand."

"You don't need to. You go in one of those doors . . . we wouldn't know which one. Just hand Old Greytooth this stick," Cross told her, proffering the item retrieved from Tiger's safe. "Tell him that it is a message from his friend Cross—the stick will prove that to him. The message is: 'Pekelo is the body we want.' But tell him we need that body alive—there are some questions he may know the answer to, and *we* want to ask him those questions."

"I will do that."

"BOSS . . . ?"

"Buddha, what more do you want? I don't think for a second So Long was in on any plot to hit Ace."

"You don't much act like it."

"Just leave it, okay? You want it straight, here it is: I *know* So Long's a thief. I *know* all thieves are gamblers—risk versus gain, right? So Long's smart. Real smart. And no matter what she might be offered to sell us out, she wouldn't like the odds."

"I don't see a guy like Hemp dealing with those freakish people, anyway," Tiger added. "They couldn't even get close enough to him to pitch a deal, no matter what it was."

"And whoever hired Hemp—this could not have been his own idea—they now know the result of that error," Tracker said, supporting Tiger's position. Or reassuring Buddha . . . although why he would do so was knowledge he kept to himself.

"Somebody wanted Hemp dead, you're saying?"

"No," Cross cut into Buddha's question. "Be easier to just dust him. But how would they get Hemp to put out a hit on Ace? The man's not insane."

"Then *you* explain it," Tiger challenged. "We know the contract was to kill Sharyn—at the *least*, kill Sharyn, maybe her children, too—just to bring Ace out into the open."

"Had to be Hemp's own idea," Cross said. "It's the only thing that adds up. Nobody'd have to pay Hemp for Ace's body, not if Hemp believed somebody had already paid Ace for *his*."

AS IF by mutual agreement, the whole gang went silent.

"It wouldn't be a hard sell," Tiger finally said. "Plenty of drug gangs in this town. Street-level slingers kill each other over who gets what corner all the time, so why wouldn't one of the kingpins want to take *all* the corners?"

"For Hemp to listen to a warning that Ace had him targeted, it would have to come from someone he trusted."

"Tracker would be right," Cross said. "But this isn't some old-school crime family—those guys don't trust them*selves*. Word about a contract? Sure. But who'd know for sure Ace had that contract?"

More silence, this time one of agreement.

"Still, Tiger's just saying what happened. No argument about that. But what if it wasn't Ace who Hemp was afraid of? Maybe Hemp wasn't afraid of any of us? Or even all of us? What if *he* was the one getting paid?"

"There isn't enough money—?"

"Not money, Buddha. Remember that girl? The one whose father kept telling her he was safe forever—that 'statute of limitations' thing?"

Buddha closed his eyes and watched the film spool inside his mind. Like it was yesterday:

Cross watched the woman descend the stairs to the basement poolroom, thinking, *Who would tell a girl like her about Red 71?* The bank-security mirror the old man with the even older green eyeshade kept just inside the door showed her clearly, standing as if she didn't know what to do next. All in black, she was—but dressed for mourning, not for style.

Finally, she threaded her way through the maze of tables, a dark, slender wraith not even drawing a glance from the men playing their various games. Cross was too far away for her to have spotted what she had been told to look for—the bull's-eye tattoo on his right hand—but she walked to the far corner as if guided by a signal.

The black pillbox hat with its matching half-veil did nothing to conceal her features. Or that she was anemia-pale under the mesh.

"Mr. . . . Cross?"

"Sit down" was all the answer she got. The woman took the only empty chair at the small table, pulled off her black gloves, and fumbled in her purse for a cigarette. Cross extended his left hand, opened it, and flame flickered out. If the woman was surprised, she gave no sign.

Two men detached themselves from the wall and racked the balls, starting a game. Even though their combined bulk would have concealed a reclining elephant, that wasn't what caused everyone in the basement to keep looking in some other direction. *Any* other direction.

Cross lit a cigarette of his own. Said nothing.

It took the woman two more cigarettes to realize that she wasn't going to be asked any questions.

When she spoke, it was in a chemotherapy voice, juiceless and resigned. "You have to make him stop. He's never going to stop."

Not a battered wife, Cross thought. *Otherwise, why come here? If she knew enough to find this place, she knew about the Double-X. So those widow's weeds aren't to cover scars.*

"Just tell me," he said.

"I can pay. Whatever it costs, I can get it."

"This part, it's the down payment."

"I thought . . ."

"I don't know you."

"And you don't trust me."

Silence was answer enough. She lit another cigarette with the glowing butt of her last one.

"I could still lie to you," she said. As if she knew all about lying.

"No, you couldn't."

"Are you going to strap me into a lie detector?"

"I am one," Cross told her, holding her eyes so she'd understand, get down to it.

"My . . . stepfather," she finally said, the last word sliding from her mouth like a venomous snake crawling from under a rock.

"What about him?"

"He . . . had me. When I was a baby. When I was a girl. When I was a teenager. Now I'm away. But I'll never be free from him. I'll never have a boyfriend, never have a husband. I'll never have a baby—he burned me inside."

"There's people for that. Therapists . . ."

Her eyes were twin corpses. "I'm not talking about my mind. He burned me with a soldering iron. Right after I had my first period. He put it inside me and pushed the switch."

Cross waited for more. When it didn't come, he said: "What do you want?"

"I went to the police," she said. "They told me I was too late. Too much time had passed since the last time he . . . had me. The statute of limitations, they said. He can't be prosecuted. So I went to a lawyer. He has money. I thought, if I could sue him, take his money, it would take his power. But the lawyer told me I was too late even for that."

"So . . . ?"

"The prosecutor, he was very kind. He told me I couldn't even get an Order of Protection. You can only get one if there's an ongoing criminal case. Or if there had been a conviction, and it was part of the sentence. But he said if he . . . my stepfather . . . ever bothered me again, they'd lock him up. He said they know about him. From other things—he wouldn't tell me what."

"Would that be enough? Taking his power?"

"Enough?" she said, as if the question were

absurd. "Taking his life, that wouldn't be enough. But if he could lose his power, if he could be in prison, that would . . . I don't know, give me a chance, maybe. To be free."

A bodyguard wouldn't help this one. Her ene-my's already inside her gates, Cross thought. *And she's right about a therapist—nothing they can do when a cutter's already hit a vein. We know this guy, works with every kind of crazy you can think of, but he goes partners with his clients, says that's the only way. They team up to fight what's already inside. She's not here looking for a partner; she wants to hire a gun. The scanner didn't pick up any-thing electronic on her, but she still has to say it out loud.*

"So what do you think we could do?"

"Hurt him," she whispered.

"You expect us to take that kind of risk, for how much, exactly?"

"I meant him. He'd pay anything. He has a record," she said.

"For what?"

"The prosecutor didn't have to tell me; I already knew. For rape. Before he married my mother. A long time ago. My mother didn't find out about it until much later. He was the one who told me first. When I was just a little girl, he told me. He had raped a girl and he went to prison for it. He told me he'd never rape a stranger again. He hated prison—it was full of animals. 'Savages,' he called them," she said, her voice too acidic to be mistaken for sarcasm. "That's why he married my mother. So he could do what he does and never go to prison again."

"He has money? Where would it come from?"

"He's like some kind of . . . gangster, I think. He'd talk real hard on the phone sometimes. And other times, he'd grovel. Crawl on his knees to whoever was on the other end of the line. I heard him doing that once, and he caught me at it. As soon as he was off the phone, he hurt me very ugly that night."

Cross lit another smoke, watching her. "You want this bad?"

"It's all I want," she said. "Everything I want."

"What now?" the hard-faced cop asked, his tone making it clear even his deeply respected patience wasn't endless.

"You know a sex-crimes prosecutor? Guy named Wainwright?" Cross said, naming the man in the DA's office the girl had said was so understanding.

"He's good stuff," McNamara said. "Young guy, but you can tell he's not in the DA's office to learn how to be a defense attorney. He's on our side; every cop in the county tries to get their dicey cases to him. I'll put it so you can understand, Cross: he doesn't give a damn about his conviction rate. See what I'm saying? He doesn't expect us to bring in videotapes of some slimeball committing the crime, with a signed confession for the cherry on top. And he's not giving away the courthouse just to get a plea."

"Doesn't even want to be the DA himself, huh?"

"Nope. He's a soldier. Like us. Us cops, I mean."

"'Us,' huh? You guys are no more all alike than this guy is with his job."

"That's right. But the only guys using all the juice they have to get him on a case, they are."

The target lived alone.

In a nice house in the suburbs. Neighbors on both sides, but there was a high fence all around the property. Solid cedar, brass-braced, with a cast-iron hasp. It wouldn't keep out an amateur.

A hard, slanting rain wasn't doing much to break the summer heat as Cross rang the bell just before midnight. No dog barked. He didn't expect any, not after a week of watching and waiting.

Suddenly the door was thrown open. Standing there, a big man, paunchy, hair combed to one side exaggerating the baldness he was trying to conceal. Wearing a white T-shirt over baggy black dress pants, barefoot.

Cross politely asked the man's name, holding his wallet open so the man could see the police shield. The man looked at it closely, eyes narrowing.

"You don't mind waiting outside, Detective? Just long enough for me to call the precinct, make sure you're who you say you are?"

"No, sir," Cross said, watching the man's expression change as he felt the pistol barrel jammed into his spine.

Cross stepped inside, pushing the man back gently with the palm of his hand. He tilted his fedora back on his head, quickly pulling the brim down again as the man's eyes flashed to the Chang B tong tattoo across his forehead. He gestured for the man to turn around.

Buddha, his face covered with a dark stocking mask, showed the target a short-barreled .357 magnum, holding it close enough for him to see the copper-tipped rounds in the cylinder.

"Let's go into your study," Cross said.

They walked the target down the carpeted hallway in a sandwich, took him over to his glass-topped desk, told him to sit down, make himself comfortable.

"You know who I am?" the man asked, unperturbed.

Cross put his fingers to his lips, made a ssshing gesture.

"Look, you want money? I got . . ."

Buddha ground the tip of the pistol barrel deep into the man's ear. The man let out a yelp; then he was quiet.

Cross opened the satchel Buddha handed him, taking out one item at a time, very slowly, as if he were a salesman displaying his wares.

A pair of handcuffs.

A hypodermic syringe.

A small bottle full of clear fluid with a flat rubber top.

Surgical bandages.

Velcro tourniquet.

A roll of pressure tape.

A mini-blowtorch.

A stainless-steel butcher knife.

"Wh-what is this?"

"Just a job, pal," Cross said. "Just earning our living. Don't worry, it won't hurt a bit. Once I give you a shot of this stuff . . ."

The man watched as Cross stuck the hypo into the rubber-topped bottle, filled the syringe, pushed the plunger slightly to check that the liquid was flowing smoothly. The man's face was a white jelly of terror.

"Please . . ."

"Look, pal, you think I get any kick out of this? Hey, I don't mind telling you the score. Woman comes to see us, says you did her real bad. Paid good money to take a piece out of you, even the score. Only thing, she watches too much TV. So she wants us to bring her the proof. And no photos, the real thing."

"Proof?" The word bubbled out of his throat.

"Proof," Cross repeated. "Couple a broken legs wouldn't satisfy this broad. She wants your hand. Your right hand."

"Oh God . . ."

"Look, it don't make no difference to us. She paid full price for a body, you understand? She's paying the same for your hand she'd pay for your head. You just relax, do it the easy way. My man Fong's gonna cuff your hand to the top of your fancy desk, hold it down flat with some tape. Then I'm gonna wrap this tourniquet around your arm, find a good vein, shoot you up with this happy juice. You go to sleep. You wake up, you got one less hand. All nice and bandaged, better than they'd do it in a hospital."

Cross switched on the blowtorch. The hissing butane was the loudest sound in the room. He opened his left hand—the torch flared into life.

"What's that for?" The man was trembling so hard, his voice sounded like his mouth was full of pebbles.

"To cauterize the wound, pal. So you don't bleed to death."

"Ca-cauterize?"

"What do you think I should use? A soldering iron?"

By the time the man forced himself to open his eyes, he was all strapped down. Buddha had the tourniquet around his biceps; Cross was gently tapping a vein to make it stand out.

"Could I talk to you?" The man's voice was a weasel's whine, begging and promising in the same breath.

"Better talk quick," Cross said, calmly.

"Look, you're professionals, right? I mean . . . you got paid to do this, I could pay you more not to, okay? I mean, pay you right now. Whatever she paid, how's that?"

"You got twenty large in this house, pal?" Cross asked, sarcasm lacing his voice.

"I got it. Every penny. That's why I thought you

were from Falcone, like I asked, remember? But . . . I'll give it to you, right now."

"I don't know. I mean, we already took the broad's money."

"Come on. Please! You're a man. I didn't do anything to the bitch she didn't have coming. I mean . . . cutting off a man's hand, for God's sake, what's that tell you? I know who sent you, now. She is one sick slut. Spent years in the crazy house. Come on! My money's as good as hers."

Cross sat back, mimed thinking it over. Watched the hope grow in the man's eyes.

Looked past him to Buddha.

"Where's the money?" he finally said.

The man went through a full-body shudder before he whispered "Safe."

He wasn't lying. Besides cash, there were a dozen kilo-sized bags of white powder, shrink-wrapped in clear plastic. The bills were neatly rolled inside Mason jars, ready to be transferred.

Cross speed-counted the cash and kept counting even after he passed twenty thousand.

He dropped it all in his medical case. Cash and coke together.

"Hey! That wasn't—"

"Quiet, now. You got a good deal. You paid us to call it off, right? For the rest of this money, we'll do a job for you. How's that?"

"What job?"

"You think that broad's not going to come after

you again, pal? You think this ends it? You bought yourself one safe night, that's all."

"But that powder, I was holding it for—"

"You got all kinds of cash, all kinds of places, don't you? Hell, you got enough in this house alone—equity, I'm saying—you can make things right with this Falcone guy."

"You mean . . . ?"

"Sure. Way I figure it, for what we're leaving with, we owe you a job . . . right, Fong?"

Buddha mumbled something in an Asian language from behind the stocking mask.

Cross could see the man thinking it over.

"When would you do it?" he finally asked.

"Tonight."

"And that's it? That would end this? Forever?"

"Tell her yourself," Cross said, handing him a cell phone. "Her number's already on this."

Toxic waste bubbled out of the man's mouth, hard, evil ugliness dripping into the phone. Telling her that her little scheme had backfired. How he had her once; how he'd always have her.

"You listening to me, you little piece of garbage? You understand the way things are now? I'm coming to see you, bitch. And when I'm done, you'll crawl back whenever I tell you. On your knees. I'll have my mark on you again, you . . ."

He hung up, bathed in sweat, licking his lips.

Cross nodded to Buddha. A hard hand clamped down on the back of the man's neck as the hypo slid home. He went out in seconds. Cross gently taped his right hand into a fist, watched as Buddha took the man's elbow in one hand, held his wrist in the other . . . and slammed the target's hand into the glass desktop until the knuckles were bruised and swollen.

Methodically, Cross removed a wax model of a woman's hand from the satchel. False red-lacquered nails gleamed. He held the wax hand carefully, then scratched some long, deep gouges in the man's cheek.

In the car, Cross used a packaged wipe to remove the tattoo from his forehead.

Buddha pulled off the stocking mask, popped the rubber wedges out of his cheeks, took off the padded jacket . . . and lost fifty pounds. The latex gloves they'd been wearing were shredded with serrated scissors, tossed out the window at intervals.

An hour later, the two men pulled behind the woman's house.

"You get it all?" Cross asked her.

She nodded, pointed to the tape recorder attached to her phone.

"Play it back, make sure," Cross told her, handing her the cell phone he'd let the target use. "If anything went wrong, it's all on here, anyway."

At a gesture, she held out her hands and stayed perfectly still while Cross attached the false red nails.

Without another word, he slapped her in the face, hard. Her eyes flared into life, focused and waiting.

"He came here about a half-hour ago," Cross told her, his tone hypnotic. "You opened the door, didn't expect him. He punched you in the stomach. You went down. He punched you in the face, over and over again, twisted your arm so hard you thought it was going to snap. You scratched his face. You remember doing that, you felt your nails go in. Deep. Then he beat you some more until you passed out. When you come to, dial 911."

"Thank you," she said.

Then Cross went to work.

"THERE'S ONLY one way we're gonna find out," Cross told the crew.

"What if Old Greytooth doesn't deliver?" Buddha said.

Cross shrugged, unconcerned.

Rhino stepped in with his agreement: "He would lose face."

Buddha felt himself go calm—the mammoth's logic was impeccable.

"WHY AM I here?" an immaculately dressed Asian asked, his dark eyes playing across the man seated on the far side of a sawhorse-supported desk.

The Asian's voice was controlled, but his gaze was a weak

flashlight in a coal mine cave-in, frantically seeking an exit before its batteries died.

"Because we're trying to solve a riddle," Cross answered. "And you're going to help us do it."

The Asian said nothing, as if waiting for the rest of the answer to his question. His regularly dermabrasioned face, manicured fingernails, and stylish haircut would have fitted a well-paid consultant of some kind. The heavy ring of white jade, the oversized, multi-dialed watch, the platinum bracelet . . . all attested to his success at whatever profession he practiced.

Cross lit a cigarette. The flame was sufficient to display the bull's-eye tattoo on the back of his hand.

"You know at least half of the answer," he said. "You'll tell us that for free. If you know the whole thing, *that* you'd get paid for."

"Do you think I don't know where I am?"

"What difference? All that matters is you solve this riddle for us."

The Asian went silent.

Cross took the third hit of his cigarette, then stuck it into what looked like a dinner-plate-sized glass saucer filled with some sort of ash-gray material.

"The first part, the one you give us for nothing, is the name of whoever hired you to kill Hemp."

The Asian didn't move, but Cross could feel he was calm and relaxed inside that stiff posture.

"You think silence is in your best interests? Or you're more afraid of whoever paid you than you are of us?"

"I have something you want," Pekelo said, the tension leaving his voice as he recognized that the bargaining was about to begin. "Something of value. You offer to pay for *part* of what I have, but I cannot parcel it out in bits and pieces—you must buy the whole thing."

"Something of value . . . What value do you place on it, then?"

"My life. Nothing more."

"We don't sell insurance."

"As you said, I know where I am. I know who you are. I know who ordered me brought to this place. If all you wanted was my life, I would already be dead."

Cross shrugged, acknowledging the truth of the captive's words.

"You already know I was paid to do something. Is there anything I can tell you, anything at all, that would convince you that I do not know who commanded me?"

Commanded? Cross thought. Aloud, he said, "I guess that depends on how you got your orders."

"Do you think I fear pain?"

"I don't care what you fear. I only care about what you know."

"I know So Long is Hmong."

"That's just a fact," Cross said, trying to cover Buddha with the blanket of gentle assurance his words projected. "Like you being Lao. Doesn't mean anything. And not what we need to know."

"I will tell you *all* I know. It may not be enough to satisfy you, but it will be the truth. Torture would not—"

"Nobody said anything about torture," Cross said, mildly. "If torture was what we thought would get us what we need, do you think we couldn't have gotten that done a lot easier by the people who brought you here?"

"I doubt you would believe me. I doubt you would even understand what I could tell you. *All* I could tell you. I cannot tell you more than I know."

"Let's see."

"I want some—"

"This isn't about what *you* want. Stalling for time would be stupid—no one's coming to rescue you."

"I know."

"So let's get it done. Tell us what you know that we *don't*. Then we'll decide what it's worth."

The Asian closed his long-lashed eyes. Fifteen seconds passed.

He might have heard a distinct *click!* sound—perhaps Cross lighting another smoke? He would not have seen Cross shake his head "No!" nor Buddha soft-release the hammer on his pistol in response.

"I will tell you what I know. I realize it may sound . . . implausible to you, but it is all I have."

The Asian opened his eyes. Took in a shallow breath. "We are all fatalists—our destiny is already written." When there was no reaction, he said, "I was commanded from the Cloud. I followed the instructions. There is no more. Do you understand what I just told you?"

"You accessed a clouded site," Rhino's voice rumbled softly—the sound did not encourage the Asian to turn in his chair to locate the speaker he had not known was present.

"No. The site appeared on my computer while I was—"

"You are lying," Rhino said. Not angrily, stating an indisputable fact. "The only way a Cloud contact could have happened is that you were *already* visiting a Web site. How you found *that* one doesn't matter. But whatever accessed *you* was

AI. So it was set up to find you. Not you, particularly. But people *like* you."

"It isn't what you . . ."

"Just stop," Cross told him. "This isn't some court. We don't care what you are, only what you do. What you can *still* do. When you said you were a fatalist, you also said something else. About yourself."

"I only meant—"

"What you told us was that you're a gambler. That's what you'd call yourself, too. The dice bounce, but there is no skill involved in the toss—only fate controls what they finally show."

"Yes. Our destiny is written before we—"

"No. Your destiny isn't written, not yet. And we're the ones holding that pen."

The Asian nodded his acceptance of what he could not deny. "It was some kind of competition. The winner was to receive what you would call 'something of value.' American dollars, precious stones—"

"You trusted that?" Rhino dropped a meat cleaver into whatever else the Asian was going to say. "That means the AI was set up a while ago. Set to deliver to winners of other . . . competitions, in the past. And it had. So you expected the same."

"Yes."

"Only this was no 'competition,' right?" Buddha said, his voice almost reptilian. "You already held the winning hand. It was us—all of us—this . . . thing wanted. But the plan—how to get it done—that was yours. Because you had the information to solve the puzzle. *Just* you. Hemp could not have been hired without you proving to him you knew something nobody else did. Ace's house. And there's only one way you could have gotten that address."

"What was the prize?" Cross said, his voice the same volume as Buddha's, but almost soothing by comparison.

"Three million euros," the Asian said, the emptiness of his voice showing he was telling the truth.

"But not in cash, right?"

"By wire. To Macao."

"Three mil to take down all of us?"

"Just for one. Any one of you, it didn't matter. The first one to . . . complete the task, that would be the winner."

"You can't contact this site?"

"Only the one I visited at first. I was contacted that one time, but I can't contact the—"

"The one you visited 'at first'?" Cross said, making it clear he wasn't asking a question. "So you had to be a regular on *that* one."

"Rape tapes," Rhino said. "A back-channel site. One you found on your own. But you must have been looking at it plenty of times—that's what kicked in the AI program, the number of times you kept going back."

"Is there any way I could leave this place alive?" the Asian asked.

"Already told you that. There's *one* way," Cross said. "You tell us what you know—*everything* you know—and you walk away. You're no threat to us. But you still have to pay. That three mil waiting on you to cyber-transfer it out, you'll send it where we tell you to. That'll square it.

"But when I say 'everything you know,' that's what I mean—you empty out, understand? Even if we don't ask a question, you keep draining until you're dry."

"I will do that. All of that. But what assurances do I—?"

"Enough," the gang leader said. "You can't contact some AI program, but it can contact *you*, right? That's part of the 'everything' I just told you about. We need you alive—how else could we track it down when it comes up with another 'competition'?"

The Asian closed his eyes again.

"Where shall I begin?" he said.

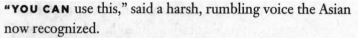

"YOU CAN use this," said a harsh, rumbling voice the Asian now recognized.

A laptop was placed before him. It was state-of-the-art, full-screen-sized. But the hand holding it made it seem like a child's toy.

"Sign on," the voice said. "We don't even need to see your password."

The Asian's laugh was thin. "But once I give this back, it would only take a few minutes to—"

"Take it with you," Cross said. "It's top-shelf; a gift from us. Nothing on the hard drive but OS—Mac, Windows, Linux, Chrome."

The Asian tapped keys, lightly and rapidly. "I am logged on," he said.

"See if the money is in that Macao account. You earned it as soon as you gave up the address of the house Ace bought for his wife and kids, right?"

Pekelo nodded. Keys tapped.

"Yes. All of it."

"Transfer it to this one," that terrifying voice said from

behind him, dropping a slip of paper onto the laptop's keyboard. The Asian's brief glimpse of the hand that held the paper showed him the fingers were the size of the same fine cigars he kept in his office humidor. And the tip of the forefinger was missing.

Tap-tap-tap.

"Done," the Asian said.

ANOTHER NINETY minutes passed.

"That's all there is," Cross said, assuring those in the darkness that nothing was to be gained by asking the same questions over and over again.

"You sure, boss?"

"Yeah."

Buddha stood up and walked over to the desk, where he turned to face the Asian, his features barely visible in the gloom.

"You know what this is?" he asked, pointing at the large glass saucer on Cross's desk.

"An ashtray," the Asian said.

"So you know what's in it."

"Cigarette butts."

"And ashes," Buddha's subzero voice added.

"Yes."

"You like the color?"

"It is just gray ash of some kind."

"The kind you get from an incinerator," Buddha said.

The Asian had opened his mouth to say something when a pair of boa-constrictor arms wrapped Buddha's biceps on

was killed. That would expose us all. Pekelo, by then,
[...]ow that. That's the flaw in all Artificial Intelligence—it
[...]o outside its own data."

GANG leader's summation was blunt.

Whatever he told the AI, that ended it. There's no way
[f]another player to enter the competition. It's over."

The silence lengthened, as if waiting for darkness to
e[m]erge.

"The AI is gone. It did its job. Or at least it computed
that it did."

"I *get* it, okay?" Buddha snapped. "I screwed up. But that's
done, and there's no way to fix it. We'll never get to question
those other ones now."

"They wouldn't have known the answers." Cross shut off
the faucet. "The only one who could have told us anything,
that . . . whatever it was Tracker and I found . . . we didn't
have time to listen. And we wouldn't have known what questions to ask, anyway."

"We have to work with what we know."

"No, brother," Cross answered Rhino. "We have to work
with what *he* knew. He might have been smart enough to
create that AI, but it couldn't hold more than he poured in."

"You all can stop," Tiger said, stepping out of the darkness and tossing her mane. "I wasn't there before, but me,
now, *I'm* in."

Cross was very still for several seconds. Then he said, "To
get off on rape tapes, you have to be a certain kind of maggot.
That's the only requirement."

both sides. "I'm sorry, Buddha," the armor-muscled man
said, his shiny skull reflecting the dim light. "Rhino told me
not to let you—"

Buddha slumped in his chair as if surrendering, but Princess slipped his hands over the blank-eyed man's as if he
expected the move.

"We promised to let him go," Cross said, quietly.

"He will be our ally," Tracker added.

The Asian's flat demeanor was stress-fractured, as if his
face had been coated in aged-out pancake makeup.

"We need a time line," Cross told the Asian, as if nothing
had interrupted an ongoing conversation.

"It just . . . It just burst onto the screen."

"Not just your screen, everyone who was qualified to log
on, too."

"Yes. It must have been so."

"So there was nothing special about the target, was
there?"

"The woman, you mean?"

"Yeah."

"No, no. It was just . . . like those old 'Wanted' posters
they used to hang in the post office. Her face wasn't on them.
No woman's was."

"Whose, then?"

"Yours," the Asian said, not even hesitating a microsec-
ond, as was his habit when confronted with any request for
information. *What answer would best serve me?* "And one
more. An Indian."

Tracker stepped next to Cross.

"Yes," the Asian said.

"Just the two of us?"

"Yes."

"What else?"

"Nothing. Just height/weight estimates. Not names, addresses . . . nothing like that."

"When?"

"It was less than a month ago. I would have to access my own computer to be exact."

"You can do that when you get back to your place. We'll give you a way to make contact to get us that info."

"I promise I will—"

"Let him go, Princess," Rhino's even quieter voice rumbled.

The Asian was almost to the back door when he realized that the behemoth wasn't referring to him. It was his last thought—Buddha's .177 hardball round was tumbling inside his brain before another synapse could complete its circuit.

⊕

"HE MUST have put in a lot of work," Cross said.

"Boss, you're really saying this had nothing to do with So Long?"

"Not what *that* guy was doing. He was trying to win a game. Gaming, he'd call it—competing against others. But it was a fixed fight. His edge was huge, but it was an accident—it wouldn't be enough for him to get paid. The tracing, from the pictures of me and Tracker, that was all his work."

"I don't get this AI—"

"Buddha," Rhino said gently, "a man with his intelligence, confined to a prison but given outside access through the Internet, he might . . . amuse himself in a [...]. He chose those . . . tapes. He probably even g[...] foul things the idea of hitting minorities to [...] more beyond the reach of the 'profilers' than [...] were. Misdirection."

"But So Long—"

"—knows me," Cross said. "She's never seen Tr[...] she knows my face. Knows it good."

"Boss, she'd never—"

"I don't think so, either. What would be in it for he[...] this Pekelo was just in the paper trail she needed to tra[...] all those properties, set up those bank loans, all that."

"If he—that man in the house we exploded—if he did[...] signal the Artificial Intelligence to hold off at some pre[...] set interval, it would go to work on its own," Rhino said. "Revenge programming. It would target whoever was on its camera-feed. A *live* camera-feed, captured. That . . . man, he probably had the whole place rigged with lenses. Infrared, so even a full-black wouldn't stop it. Backup generator[...] in case whoever came for him cut the electricity first. Yo[...] and Tracker, the cameras would have your images. Nobo[...] else's."

"That's where the work came in," Cross said, noddi[...] "This Pekelo had to find out who I was, first. Once he[...] that, then he could poke around until he got a lot of [...] sible targets. But none of that would have meant a thing[...] hadn't seen Ace's name—or Sharyn's name, most likely[...] one of those transfer deeds."

"So he set Ace up. . . ."

"That was what the AI paid off on. Ace would go i[...]

He took a deep hit off his cigarette. "But to *find* people who actually want those tapes, not so easy. And to find a whole damn *market* for that product, that's much harder yet. You'd have to be inside . . . inside *them*, I'm saying. It's not like a kiddie-porn ring. Not that hard to find one of those. Hell, find a *lot* of them, you want to—that's just computer forensics.

"But *this* guy, the one in that house, he was a different species. He had to find a market. Not a network: all individuals—they probably didn't even know each other. And he also had to find a gang who wouldn't want to just watch those tapes—they'd want to *make* them. Plus, he had to do all that without ever leaving his house."

"Prison."

"Huh?" Tiger suddenly erupted. "You said he was working out of his house."

"No," Rhino told the Amazon, the squeak re-entering his voice. "Where he was, it wasn't *his* anything. He couldn't leave. Ever."

"If he was smart enough to—"

"He couldn't leave his own body," Rhino said, more softly, but no less despairing. "The longer he stayed trapped in it, the less he could move under his own power, even if the door was wide open."

"I was there, remember?" Cross spoke to Rhino, his voice pitched at the same volume as the behemoth's, but the thread running through it lacked even a trace element of Rhino's empathy for the man they all thought of as some kind of creature. "And whatever in hell that thing was, however he got where we found him, he was *some* kind of genius, right?"

"So what?" Buddha said, still defensive. "The only thing

we know for sure about him is that he's gone. And he's not coming back."

"Neither is the guy you just killed. But there's one difference between them. And that's the one we have to focus on."

CROSS OPENED his left hand and lit another cigarette.

"You know those clowns who do 'threat assessments' for people with enough money to make them walk around scared? That's a nice racket, but we're not customers."

"What are you saying?" Tiger snapped, irritated.

"We know there's a threat out there, we *take* it out," Buddha snapped back. "You got a thousand cockroaches in your house, what's the point of killing nine hundred of them?"

"I'm glad you said that, brother," the gang leader said, not even a touch of sarcasm tainting his speech. "Because now we've got to talk to So Long."

"WE NEED your list," Cross told Buddha's wife. "The whole list."

"Why? This 'list' you call it, not valuable? You want something that is valuable, it is only good manners to—"

"No bargaining, So Long. Just give it to him, okay?" Buddha said, his voice empty of anything but words.

"Now *you* give orders?"

"This isn't about that," the pudgy killer said. "There's no choice."

"Always a choice."

"For you, only two," Cross said, his voice as quiet and uninflected as when he first spoke.

So Long looked at the man sitting in one of a matched set of armchairs. *Always the same*, she thought to herself. *Cross. This is a man with no blood in him.* Aloud she said, "You come to *my* house, to—what?—give me orders, like this is some restaurant, maybe?"

Cross didn't respond.

"Well?" she said, turning to her husband.

"So Long, you remember when Cross got us out of that jungle? Saved our lives?"

"Saved *your* life. You told this man, if he wanted to take you back, I have to come, too, yes?"

"Sure. That makes me a bad guy now?"

"You? No, husband. Not you. But to . . . him, I was baggage. Extra baggage. And now he gives you that same choice, yes?"

"No," Buddha said, in a voice his wife rarely heard. "There's something out there. We don't know if it's *still* out there, but it was trying for a kill. We've got it narrowed down to maybe just two targets—Cross and . . . a guy you don't know."

"Yes?"

"That note you got. It was from some degenerate freaks. And they would have done what they threatened to do, only now they won't be doing anything like that. They won't be doing anything, ever. The man I had stay with you one time?"

"Black man. True gentleman. Like that giant. Very fine manners. Very respectful. Not like him," she said, tilting her head slightly toward the man with the bull's-eye tattoo on the back of his right hand.

"They don't know you," Cross said pointedly.

"Huh! Very nice. But I told you already: Pekelo."

"He's not here."

"Another of your riddles? Better to do business. Like always, yes?"

"Pekelo told a killer where to find Ace's wife, So Long. And that killer came over to the house—the house you did all the paperwork on—to kill her. Following orders. Not because his boss needed her dead—he wanted to drive Ace insane, rage him to stepping into a trap. Then kill *him*."

"How is this—?"

"Listen," Buddha said, his tone so softly penetrating that even So Long shrank back in her chair. "The first target wasn't Ace's wife, it was *my* wife. You, So Long. And it worked. The trap, I mean. Only not like they thought it would. That Circle of Skulls gang, it's gone. Every one of them. It didn't have to be that way, but I lost it. They were dead before we could ask them any questions. And that's on me."

"They wouldn't have known the answers," Cross said, hearing the bitterness of self-blame in Buddha's voice. "But we all worked on this. Every single one of us. Because our brother's *wife* was under threat. No other reason—he's one of us, and that was enough.

"That was all we had, to start with—that threat to rape you, So Long. And Buddha didn't make the first strike; he didn't even know about it. This drug boss, he was going to panic Ace out into the open, but he didn't live long enough to make it happen.

"That one is gone. His gang is gone. Pekelo was playing a game; that's what he thought. If someone had to die for him to win, that was okay—no problem for him. You gave him the information he needed to win the game. Now he's done, too. He won't be playing any more games.

"There were only two targets. Me and . . . this other guy. At least, that's what we thought. Now we're not so sure. And we have to *be* sure, understand?"

"You were a target, So Long," Buddha said. "That brought us *all* in. If Cross had refused to take you when we left that damn jungle, I would have stayed—I wouldn't have left you—that's true. But this is different. Don't make me—"

"She's not going to, brother," Cross said, cutting Buddha off before permanent damage could be done. "She knows how that would play out."

"Huh!" So Long snorted. "You would kill me?"

"It wouldn't get that far," Cross said, in the same dead tone he'd been using since So Long stepped into her living room and realized her husband had brought company. Unwanted company. "Buddha could never let us do anything to you. But he couldn't let anyone do anything to *us*, either. Only one way for him, then."

"Husband . . . ?"

"He's right, So Long. I couldn't kill my own people. I couldn't let anyone kill you. Or kill me, either. So, you and me, we'd both have to . . . go home."

A long second passed. "I get you the list," the hard-faced Hmong woman told Cross.

"BOSS . . ."

"It's nothing, Buddha. So Long was always going to give

up that list. It's not like they were her own people or any-thing. But your wife, she is what she is. She had to test. If she saw any way she could get paid . . ."

"But you took it so far."

"Someone always blinks first."

"Sure. Unless they don't. Then what—?"

"I would have come up with something."

"Yeah," the pudgy man behind the wheel said, resigned to a truth he already knew.

IF BUDDHA thought the next hour of silence would give way to the thread of the original conversation, he was disappointed.

Expertly sliding the Shark Car between pools of shad-ows made the trip back to Red 71 longer than usual, but Cross was apparently comfortable with it. *Safety first*, Buddha thought. *Safety for us, no matter what it costs anyone else.*

As he slid the gang's car into a U-turned tunnel behind the building, Buddha tried once more. "Boss, you know *what* you would've come up with?"

"No."

"But . . ."

"Brother, I don't have a crystal ball. I can't answer 'What if?' questions. Let it go, okay?"

AS THE two men walked through the unlit tunnel, Buddha held back slightly, then moved to Cross's left side.

He can't shoot worth a damn with his left hand, Buddha thought to himself. And then stopped in his tracks.

Cross stopped, too. He didn't know what Buddha had seen ahead of them, but he wasn't going to break silence to ask.

"What the hell is that thing doing *now*?"

"Where? I don't see—"

"Not ahead, boss. On your face. Just below your eye. That . . . blue thing. It's blinking on and off."

"Wait till we get back inside," Cross told him, puzzled. *How come it didn't just burn steady? And how come I didn't feel it this time?*

"GO LOOK inside the poolroom," the gang's leader told Buddha. "If any of us are out there, ask them to come back."

Before Buddha could return, Princess burst through the curtain face-first, as if the black steel ball bearings were cobwebs.

"We won!" he burst out.

"You got people to play nine-ball with Rhino?" Cross said, surprised in spite of himself—getting people to even *approach* the Goliath was never an easy task.

"No! It was Sweetie! He did it! I've been teaching him. Like you said, Cross. When he does something good, I give him a command . . . and a chunk of meat. Like that was what I wanted him to do all along. That's all. It just took a lot of . . . patience. Like you said. Nobody believed he could do it. But . . ."

Rhino came through the curtain, his bulk parting it sufficiently to let Buddha pass through untouched.

"Where's that damn—?" Cross began, but caught Rhino's gesture and clipped off whatever he had been going to ask.

The subject of the uncompleted question followed Rhino inside. As calm as a man who chewed Valium to alleviate boredom, the big Akita walked over to Princess, scanned the room quickly, and flopped down at his armor-plated friend's feet.

"Boss, I swear, I never saw anything like—"

"Rhino, can *you* tell me what in hell everyone's going on about?"

"Physically, it was impossible," the behemoth said. "The dog—Sweetie," he added quickly. "Sweetie stood on one side of table twelve. Princess bet everyone in the place that his dog could jump across, from one side to the other, long rail to long rail. We've got more room between the tables than in most poolrooms, sure. But not enough to get a running start."

"You saying . . . ?"

"Yes. Sweetie went into this crouch, as if he was transferring all his muscle mass to his back legs. Then he just *launched* right over. If I'd seen that in a movie, I'd know it was faked. But he actually did it."

"Who collected the money?"

"Princess. You could see they all thought he was out of his mind, but here—in Red 71, I mean—they knew they were safe. If we had lost, they knew they'd have collected, too."

"You guys cleared—what?—ten G's minimum, am I right?"

"I don't know, Buddha," Rhino said, without interest. "Here, you want to count it for yourself?"

"Duh-*am*!" the pudgy man exclaimed. "Closer to fifteen. What a score. Hell, I would have taken that bet myself."

Cross held his head in both hands.

"I will ask what Buddha really wants to know," Tracker spoke from one of the pools of darkness that made it impossible to gauge the size of Red 71's back room. "How did you cheat?"

Buddha shot a look in Tracker's direction but didn't pretend to be insulted.

"There was no cheating," Rhino said, almost pedantically. "We use professional-standard tables. The playing surface is nine by four and a half feet, but there is some additional room for the wood surrounds . . . where the diamonds are inset."

"Diamonds? You mean those are real?"

"No, Buddha," Rhino said patiently. "The inlays are diamond-*shaped*, always in a contrasting color, usually a pearly white. Players use them to calculate angles. They must be precisely set, just as the slate bed is. Variations in a particular table would give an advantage to anyone who knew them."

"What's that got to do with—?"

"Most poolrooms have the tables too close together, in order to squeeze an extra table or so on the available floor space. But in, say, a tournament, this would not be the case. You wouldn't want players getting in each other's way."

"So you had it fixed?"

"There was no 'fix.' Our tables are about thirty inches high. Even with the extra space we added, it's not enough for Sweetie to get a running start. He had to—"

"He was like a goddamn helicopter," Buddha interrupted. "Just took off and kind of . . . floated over the whole thing."

Rhino's patience was never tested by interruptions. He continued at the measured pace of an engineering professor explaining a concept to a vaguely attentive class. "Roughly, a parabolic arc of less than three feet at its peak is required. It's simple physics."

"We started him on two feet," Princess said proudly. "Once Sweetie got the idea, we added an inch every few weeks. His back legs, they're like steel springs."

"Yeah, well, it's a good hustle, but you can only use it once. It's not like you and Princess could pick up a pool table and carry it around with you."

"We could, too!" Princess insisted. "Me and Rhino, we carried all the new tables in through the back. If we wanted . . ."

"Ah" was all the Amazon said.

"Boss . . ."

"We're not going into business with this, Buddha," Cross said, his tone clearly communicating that the subject was closed.

"Sure. I wasn't gonna say anything about that. I just wanted to know why that little blue mark is back again."

"I see it, too," Rhino said. "Princess and I both."

"Ace?"

"Same for me, brother."

Cross drew in a deep breath through his nose, held it for a count of sixty, then slowly exhaled. "Only this time, *I* can't feel it. So something's happening," he finally said. "Changing. But nothing is adding up.

"I thought it was some kind of warning. I could *feel* it—

that's what made me look in the first place. But now you see it when it flashes, but I don't feel a damn thing."

"THAT'S WHERE it all started," Cross said, recapping. "No reason I should have gotten out of that basement alive—whatever it was had to know I'd put the whole capture-trap in place.

"And ever since, I've had this little . . . brand thing under my eye. When I can feel it, it's always some kind of warning. So, whatever put it there, it's still got some use for me.

"Remember when Blondie was running down all the info they had collected? First, those government morons thought some serial killer was responsible. You know, all those 'profiles' they had worked up? But the load of slime who confessed to the Canyon Killings out in California blew the covers off that—he was just playing the Henry Lee Lucas game."

"A professional case-clearer," Tiger said. "That's what this clinical psychologist told them. And he was right."

"Lucas was the model," Rhino added. "And the same tune's been on the fake hit parade ever since. Turns a lot of 'Unsolved' into 'Closed.'"

"It's a damn TV show," Buddha spat out. "You know, where the cops get to stand over some grave and tell the camera how they made a promise to the dead kid's parents. It's a good deal for everyone," he sneered. "The maggot's already been sentenced for a killing that was actually his—so he's either on Death Row or doing Life Without—it don't cost him nothing to confess to a few dozen more. Even that Ottis

Toole—now, *there's* a guy with a name that fits; his mother couldn't spell 'Otis' and he was a tool from that day on—picked up the trick, right from Lucas himself. Toole for sure: the IQ of an imbecile for openers, with his brain fried from Sterno on top of that."

"What makes you so sure of that, Buddha?"

"Rhino, come on! Man dies of cirrhosis of the liver before he's fifty? As long as he kept confessing, they kept him oiled."

"Okay, that's enough," the gang's leader said. "What difference does some damn guess make? There's things we *know*. What I told Blondie about the Simbas, that was all words carried on the wind. The whisper was that they were supposed to be a tribal mix. And in Africa, that just doesn't happen. At least, no one had ever heard of it. When whites invaded Africa, maybe that intensified the tribal separations, but it was *always* that way."

"Here? You mean, in America?" Tiger asked.

"How many black gangs on the South Side?" Ace half-snapped at her. "Or the West? Too many to count, growing all the time. When they get *too* big, they split into sets. Next, they turn on each other. Who wins *those* wars? Same with the Latinos. How many Mexican gangs on the East Coast? How many Puerto Rican crews on the West? Sure. But it don't make no difference—they all go the same way, no matter where they are."

"Chinese, too," Buddha cosigned. "They been having all-outs between themselves in New York for—what?—damn near fifty years."

"Sure," Cross said, quietly. "Africa, you could almost understand it. That continent, it's always been fertile territory—first it was slaves, now it's gold, diamonds, oil.

The only time an African country is 'politically stable' is when the dictator is such a degenerate that he kills people for entertainment.

"But it wasn't until the same signature kills all got connected that they started talking about this 'entity' thing—the G may not be good for much, but they're great at making charts. What we heard called 'Simbas' in the Congo, they were called 'Natt Krigere' in Scandinavia."

"What does that mean?" Tiger asked, frankly curious.

"In Norwegian, it means 'Night Warriors.' You go far enough north and half the year you don't see the sun at all. But they still found the same kill-signature in places where every single native was as white as people get. And the *language*, that's the big clue."

"Why?" Tiger asked, not so gently. Standing with both hands free, as if she wanted to close the distance between this unknown entity and the twin throwing daggers strapped to her muscular right thigh.

"I'm no historian," Cross said tonelessly, "but I always read a lot—I had the time to do it. We know there were a lot of Finnish collaborators in World War II. You want Norwegian, just look up 'Quisling'—the Nazis put him in charge, and he was convicted of being a war criminal. You know where he was executed? Oslo.

"Why there? Well, the Norwegian *people* never made any deals. They just gathered their forces and rolled up north. For them, 'north' means above the Arctic Circle. Then they told the Germans to come and get some. Which didn't happen.

"Now, that was strange, right? Where's the access to oil? Right off *their* coast, yeah? And they don't come much whiter than Norwegian. But even the German generals weren't dumb enough to swallow that Master Race crap—Hitler looked about as Nordic as Malcolm X.

"The Norwegians, they didn't trust the Holy Church any more than they did the Swiss government. They didn't need to join some Crusade to reach the Pearly Gates—dying in battle, that was their guaranteed ticket to Valhalla.

"Now even the AB is under fire from the Odinists inside the walls—Vikings are as feared warriors as the Mau Mau ever were. And they've been around a lot longer."

"Maybe I can't follow that. Not *all* of it, anyway," Tiger spoke softly. "But I think I know where we can find out some more of it."

"Where?" Tracker asked.

"Mural Girl," the Amazon answered. "But we'd have to actually make contact this time. That camera we set up, it never holds an image for long. And all it ever shows is some kind of . . . explanation, maybe? I don't know. But maybe she does."

"TWO RIDES," Cross ordered. "Buddha, me, Tiger, and Tracker in the Shark Car. Rhino, Princess, and Ace in the backup."

"Why can't—?"

"There isn't room, Princess."

"There is, too! Plenty of times we all—"

"Don't you want Sweetie to come along?" Cross said, ending any discussion. Explaining the tactical reasoning intuitively understood by Ace and Rhino to the muscle-massed child would have taken hours. "Mural Girl works in daylight. It's already getting dark, so tomorrow we move. First light."

"Let *me* ask her," Tiger said.

"Ask who?"

"Mural Girl," she told Cross. "First light, like you just said. But let me do the talking, okay?"

"ONE QUESTION?"

"Worth what?" the Chicago detective said into what he called his "CI phone."

"Can't tell until I get an answer," the gang boss said in response.

"Gonna spook the paying customers if they see an unmarked parked at your joint?"

"Might. Only they won't see it. Just pull up to the gate— you'll be met."

"IT WOULD be you," the detective said, later that night.

"You know a better driver?" Buddha said. "Besides, I'm the only one that could fit in this seat."

"Rhino isn't the only—"

"Yeah, he is. You'd want Princess driving your car?"

"I was thinking about—"

"Don't waste your time, Mac. We won't pretend to know what you know, but, trust me, it ain't as much as you think it is."

"Trust *you*?" the detective retorted, as he slid out from

behind the wheel of his unmarked. "I've taken a few hits to the head over the years, but never *that* hard. I got the odometer memorized, so don't even think about—"

"It's not going more than a couple of hundred yards," Buddha promised.

CROSS MATERIALIZED next to McNamara while the cop's unmarked was still moving slowly away.

"Only one question, Mac," he said, firing a cigarette from the flame in his left palm. "No reason for us to go further than that dark spot over there."

"Then you could have met me."

"I don't know what's in your car. What I got is for you, not some audio pickup the cop shop installed."

"They'd never—"

"Sure. You don't trust Buddha, but you trust *them*, right?"

"One question, you said. Get to it."

"The Rejuvenator."

"That's not a question."

"This is: You *sure* he's dead?"

"He was a . . . Ah, pick your own words. 'Narcissistic psychopath' is pretty much what the department shrinks decided on."

"Not you, huh?"

"What difference? 'The Rejuvenator'? Fine. You know how it works: once the damn media gives any of these dirtbags their own special name, they never drop it. 'Son of Sam.' 'Hillside Strangler'—like that. Only reason Speck didn't get one is because he was nabbed too quick."

"This time, though, there was some reason. . . ."

"Sure. He copied every serial killer's work, like those guys who copy Rembrandts. They know their 'creation' is just gonna end up in some collector's private gallery, so they always leave some little hint that it was *their* work. Same with this freak; he couldn't resist leaving a tiny piece of himself at the crime scene. That ® brand. Cute, huh? That's the symbol for 'registered trademark,' so he was doubling down on his bragging."

"I know. He got all the usual props for a serial killer: fan mail to the Internet, like that. Even book-and-movie deals, only he never got to sit in a cell and read them. My question's still the same: You sure he's dead?"

"The man who left those ® brands on all those kills? Yeah, I'm sure."

"Then you're sure the man you beat to death was the Rejuvenator? None of those 'true crime' writers scored an interview with you. None of the TV shows, either."

"I didn't beat anyone to death," McNamara said, unconsciously dropping his voice into the toneless recital he always used when speaking with Internal Affairs. "I followed him to where he was holed up. When I saw him coming down the stairs, I drew my service weapon and told him he was under arrest. He kicked the gun out of my hand—I guess he'd been some kind of martial artist—and came at me all in the same move. I defended myself."

"You didn't have a search warrant."

"I never entered his place. He was still on the staircase when—"

"You didn't have an arrest warrant."

"No time to get one. I was—"

"—acting on a tip from a CI that the man you'd been looking for—the one who wrote all those notes, like 'Heirens Is Innocent,' and mailed them to the papers—he was on his way back to his hideout, right? Pretty good CI . . . even gave you the address."

"What's your point?"

"You don't even know who the CI is—all he ever does is call, always from a different number."

"Uh-huh. That's the way it usually works."

"And the phone you kept for those calls—the one you paid for out of your own pocket—it got smashed so bad during the fight that even the SIM card was destroyed. So all the IAD investigators could recover was an under-a-minute call to your phone. Made from a burner cell—bounced off five towers within a half-mile. So there was a call, but whatever was said, only you know."

"That's the way it happened. And that's what was in their report. Although how *you'd* know about that . . ."

"Come on, Mac—databases get hacked all the time. Those boys always talk about their 'exploits'—all you have to do is listen. But it's still the one question."

"How would it help *me*, like you said it might."

" 'Might' *is* what I said. If you've still got copycat crimes unsolved, and this 'Rejuvenator' guy is definitely dead, I've got something for you."

"No copycats for years. And *definitely* not one sending love notes to the papers."

"So the one you were looking for once, he's dead. And you'd know, because you killed him yourself."

"I defended myself," the hard-core cop said, nothing in his voice but relentlessness.

"Must've been a hell out of a fight, the way the guy got his neck broken, ribs driven into his lungs, too. And—"

"You got a point you want to make?"

"Not anymore, I don't," Cross said.

"SHE'S THE one who's gonna be doing all the talking, so what do you need me for?"

"Drive the car, Buddha. Like you always do."

"You're keeping the others back, right? Whatever this . . . thing is, you know what it can do. So you're keeping them out of range."

"Whatever this thing is, it's got a longer range than any distance we could run to."

"So why aren't we *all* going?"

"You know damn well we can't all fit in the car. Even if we could, any of the others get out, it's gonna attract attention. We don't need any cell-phone video on some idiot's Facebook page."

"Tiger's the only one who's gonna go over to that ladder. Why can't she just drive over there by herself?"

"Tiger's not working with a cold back."

"Then the more the—"

"Buddha, what the hell's wrong with you? We need the car to slip in quiet. And maybe get out fast, things go wrong. Sure, I could drive this beast, but not like you can. I can't shoot like you, either. But I can cover one side, launch a message out of one of the tubes, if I have to do that. This makes sense, brother. It's the right play, the right tactic. . . ."

"Boss, ever since . . . Hell, I don't even remember exactly

when it started, but . . . I'm just spooked, I guess. We don't know—"

"We don't and we *won't*. Not unless Mural Girl knows something, and right now she's the best bet we have."

"Why should she talk to us?"

"I don't know why. But Tiger's right—if there's anything Mural Girl wants to say, Tiger's the one she'll say it to. Look, I don't like it, either, okay?" Cross said, feeling the tiny brand below his eye suddenly flare—one flash-burn and then it was gone. "But I don't think we could do anything about the Simbas, even if it *is* them. This is just to make sure that this AI stuff is legit. It doesn't feel like anything they'd bother with, but we've gotta make sure—*dead* sure, brother—that whatever we blew up inside that creature's house doesn't have any friends left."

"Sure. What you're saying is, besides the ones I—"

"Buddha, will you *drop* it? No one's blaming you for blasting that car. I finished them off myself, remember? Those guys, they were flunkies. We could've questioned them for days, they still wouldn't have had anything to tell us. We had all the time in the world to talk to that piece of work Old Greytooth delivered to us. And *he* was dry, okay? But if there's any chance Mural Girl knows something, we can't pass it up."

Buddha lit a smoke, took one deep drag, and snapped it into the darkness before he nodded his head toward where the Shark Car sat waiting.

"First light, we want to already *be* there, right?"

TIGER'S ONE-PIECE spandex outfit was a city-camo match for the Shark Car's skin, and pulled almost as tight.

When the back door popped open, she slid inside.

"Hey!" she said softly when she realized the seat was empty. "What am I, a passenger?"

Cross turned his head to face her. "You're the only one getting out. We're your cover, just in case some stranger gets stupid."

"I don't need any cover. Nobody ever bothers Mural Girl."

"You're not Mural Girl."

"Oh, I *know* that," Tiger whispered, taking in a deep breath to emphasize the difference. "Anyway, in this outfit, nobody's even going to notice me."

"Sure, they won't," Cross said, without a hint of sarcasm. "You couldn't have capped your hair?"

"Not unless I cut it real short first. And who'd want that?"

"You could shave your head, it wouldn't make any difference," Cross said, already riding the tide. "Nobody watching you climb a ladder would ever forget *that*."

"Ah, you're so cute when you're trying to be a player."

THE SHARK CAR passed through areas of the city where people who might be awake at that time of night could never be sure exactly what they'd just seen.

Not an unusual situation for most of the watchers: those on their way to work auto-blurred their eyes whenever they saw something the police might question them about later. Curiosity had long since been deleted from their senses.

They moved stolidly forward, one foot in front of the other, walking a treadmill that discharged meager paychecks, a health plan that covered everything but illness, and a pension that made them pray Social Security would survive federal plundering long enough for them to collect it.

"CAN I ask you a question?"

"Sure," Cross told Tiger, his tone clearly communicating that she should not mistake his affirmative for anything more than "ask."

"Princess . . ."

"Princess what?"

"I love him, you know that. But . . . this has been just *killing* me for a long time. I would never ask Rhino why he dragged Princess along on the way back from that job down south. I can tell it's not something he'd want to talk about. Not to me, anyway. But I know he—Princess, I mean—he was some kind of . . . 'cage fighter,' right?"

"Yeah."

"Well, what *is* that? I mean, it couldn't be a sport or any-thing. Princess doesn't *like* fighting. All he ever wants to do is make friends. He never even gets mad. Not unless—"

"Not unless someone 'starts it,' I know."

"Well, if you're a fighter—I don't care what you call it; 'cage fighter,' that could mean anything—if that's the way you make your living, you don't have to *like* it, I guess. But I can't see Princess doing it. Not at all. That's just not him."

"You know how old he is?"

"No. I mean, who could tell? He *acts* like a kid. A sweet kid. But he's been with the crew a good while, and—"

"We don't know how old he is, either. Rhino taught him English. All Princess can *remember* is fighting. From the time he was a baby, some kind of fighting. Rhino says he was probably abandoned by his mother. Or sold. But he must have gotten away somehow. When the soldiers found him, they knew he was worth money. You know why? Even when they had him netted, he fought like a wild animal. Scared them, serious.

"They brought him to *el jefe—el rey*, more likely. That's when he got trained for fighting. Once he was ready, they put him into one of the cages. Very simple deal: the one who kills the other one gets to walk out.

"Princess always tried to make friends with the other guy. That never worked, but he kept on trying. For *years*, this was. He got so damn good at fighting, he figured out he could cripple the other guy bad enough so that he couldn't move— that way, he wouldn't have to kill anyone.

"But he's not stupid. The first time he heard the gunshot behind him, he knew the other guy was going to end up dead, one way or the other. One time, he told Rhino, he just refused to fight. Just stood there. But that didn't work, either—he'd do that, the other guy would always attack."

"That must have driven him crazy."

"He's not crazy, he's . . . damaged. When he thinks someone else 'started it,' he's going to start breaking bones. How's he supposed to know any better? In his mind, once he's in a fight, he wins or he dies. If that makes him crazy, it makes us *all* crazy, right?"

"But . . ."

"But what?"

"I know about that degenerate who got harpooned to a wall. Everyone in Chicago knew about it. That was you delivering a message, I get that. But how could you convince Princess that this guy 'started' anything?"

"We told him that the guy was a buncher."

"A what?"

"Guy who goes around to the animal shelters, adopts as many dogs as he can. Then he sells them to the people who need live dogs for their pits to practice on."

"If Princess thought anyone was getting puppies ripped to shreds . . ."

"Yeah."

"So you used him," Tiger said, her husky voice suddenly just short of a feral snarl.

"Don't be stupid. That sack of waste was already dead. All Princess did was pin him to that wall. So he had nothing to do with bunching dogs, so what? He was part of that gang that was raping women, and making tapes of it for sale. You think Princess wouldn't consider that 'starting it'?"

"But, Princess, he's just a—"

"He's a maniac," Buddha cut in. "So what? He's one of us. It took me a while to understand that. And, yeah, he gets on my nerves sometimes, but—"

"Chop it, Buddha," Cross said. Just in time.

"Was it a real cage?" Tiger asked, as if Buddha hadn't said a word. "I mean, with bars and all?"

"Sometimes it was. Sometimes it was down in a pit they made with a backhoe. And when the big shot wanted to show off, they'd make the cage real small, and use a crane to hoist it into the air. That way, the kingpins and their women could all sit up high above the rest of the crowd and have a perfect view."

"I never even *heard*—"

"The narco-reyes didn't invent it—you can thank the Japanese for that. There's a breed of dog over there. Tosas, they call them. Only the Emperor was allowed to own such dogs, going back hundreds of years. But no emperor could really control all the territory, so it was the Shoguns who did most of the breeding.

"Those dogs are *huge*. Three, four times the size of any pit bull. In those little cages, they'd lock up right away. The dog who died, so did his trainer. The dog who won—even if he died later on from his wounds—*his* trainer would get some big reward.

"I heard they still do it. Not like before. No emperor, not in public. But yakuza obyans put on those same kind of fights, even today."

"Too bad we couldn't have tested those A-bombs on *them*," Tiger said, grimly.

"Yeah. Well, that's the thing about bombs—they don't cherry-pick."

NO ONE else spoke for a while.

The Cross crew knew Mural Girl didn't work every day. The permanent camera-feed was downloaded every hour. That's how they knew she had no fixed schedule; how they knew she was never interfered with by any of the gangs warring over that single block of unclaimed turf.

And how they knew that whatever had branded Cross was always around. Its last message had been that full-house version of the Dead Man's Hand. Whatever was protecting Mural Girl wasn't something they could contact. The chance that *she* could reach out that far was what had brought the crew to her.

"**POSSE CAR** at three o'clock, boss."

"Yeah. I hear them. Rolling slow, working the muffler bypass just enough to represent. That thumping, some kind of rap?—probably heavy bass out of a trunk-speaker setup. They shouldn't be a problem."

"Oh, they *won't* be," Buddha promised, slowly pulling a long-magazine 40mm semi-auto from his jacket and resting it on the seat to his right.

"Buddha, stop. Stop the *car*, okay? There's no reason for us to cross paths. Cut the lights, they'll roll on past, never even look our way."

The pudgy man behind the wheel muttered something under his breath but followed orders.

Less than two minutes later, Buddha touched the button that re-started the Shark Car and motored down the road for another few blocks. Finally, he shifted into neutral and cut the engine, letting the big car glide to the vacant lot next to the slab-sided building where the woman they called Mural Girl did her work.

"SHE'S NOT here," Tiger said, not hiding her disappointment.

"It isn't quite first light yet," Cross said. "If she's coming, she'll be here soon enough. But if she rides up and sees *this* car, she might think one of the local mobs doesn't want any tags in their territory.

"Only she's not tagging, Tiger. She's painting. And there's no way she's gonna be scared of *any* damn car. She couldn't have been working this long without all the gangs knowing she's covered."

"You think she actually talked to—?"

"I don't know. The nearest I can figure it is that they . . . or whatever it is . . . they can *send* messages, but—*damn!*"

"What?"

"I *felt* that one. Right here," Cross said, tapping just under his right eye. "They don't miss much. Wherever they are, they can see us. Hear us. So Mural Girl must be—"

"Bicycle coming, boss. Riding the street, not the sidewalk. Hear the hum?"

"I do *now*. Okay, remember, Tiger's the only one leaving the car."

A trail bike came into view. All they could see was the knobby front tire, illuminated by the bike itself; it looked as if every downstroke of the pedals flashed an orange glow from its heavy frame. As the bike pulled up, its rider jumped off, floating to the ground. The bike itself rolled toward the freshly whitewashed wall, turning at the last second so it was leaning upright as it came to a stop.

The dismounted rider pulled off a black helmet, shook her hair loose, unsnapped knee and elbow protectors, and strolled over to the wall. There was a ladder with a platform coming off the top shelf standing there—none of the car's occupants had seen it before Mural Girl's arrival.

"Did that ladder just show up?"

"Damned if I know," Cross said to Buddha. "But she's acting like it's been there all along."

"My turn," Tiger said softly as she stepped out of the back.

BY THE time Tiger had covered the distance to the ladder, Mural Girl was already at its top, holding a brush as if deciding what to create on that giant easel.

"Could I talk to you?" Tiger called up.

Mural Girl looked down. Studied the big girl with the trademark hair that announced her name. "How are you at rock climbing?"

"Good enough," Tiger responded.

"Come on up, then," Mural Girl said, pointing at a series of pegs emerging from the wall.

Tiger's face showed no surprise at this development. Her spike heels proved no handicap as she pulled herself up using only her hands, as easily as a gymnast climbing a rope. When she was level with Mural Girl, she carefully felt for toeholds, then planted herself.

"You do beautiful work," Tiger said.

"Haven't done *any* work today."

"I've seen some. Before today, I mean."

"Camera's still working, huh?"

"You know. You've known all along, right?"

"Yes."

"How do your murals disappear? It seems a shame, they're so—"

"They just disappear from *here*. When they leave this wall, they end up on other walls. All over town."

"Oh."

"Now you want to know if they get over-tagged in *those* spots, right?"

"I . . . I guess so. Yes."

"No," Mural Girl said. "Never."

Tiger frankly studied the woman standing just to her left. *Dark-skinned enough to be almost anything*, she thought. *Could be Italian, Greek, Spanish, African . . . probably a whole bunch of roots went into that face. Sharp features, heavy hair . . .*

"I pass inspection?" Mural Girl said, her tone underscoring that she didn't care about the answer.

"You're a beautiful woman," Tiger said frankly.

"To some, I suppose I'd be."

"I'm not hitting on you."

"I didn't think that. Although"—looking Tiger over—"if you were, it wouldn't shock me."

"Fair enough. I can play both ways. But what I said, it was just a . . . I don't know, just an honest answer to that 'inspection' thing."

"You must be here for something, yes?"

"Yes. Do you know how your murals get moved? Or why no gang ever defaces them?"

"Not how. And the 'why,' that would only be a guess."

"The same guess covers how you can work here all the time and never get hassled?"

"Yep. I'm not a painter, I'm—"

"An architect."

"You did some research, huh?"

"Not trying to get into your business," Tiger assured her. "It's just that this whole thing you do, it's a mystery. Not the kind any of us would try to solve, except that we think whatever's looking out for you, it's looking out for us, too."

"And . . . ?"

"And we don't know why. It started with . . . a tiny little symbol. On the face of one of us."

"Cross."

"Yes," Tiger answered, nothing in her neutral voice revealing surprise.

"They make their own decisions. I don't have a clue who . . . or what they are. It's not like I could talk to them, or anything. I was riding by this spot a few years ago, and I noticed this huge white wall. That's when I started. And I've been doing it ever since."

"You didn't whitewash the wall yourself?"

"No. One day, it was just dirty brick. The next day, it was as white as a fresh canvas."

"How did you get the ladder over here? And all the paint?"

"I've got a friend with a pickup. He didn't want me doing this, but he didn't try and stop me. If he'd said 'no,' I'd have just asked someone else."

"Which he already knew you'd do."

"Yes," Mural Girl answered, flashing a smile that could only be measured in kilowatts. "He helped me get everything set up, that first time. He didn't want to leave me here, but he has a job. When he came back to take me home, I was just about finished. With the first one, I mean. I don't know why, but I can paint *fast* here. It's like it goes from my mind to the brush, zip!"

"Nobody bothered you?"

"That first day? Oh yeah. Some boy standing at the bottom of the ladder. 'Hey, girl, the view from here is something to see!'—that kind of play-pimp rap."

"He was the only—?"

"No. Just the first one to show up. I ignored him and he went away. At least, he wasn't there when I turned around a few minutes later. But a whole car of gang boys came later. Told me I couldn't work on this wall without getting a 'pass' from them."

"What happened?"

"I don't know. And that's the truth. They just . . . disappeared. Right in the middle of them waving their guns around, like they were posing for one of those lame TV shows. I *think* I heard this sizzling kind of sound, but . . . I'm just not sure. That wasn't the last time. Other people came by. Some just watched—that was fine. But every time anyone got stupid, something happened. Different things. Nobody's even *tried* to stop me from working for a long time now."

"You just see something in your mind and ride your bike over here, and it goes up on a white wall? And the *next* time you get an idea . . . a message you want people to see . . . when you come back, everything's all ready for you?"

"Sounds crazy, huh? I wouldn't have known what happened to the murals except that I saw one on a building we were gutting a half-mile west of here."

"You must have gone back to that one. I mean, just to see—"

"It wasn't touched," Mural Girl said. "None of them have been."

"How did you know Cross was the one they branded?"

"I didn't. Not until I saw you."

"Me?"

"Don't come at me sideways, lady. You think I'd have to be connected with . . . whatever they are . . . to know *you*?"

"But you never—"

"What? Visited Orchid Blue? That's right. And so what? Here's what *everybody* knows, okay? Cross doesn't look like much of anything, but you can't miss that big bull's-eye tattoo on the back of his right hand. Buddha, he can look like *less* than nothing, but word is, he's a magician with a pistol. Or a car . . ."

Mural Girl turned and deliberately looked into the shadow where the Shark Car lurked.

"Yeah. Never far away, are they? I don't know any of them, except by street talk, and that's never worth more than *who's* talking. There's one I don't know by name, but word is he's twice the size of an NFL offensive lineman. And Princess, now, *that* one's a pale gorilla with so much muscle he looks like he's armor-plated. He gets his hands on you, you're gone. Only he dresses up like some idiot's version of 'campy.' Lays that makeup on *heavy*: rouge, eyeliner, lipstick . . . the works.

"And you think there's a lot of Amazons walking around in neon bodysuits? With daggers strapped to their thighs? And black and gold stripes in their hair? If that's supposed to be a disguise, it's a beaut." Mural Girl chuckled. "All I'd have to do would be to drop word that you climbed this ladder in four-inch heels, street-talk would have them be six-inchers in a few hours."

She doesn't know about Tracker, Tiger thought. *Or Ace, either.*

"A lot of people—"

"—talk. I know," Mural Girl said. "The more they talk, the more outrageous they get, like some kind of multiplier effect. But they *do* talk, and it's not hard to hear what they say, if you're in places where they say it. That's how you can tell the natives from the tourists. Ask a cabdriver to take you to Red 71, you get a blank look, that's one thing. But if it's 'Are you out of your mind?,' that's all you need to tell them apart."

"That's why you're not worried?"

"About what?"

"About why I'm here? About why the car's over there?"

"You mean, because I think all that talk is so much BS? No. I know better. A lot of people know better, probably more than you think. But if you were here to try and do something to me, why even get out of that car?"

"That's not it," Tiger said, eyeing Mural Girl's face as if trying to memorize it. "You got . . . *them* watching your back, right? Whoever they are, they wouldn't let anyone do anything to you."

"I can take care of myself."

"We know that. You're supposed to be real good at some kind of martial art. And anyone who goes on one of those thousand-mile bike rides has got to have legs of steel."

"You know stuff? Or you *heard* stuff?"

"If the source is reliable, those are the same."

"Is that right? And *your* source . . ."

"An undercover. Infiltrated a major gang. Not some cop looking for a big drug bust; a fed. Working his way close enough to see if it's a true clue that one of the gangs actually took money from people who'd like to see Sears Tower fall down."

"Why tell me?"

"Because you asked. This . . . source, he saw you kick a banger in the knee. The one who walks with a cane, now. Not some Snoop wannabe—it's the only way he can get around."

"That's enough."

"Sure. You told us stuff we wanted to know, I figured the least I could do was—"

"You get it? Good. Then get on your way—I've got a lot of work to do."

Without a word, Tiger leaned her long-nailed hands against the whitewashed wall, pushed off, and butterfly-floated to the ground. Mural Girl never turned around as the Amazon stepped into the back of the Shark Car.

TIGER WAS silent as they slid through the treacherous streets, heading for the Badlands.

Buddha killed the headlights and switched to the laser light-bar behind the mesh grille as they rolled past the rusted out hulk of a de-wheeled semi that marked one of the entrances. Very few would take that route; even fewer would make it a round trip. There were other entrances, one to the Gangland version of Chicago's famous Commodity Exchange—an outlaw menu of bartering transfers, black-marketing, drag racing . . . and, if you knew the way, a path to Red 71. Buddha had already hit the "come home" signal to a network of one-use cells.

Hearing Tiger take a deep breath, Cross said, "Wait till the others get here. No point telling the same story twice."

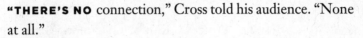

"THERE'S NO connection," Cross told his audience. "None at all."

Silence.

"What I'm saying, whatever that creature in the house was, he didn't connect to Old Greytooth's present for us. Pekelo, that one, looks like he was telling it true. It *had* to be AI, set to trigger if that creature didn't tell it to stand down. Whether he had to send the signal every hour or every month, it doesn't matter.

"It wasn't Hemp who was playing that 'game,' that was the Lao. To win, he had to draw us out. And what better way? I won't miss him. Or Hemp. But this wasn't the same kind of . . . Hell, I don't know. The Simbas, maybe? What*ever* they are, what*ever* we call them, we know this isn't how they work."

"Mural Girl told you all that, right?" Cross asked Tiger, no hint of skepticism in his words.

"Pretty much," she answered. "Mural Girl knows something's been watching her back. Something that can give her a fresh canvas to paint on. And—here's the thing—those murals of hers, they don't get erased, they get *moved*. She's seen them all over the city. Places where you'd expect them to be X-ed out, over-tagged, *something*. But once they go up, they *stay* up.

"She's used to it, by now. And this is one tough girl, no

question. But she knows she couldn't do what she does without cover. Why they picked her, I don't know. But she knows us. Knows *of* us, anyway. And—"

"All of us?" Tracker interrupted. This was so uncharacteristic of the man that the room went quiet, waiting for Tiger to answer.

"Cross, Buddha, Princess, Rhino, no doubt. Me, she knows, but from the way she was talking, I'm not sure if she knew I was always part of the crew. Until this morning, anyway."

"So not Ace . . ."

"And not you, either," Tiger told Tracker.

"What about—?"

"Oh, she knows all about Sweetie," Tiger smoothly assured Princess.

"What they could brand, they could kill," Rhino cut in, hard. "So something else must be in play."

Tracker cleared his throat. "When we got that message about what Hemp had sent a man to do, we deployed. I found a roost and waited. But . . . this is difficult to explain. I had a clear sight line, working off a bipod. I was going to make it rain .50-cals, but I opted for a head shot first because I needed time for the armor piercers to find the Semtex, and Hemp was Job One. A man taking a body hit could get lucky—he might have been wrapped.

"I didn't miss. I know I didn't. But . . . this sounds insane, but I swear Hemp's head just *exploded* at the same time I squeezed off the round. I saw it in the scope. This is all inside little tiny pieces of a second, but I'm sure it wasn't my round that took him out."

"They could do that," Cross said. "Stuff like that, they've

been doing for centuries. At least, I think so. Nothing else explains what Blondie and his girlfriend were putting together a capture-team for. Those two didn't know Tracker and Tiger were really with *us*. And they never found out.

"So whatever put this brand on me, it had its own reasons. But, whatever those are—whatever *it* is—just like Rhino said; if they wanted us, they could take us. I think Tracker saw exactly what he described. Maybe Hemp wasn't looking for us to move so fast, but he had to know what was going to jump off if that hit on Sharyn—"

"And my *children*," Ace said, his deep voice throbbing.

"So they took care of the problem to keep us from acting," Cross went on. "And what Mural Girl told Tiger, that's enough to confirm. There's no connect."

"Swell. Now we don't have an enemy in the world. Not in *this* world, anyway," Buddha sneered.

"If Blondie's alive, we do," Cross said. "I doubt the feds would answer our letter. Hell, the way things turned out, they could be looking for him themselves. And that Wanda girl, too, maybe . . ."

"What about that other—?"

"Percy? He's stone-to-the-bone loyal," Tiger answered Tracker. "You watched him, right? He didn't like those two any more than we did. Percy, he's no analyst. A pure hunter-killer team in one man's skin. He couldn't find them on his own, but, if the G does, he's the man they'd send to clean up the loose ends. If they've got any more like him on their payroll, they're already in some desert, laying waste.

"No, it's just Blondie and Wanda. A lethal cocktail, true enough. But do-it-yourself wouldn't be their style. Those kind, they push buttons to launch missiles. Percy *is* a damn missile, but he's not theirs to use, not anymore. Whatever they do, it would have to be on their own."

"All that is what I saw as well," Tracker added. "Percy is no danger to us. So we must either find those two, or confirm they're dead."

"We find them, we *make* them dead," the gang's leader said, passing the final judgment.

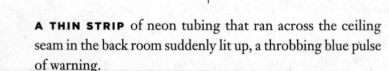

A THIN STRIP of neon tubing that ran across the ceiling seam in the back room suddenly lit up, a throbbing blue pulse of warning.

"Strangers," Cross said. Meaning that the ancient man who sat at the front desk of Red 71's basement poolroom hadn't recognized whoever had just entered.

"Didn't come here to shoot a game of pool," Buddha said, unnecessarily.

Cross toggled a switch that sent a visual feed to a flat-screen monitor. "Russians" was all he said.

"I thought we sent all of Viktor's mob to—"

"That's the problem with blowing things up," Tracker said to Buddha. "You can't get an accurate body count."

"And we could never be sure they were all there when you RPG'ed their joint, anyway," Cross added.

"How many?" Rhino asked.

"Looks like four," Cross answered. "All at the same table."

"I'll bring them over to *your* table," the behemoth said.

"No," Cross said. "Too messy if they get stupid."

"You boys all forgot the most important ingredient in any

successful club," Tiger said, standing up as she spoke. "That would be the hostess."

"No," Rhino said to Princess, who was already on his feet, the Akita at his side. "You and Sweetie have to wait now. Tiger will be fine."

"Already *is*," Ace said, as he reached for the sawed-off 12-gauge he always carried on a rawhide thong around his neck.

"HI, BOYS," Tiger purred at the four men. "Welcome to our little club."

The men froze. Maybe it was the sight of Tiger's outrageous torso threatening the camo spandex. Or her striped mane. Or the fact that she was taller than any of them.

"My name's Tiger. Can I help you with something? Anything you want?" she innocently asked, her voice going throatier with her last three words.

"We play pool," one of the Russians finally said. "Eightball. Two teams." He was medium-height, stocky, in a black leather jacket and dark jeans. Heavy cheekbones, thin lips, short haircut. Nothing to distinguish him from the others, except that he had spoken first. And the crude tattoos on his hands. *Cross will know what they mean*, Tiger thought, taking a mental snapshot.

"Playing for money?" she asked, a slight smile dancing over her lips.

"Sure," he said, tossing a rubber-banded roll of bills on the green felt of the tabletop.

"That's against the rules here," Tiger said, pointing a long, black-gelled nail at the sign against the far wall.

NO GAMBLING

She put her hands on her hips, as if the matter was settled.

"There are many more of us," the Russian said. "We lost some people. Viktor is gone. But we are here. The money I show you, that is to explain ourselves. Viktor did not understand there is always a tax to pay. We understand. We pay the tax. Every week. Right here, we send a man with the tax money. And your . . . people, they leave our business in peace."

"How much do you think this tax would be?"

"That is for you to say. But we do not haggle like some fishwives. We—"

"Do I look like a fishwife to you?"

"No, no. My English is maybe not so good. You tell us the tax. Flat only. No . . . percentage, nothing like that."

"Come back in a week," Tiger said, turning on one heel and walking away.

The Russians watched her until she disappeared from view. Then their leader nodded his head sharply, a clear signal.

They left their pool cues on the table. And the rubber-banded roll of bills.

WHEN THE neon tube went blank, Buddha and Tracker entered the poolroom, pistols held loosely at their sides.

Upon returning, Buddha tossed the roll of bills at Cross, who caught it in his right hand, opened his left to start a flame, and lit the cigarette that was already in his mouth.

"No Kansas City bankroll," he said. "It's all hundreds. Five large."

"Not bad for once a week, right, boss?"

"Very bad," Cross answered. "We take that, we're letting one of them in here once a week, too. Probably a different one each time. Enough time passes, we get used to that. These guys, they already know Putin's got his own problems now. Never mind the Ukraine, it's the Chechnyan rebels he's *always* got on his mind. The Ukrainians aren't going to invade Russia, but they could learn from the Chechnyans—suicide bombings are convincing propaganda.

"Putin can't have that. He's got to be in control. Somebody whispers in his ear that we—our whole crew—that we're negotiating with the Chechnyans. Hard contract, huge money. Not a contract for some movie theater or train station. For *him*. He doesn't have to be a mind reader to know they'd empty their pockets for his head."

"Come on, boss. We don't take any out-of-country work anymore. And even if we did—"

"How would Putin know any of that, Buddha? And I can think of one way he could believe we've already taken the contract."

"So these new Russians, they go back into the bear-claw business? And, one week, the guy they send with the taxes, you're saying he's gonna be wrapped?"

"Yeah. Some true believer Putin sends over. Might not even be Russian. There's a whole horde of ISIS-style dummies running around. Chump kids, recruited on Twitter.

The G keeps saying it's the Arabs who're supplying them with weapons. Maybe that's so. But cash is easier to smuggle than ordnance. And the Russians, they've been arms dealers for a *long* time now. Where do you think Saddam got those SCUDs?"

"One had tattoos on his hands," Tiger said. "Would that tell us whose side they're on?"

"One of those tattoos, it had some kind of crown showing? Or a playing card, a king of clubs, maybe?"

"The crown—that one I saw."

"Whoever had that one, he did the talking?"

"Yes."

"Some kind of 'authority' when he was in prison. But once he said 'Viktor,' we knew that much, anyway. He's the new boss. However he got to be that, it doesn't matter."

Buddha stirred. "Even if they've taken over Viktor's racket, I can't see Putin buying that Chechnyan story, boss. Not from them. They're nothing but animal-parts traffickers. Putin, he's ex-KGB, right? He might be a maniac—hell, he might be crazier than a psycho on angel dust—but he'd want actual intel, not some rumors. There's no way—"

"The blond man," Tracker interrupted. "He would do such a thing in a heartbeat. And that woman with him, she would know how to make contact with a foreign power."

SILENCE REPLACED SOUND.

Cross went through three more cigarettes before he finally spoke.

"The only way it adds up is if Buddha's right. This new mob, all they did was take over Viktor's business. Different gangs come to this country, they pick up on how we do business here. And that's easy enough, right? Because all over the world, it plays the same. No matter where you are, politics and crime, they need each other to survive, like air and water.

"You see that book?" Cross said, pointing at the single wood shelf against the wall behind the desk. "*Casino*. Nicholas Pileggi. You want to understand, you don't need to take some course. Just read that man's books. He knows. Now let's just get back to— *Damn!*"

"What was that?"

"Just that little brand on my face, Princess. It hit me with a real burn in the middle of what I was saying, that's all."

"Sweetie didn't even growl."

"Why would he? It was a message, not a threat. Whoever's doing it, they wouldn't need to threaten anyone. Sweetie's smart, right?"

"Sure!"

"Well, there's your proof. He knew there was nothing to worry about. From that burn, I mean."

"If they wanted to kill Cross, they could have done it when he was down in that prison basement," Rhino explained. "But they let him live. We don't know why. Maybe we never will. But they're not *our* enemies. A different tribe, maybe. But not one we're ever going to war against. You understand that, yes?"

"Sure! Sweetie, he knew all this—that's what you're saying?"

"Yes, honey," Tiger said, assuring the armor-plated child. "And Buddha *has* to be right. Forget those Russians who came in here. Putin wouldn't trust intel from anyone who works on our—I mean, the Americans'—side. But if Blondie and Wanda are still out there, they've gone rogue to the max. Who knows what they're trying to peddle. Percy's not with them, but he's still every movie-merc's fantasy. Macho and merciless. A one-man spike team."

"He's also loyal," Cross reminded her. "And he's not what you'd call subtle."

"He would never go off on his own," Tracker agreed. "He may be a human missile, but he's a *guided* missile."

"Then that's what we've got to do," Cross said. "Find him."

"Boss? I mean, what's the point?"

"Buddha," Rhino said, on the fringe of impatience with the pudgy killer's failure to understand—or admit—the obvious, "if the blond man and that woman went off together, people would be *looking* for them. You know which people. And who would know them better than Percy?"

"He had no use for either of them all along," Cross agreed. "If it was us the G wanted, they'd have tried way before now. Percy's a machine. If you don't give him work, he could rust. He may not like us much—I don't think he likes anyone much—but he's got no real problem with us, either. We—that's just me, as far as Percy knows; Tiger and Tracker, they were supposed to be hired hands *before* they got me involved. And me, I came through, right? I got the job done. It was *Blondie's* plan that was hosed from the start."

"So now we—?"

"We wait, Buddha. But there's no reason why we can't wait and work at the same time. Rhino?"

"I'll try and see if I can pick up his tracks," the behemoth said.

"And me and Sweetie, we'll help. I mean, I bet Sweetie would be better than any bloodhound if he wanted."

"That's perfect," Cross said, lighting another smoke and closing his eyes.

"YOU WANT . . . you want my *wife* in on this?"

"There's two possibilities," Cross said to Buddha. "Just two."

"Boss, I—"

"One," the gang leader interrupted, holding up his index finger, "the AI program was the end of the story. That lunatic in the fancy house had it on negative option—if he didn't call it off by some specific time, it would activate. The cameras in his joint were set to feed the program its target."

"The last ones in his house, you're saying?"

"In his *part* of the house. Nobody went up there. Ever. So anyone who did . . ."

"Yeah, I get it. So the only targets were you and Tracker."

"Right. That AI program had the capability of doing its own work. We know it put my picture up, with all that prize money for bait. You still with me?"

"I guess so, but . . ."

"Just *listen*, then. You get lost, you stop me. Otherwise, just ride."

A nod was his only response.

"Okay, next move is from that Lao, the one So Long used for the paper on those houses. He sat down one night to watch those rape tapes he liked and—*bang!*—that 'game' pops up on his screen. If he wasn't warped to start with, the AI program wouldn't have allowed him to see the game."

"So the one in that house we blew up—?"

"Buddha, that psycho didn't have to be interested in those rape tapes himself. But he'd know the kind of people who wouldn't hesitate to do . . . damn near anything. Not when so much money was on the table.

"And I'm thinking, me and Rhino, we have it right. So the Lao sees my picture. I don't look like much of anything, but this, this would show up nice and clear," Cross continued, holding his hand up to display the tattoo known throughout Gangland.

"From there, he could follow the trail. He knew So Long was putting together a big score. She wouldn't have said my name, but if she described the tattoo, that would be enough. So: me to Ace, Ace to Sharyn. After that, no more complicated than paying Hemp to call a blackout on everyone in that house."

"But So Long was on their hit list before any of that happened, boss."

"Yeah, she was. And *there's* the link between the Lao and whoever set up the whole rape-tape online game. She wasn't picked because of any connection to us—it was just her skin color."

"So . . . ?"

"So remember what the Lao told us? Remember what Rhino figured out? Pekelo was a miserable pervert when it came to his idea of 'entertainment,' but he wasn't stupid. He must have been good at whatever he did—he didn't get all that jewelry playing real-estate games. And that offshore account, not so easy to set up securely, not today."

"Boss, I can't—"

"Yeah, you can. So Long's got her own rep. Her own network, too. Pekelo, he was on the fringes, but he knew So Long was a big-money player. And he knew this rape-tape crew was operating out of somewhere close. Remember, he was *watching* those tapes. That wouldn't be for free.

"He couldn't get to whoever set it all up. But he *could* send a message to that back-channel site. Those rapes, they weren't random. Had to be scouted out. And that 'pattern' crap, it was just to throw off those profiler clowns. Like with that 'Rejuvenator' thing. But So Long, she fit, right?"

"*He* put So Long in the crosshairs? The Lao?"

"Could have," Cross said, meaningfully. "But there's no way to ask him. Not anymore."

TIGER SLID into the back room.

This time, the spandex was all black, the shoes were crepe-soled flats, and her hair was rolled into a French braid inside a black Unabomber hoodie. Working clothes.

"We got a target?" she asked, speaking very softly but unable to hide the hopefulness in her voice.

"The boss said two. And, thanks to me being a . . . damn chump, we're down to one," Buddha said soberly, holding up one finger. An index finger to most, a trigger finger to him.

"Pekelo?" Tiger guessed.

"Yeah," Cross answered. Then he quickly ran through everything he had gone over with Buddha.

"You're saying, if he hadn't . . . ?" Tiger said, pointing a finger of her own, the talon's nail now a dulled matte black.

"I'm saying, if it was an AI program, there's only two of us it could target—it couldn't go beyond whatever those cameras in his attic captured. The AI program had to be set up in front: once activated, it could only run on autopilot.

"A 'spider' is what Rhino called it. The program would reach out to everyone who'd been paying for online access to the rape tapes. Make it a competition, with a monster payoff. Pekelo was a fatalist. Dao equals destiny. So, when the program found him, he already 'won,' see?"

"No" was Buddha's flat reply.

"It wasn't personal," Cross said. "It *couldn't* be. How could that psychotic know *who* was gonna show on one of those cameras he had set up?"

"It's glowing," Tiger said, pointing again, in a different direction.

"You see it; I *feel* it. The G has all kinds of surveillance equipment, but the Simbas, they're a few thousand years ahead of anything on this planet. *That's* the message."

"Boss . . ."

"I got this brand in that basement slaughterhouse," Cross said, as calmly as he would recite any indisputable fact. "That was *their* choice. But who sent me there in the first place? Who hired Tracker? And Tiger? Who wanted that 'specimen' they sent me after?"

"Blondie and that little bitch," Tiger summed it up.

"There's also—"

"Percy? He didn't like Blondie and Wanda any more than you did. They each had their own smell."

"What?"

"Smell, Buddha. Percy's was like a testosterone overdose. I dropped a pen once. Bent over to pick it up. Little test. Percy's perfume snapped out so heavy it clogged the air.

"Wanda, I got *real* close to her anytime I could make it look natural," the Amazon continued. "She wanted me so bad it hurt her. Really caused her pain . . . because she couldn't *show* it."

"Blondie?" Cross asked.

"Neutral. Dead empty. Asexual, or whatever you want to call it."

"But him and Wanda, they were partners?"

"Why not? Everything doesn't have to be about sex. There was nothing like that between them, and so what? They'd been together a long time. I don't know how long, but that job, that 'specimen capture' thing, it wasn't their first. You could see. Little gestures, stuff that only they understood, no outsiders allowed."

Cross picked up a cell phone.

THE BACK ROOM of Red 71 slowly filled; Ace was the last to show.

Cross looked around the room. In the darkness, the tiny blue hieroglyph blazed as coldly as the neon promises of a strip club.

"It's not over," he said. "The G expects to get what it pays for. But I don't see them blaming us. It had to be Blondie and Wanda—probably just Blondie—who sold them on the 'specimen' thing in the first place. It's like chronic liars—they're sure *everybody* lies, just not as good at it as they are. Same thing goes for people who're for sale—they think *everybody* is, only a question of the price.

"Understand? Blondie for sure was on the G's payroll at one time, so he could have run across Percy. Who'd *you* rather have handling rough stuff? And the G would want Percy in there, too. Someone *they* could trust.

"But Blondie wouldn't have thought of that. He's about as superior a weasel as you'll ever meet. To him, Percy would be some kind of robot. Ten kinds of killer, but not too bright. Blondie, he'd sell the Simbas as a 'terrorist' story. More than enough to convince Percy to go along for the ride. They'd all be heroes."

"They *could* all be dead," Tracker said.

Buddha nodded, taking the Indian's words as prophecy.

"Sure," Cross agreed with Tracker as if in past-tense speculation. "But if they're not, there's two hunting parties out there."

"Two?" Tiger said.

"No matter how it's spun, the blond man and the Asian woman would be failures," Rhino squeaked. "The government doesn't trust failures. Especially those who don't share all their information."

"They did not share how to find that apartment Cross had," Tracker said. "They were *very* secretive. Perhaps a bargaining chip in case . . ."

"Not enough of one," Rhino cut in. "That apartment where Cross used to live, that's gone. And Red 71's no secret. Or the Double-X. If the G had *us* targeted, they wouldn't have been so elaborate about it. What they wanted, maybe what they *still* want, is that 'specimen.'"

Cross nodded. "If those two are alive, they know it can't be for long. Without the G, they got nothing. Never had a network of their own. It was just the two of them. Otherwise, they would have known Tracker and Tiger were connected to us before they reached out and hired them. They couldn't have gone rogue for real—not then—they needed the G's backup. Which is why they couldn't stop Percy from being in on their plan."

"Those two, they're out of moves now," Tiger agreed. "But I can't see them going on the run. Especially Blondie— he'd be positive he could still pull it off. He couldn't sell the G on some 'possibility,' but if he actually made it happen . . ."

"They would not take their own lives, either," Tracker said. "They are not some form of yakuza—the concept of atoning for failure would be alien to them. They are just jagged edges who somehow fit together to make a single unit. They have some . . . bond between them. But without the government's resources . . ."

"So *we're* the target, then," Buddha said, clearly relieved that the gang had finally reached a point where homicide could solve a problem.

"Are you even listening?" Tiger snapped at him. "If Blondie and Wanda are hunting us, Percy's not with them. But if the G wants them gone, Percy would be just the man for *that* job."

"I would, too," Ace said, so softly that Cross couldn't be certain he had spoken at all. Or maybe he was just feeling his first partner's thoughts inside himself.

"WHO THE hell are *you* supposed to be?"

"What do I look like?" Tiger said to the immense block

of tribal-tattooed Maori standing between the "Valet Parking Lot" and the road leading to the back of the Double-X.

"Don't matter what you look like—nobody gets back there without word from the boss."

"This is where Cross said to come," Tiger answered, as if that should settle any argument.

"Anyone can say a name, miss."

"Then use your phone, you blockhead. I have to go on in an hour, and—"

"Who the hell is *that*?" the Maori stepped back, startled.

"This is my manager. His name is Princess."

"Hi!" said the muscleman, extending his hand.

The Maori didn't accept the offer. He was just about to reach for his phone when an almost prehistoric growl came out of the darkness. "What the—?"

"Sweetie! You stop that!" Princess chided the beast. "We're here to make friends!"

The Maori's eyes shot to the black-masked, white-bodied—*Is that a dog?*—creature. His hand slid from the pocket where he kept his phone to a shoulder holster.

"No!" Tiger yelled, reaching toward her thigh just as the Shark Car rolled up behind her.

Rhino leaped out, a meat-locker-sized blob of gray. "Freeze!" he squeaked. "Princess, come on back here. Now!"

"I'm not leaving Tiger," the armor-muscled man said, his voice that of a petulant child.

By then Cross was closing in. "You must be another one of K-2's cousins," he said, calmly. "That guy's family has got to be the size of some small towns."

"You're—?"

"Yeah," Cross answered, holding up his right hand, palm toward his face. "Just step back, and make your call."

As the Maori retreated deeper into the darkness, Cross spoke to Tiger out of the side of his mouth. "You couldn't wait, huh?"

"I thought you'd be here first. With Buddha driving—"

"But when you saw we *weren't*, you had to go all Bogart on that poor guy, right?"

"I was *sweet*, you moron."

"Yeah. I can tell. Never mind, here he comes."

"Mr. Cross? I apologize, sir. K-2 says he apologizes, too."

"He's got nothing to apologize for. He knows he can bring on anyone he wants without asking me. As long as it's family."

"Then I should—?"

"You should get out of the way," Tiger said, flashing a dazzling smile.

"TRACKER'S SNIFFING the air," Rhino said, as he fired his computer into life in the NO ACCESS back room.

"And you're sniffing the Net," Cross nodded. "So where's Ace?"

"He slipped off, boss," Buddha said.

"Damn! He thinks he's going to find Blondie and Wanda holed up in some motel?"

"I don't know, boss. But Ace, he's no dummy."

"You think you know him like I do?"

"No. But . . . I mean, he's probably up to something. Spreading the word, putting up a bounty . . ."

"Buddha," Cross said, almost wearily, "you just *had* to shoot Pekelo, didn't you?"

"Boss, come on! I mean, he almost got my wife—"

"What? Raped? Sure, I get it. What I'm saying is, *you* don't. That grown-up thalidomide baby trapped on the top floors of that house, he set a chain in motion with that AI program, sure. But the Lao, the only one who might have shown us something if we let him run—he's dead. Ace could have lost Sharyn. And some of his kids."

"But he didn't," Tiger said, gently.

"So Long didn't get raped," Cross said, opening his left hand to flame a light for his cigarette. "As soon as we knew what was going on, she wasn't *going* to. So what's left? Nobody we can talk to, nobody we can follow. You think Ace doesn't know he couldn't find Blondie and Wanda? He wouldn't even try. But if Percy's out there, *he* won't be invisible."

"If Percy's after them, and the G's backing his play, they're as good as dead anyway, right?"

"Yeah. Very logical, Tiger. Only Ace may not give a damn. He can't kill some AI program. But if he thought those two played *any* part in throwing a blackout at his family, he'd need to watch them die."

For a long minute, the only sound in the room was Rhino slamming his fingertips into an XXXL keyboard, watching the big-screen TV that served as a monitor.

"Boss?"

"What, Buddha?"

"Okay, I lost it. Twice. I get it. But . . . but Ace knows what he's doing. Just because we don't know exactly what that is . . ."

Cross took the third drag of his smoke, snapped it into a bowl of some murky liquid substance, and closed his eyes.

"CHECK THE camera feed," Rhino squeaked, not taking his eyes off the screen.

"Mural Girl!" Tiger yelped. "Is there another place where we could plug in?"

"Buddha, show her, okay?"

"This isn't really anything I know about," Buddha said, half apologetically.

"Nothing *to* know," Tiger assured him, working the mnemonic in her head as she tapped keys.

The mural was twin ribbons of blood red, not intertwined, not parallel, connected only by a huge tree bole before it branched out.

Inside the bole, humans pursuing other humans. As the ribbon branches separated, they marched through time. Mountain dwellers hunting food and cosseted-by-wealth pleasure seekers, moving in opposite directions. Thinner tendrils connected the thick branches. Within them, all they had in common was killing. Some for land, some for religion, some for wealth. And a tiny bubble off those tendrils . . . killing for pleasure.

"What the—?"

"Sssshhh" was all Tiger said.

"We have to watch," Princess explained, proud that *he* understood.

Suddenly the mural vanished. Three playing cards, laid faceup on a green felt surface: the seven, nine, and jack of clubs. Another card dropped into line. The eight of clubs. The image was static for two full minutes. Then the fifth card fell: the ten of clubs.

"Double gut-shot straight flush," Buddha whispered, almost reverently.

"Percy's here. And Ace is looking for him," Tiger said, as the cards disappeared and the mural wall turned into pure whitewashed brick.

"YOU READ it right," Cross said to Tiger. "Let's—"

"Boss!" Buddha hissed, holding up his phone. "It's So Long. She wants to help."

"Help her*self*, right?"

"Help *me*," the pudgy killer said. "She knows it's my fault that there's no way for us to work backward. She knows she can't help with Percy. But she says she knows a way this might *all* connect. A way we can find them. Maybe. But we'd have to—"

"Tell us on the way," Cross said, getting to his feet.

Buddha chewed over his wife's last words: "Hmong, we know. And we hate them all." But finally decided it wasn't time to turn that card faceup.

THE ALLEY'S darkness was neither obstacle nor friend to the monolithic war-machine as he moved carefully, inexorably forward.

Under the government-modified flak jacket, a pair of shoulder-holstered MAC-10s awaited his touch. A jungle belt of grenades circled his waist, separated from each other by the same thin film that wrapped the barrels of the full-autos.

A black bladed K-bar with extended reverse serrations was strapped to the outside of his soft-soled boots. Each pouch of his jacket held various forms of death: a titanium-wire garrote, curare-tipped darts, an aerosol of acid. . . .

And even if that entire arsenal were to be expended, Percy wouldn't be out of weapons—he always had his hands.

The neighborhood was as black as the alley's shadows, but this wasn't the first time Percy had worked territory where the entire population was a collection of hostiles. He understood the value of stealth and accepted the inevitability of discovery if he spent too much time in the same place.

But for now, he'd wait. If discovered, he knew what to do.

Probably lousy intel, he thought to himself. *Usually is. But I should be able to get close enough to see for myself. . . .*

"You know what this is?" a voice came from behind him.

Nobody gets behind me! was quickly replaced by tactile recognition of a double-barreled weapon pressed squarely between his kidneys.

Before the soldier's intrusive *I didn't even feel the flak jacket move. . . .* thought could be completed, the voice came again: "You're good. And you got the tools, too. But don't get stupid. You're not fast enough. Nobody is. Twelve-gauge, three-inch magnum shells, number two steel shot. You move, you lose your spine. Understand?"

"Yeah," the soldier said, as carefully as a man defusing a bomb. *He wanted me dead, he could've done that already.*

"You're Percy," the voice said. "Saying that so you know *I* know. Here's how it is: You're hunting a pair of . . . Ah, don't matter what I call them, just their names, right? Okay: Blondie and Wanda. Thing is, they're hunting *us.* Not sure why, exactly. And that don't matter, either, am I right?"

"Yeah," Percy said, carefully keeping his voice empty.

"I'm Ace. Cross crew. I know you saw me on some tape those two had of that dogfighting hit. Okay, now they're loose. Maybe they're still on the job, maybe they've been *cut* loose. Only one who knows is you."

"Cut loose," Percy said. "On the run."

"So you weren't with them before. And you're not with them now. But your boss—the G, I'm saying—maybe needed you on the scene to watch them. Maybe even protect them. That was then. What's now?"

"I'm not with them. I'm looking for them."

"Looking for them *here*?"

"Supposed to be on top floor of that dope house, two blocks further south."

"That's an off-brand operation. Only reason it's lasted this long is the taxes they pay. But they're on the checkoff list."

"Mine, too" was all Percy said.

"You gonna just rush that place? Kill your way to the top floor?" Ace said, unable to keep a trace of admiration out of his voice.

Percy was silent.

"Why not just make the whole place disappear?"

"Only confirmed kills."

"Okay, I get it. Only thing is, they're not in that joint."

"You sure?"

"Dead sure."

"You got surveillance on—?"

"I asked. They told me," Ace interrupted.

"Just like that?"

"A hit man went over to where my wife was. My wife and my kids. He was supposed to *leave* them all there. The people running that house over there, they know me; they know what I do. I told them the stone truth: whoever called that blackout, they're dead. What the guy running that house told me? They ain't there. He wasn't lying. He knows—they *all* know. I don't mess with dope. And I ain't no tax collector."

"You telling me to back off?"

"You want to hit that house, don't mean nothing to me. I'll just fade. You want to make Blondie and Wanda dead, I'm telling you two things: They ain't in that house. And I *am* going to kill them."

"That's my job."

"You want to come along with me, I'll let you take all the cell-phone snaps you want when we're done."

"I don't work with partners."

"Me, neither. Not when I'm . . . doing what I do. This is different. Not about business. Personal. If it's same ol', same ol' for you, go ahead and do whatever you feel like doing."

"You just happened to be here, right? And you figure, why not keep me from wasting my time?" Percy said.

"I was here for the same reason you are. Like I said, I was already at that house. So I figured you'd be along soon enough."

"That isn't any—"

"What, explanation? I don't owe you no explanation. Didn't ask you for one, neither. Why I waited was to offer you what you just turned down."

"You mean a . . . ?"

"Yeah. A partnership. You're hunting what I'm hunting. I want them dead; you want the *proof* they're dead. You're a good man in a gunfight, and you got some kind of G-man thing working for you, too. So, even if your info is half guesses, it's got some facts mixed in. I could use that.

"I got to be close to do what I do. But I got something to ante up that you don't. I can work this area. I can get *ground* info. You want them wasted; I don't have time to waste. You're walking with me or you're walking alone, your choice."

Percy did the math at combat speed, his internal Threat Level Meter dropping like an anvil from an airplane. "Let's go," he said.

The pressure between his kidneys disappeared.

"WHAT THE hell is *that*?" Cross asked So Long, pointing at a sign over a black-glass storefront over which fleeting images played, none long enough to actually identify:

NO-CHANCE GAMING PARLOR

If being wedged between Rhino and Princess bothered her, it did not show in her voice.

"That sign is a message. 'No-Chance' means this is a place for games of *skill*, not luck. The people in there, most are . . . I cannot describe them, but they know each other by something more than appearance."

The black-masked Akita nudged So Long's sleekly silked legs, as if in agreement.

"See!" Princess half-shouted in excitement. "Sweetie understands what people say. I *told* you!"

"Do *not*!" Tiger snapped at Cross, anticipating his response to a male dog nuzzling So Long.

"I could not go in there," So Long said, as if none of the

surrounding nonsense—spoken and otherwise—was any of her concern. "Not you, either," she told Cross, clearly assuming that Buddha and Rhino would not even entertain such a thought.

"Me?" Tiger asked.

"You and Princess," So Long answered. "None of those playing inside would feel out of place at ComicCon, and you and Princess would fit—"

"And Sweetie, right?"

"Certainly," So Long replied, as if this had never been in question.

THE SHARK CAR'S doors hissed open.

Princess stepped out onto the sidewalk and waited patiently for Tiger to climb over Cross from her position between him and Buddha.

Tiger and Princess entered the gaming establishment together, her hand resting lightly on the cartoon-muscled arm of her gentlemanly escort. The three proprietors, identically dressed in white T-shirts sporting the game cave's logo that draped down to the knees of their jeans, stopped whatever they'd been doing to *stare!* at the invasion. The blazing-color comic book covers that lined the entire back wall had sprung to life, leaving them stuck somewhere between fascination and terror.

Others were so deeply engrossed in whatever was on the screens of the hexagonal tables scattered throughout the room that they didn't notice. At first. But the rolling wave of gaping silence coated the room like the spray from a slow-motion tsunami—even the faint pings from the demanding screens seemed to be muting of their own accord.

"Hi!" Princess boomed, as Tiger pranced around him, whispering, "Rip your shirt off, honey," to the monster child. Princess fisted his tearaway lilac mesh shirt and stood silently, still waiting for the dumfounded crowd to respond to his greeting. He was utterly without makeup, a ridiculous .600 Nitro Express pistol holstered under one arm. His body gleamed, its armor coating flexed and popped, as if acting on its own instructions.

He's right out of Geof Darrow's pen! a few of the more sophisticated watchers thought, in one single, soundless a capella.

"You and Sweetie just watch the back wall, honey. I want to talk to those boys over there, okay?"

Princess dropped Sweetie's chain. It hit the floor like the sixty-pound linked iron it was, but all eyes remained glued to Tiger as she stalked over to the counter. Her every move threatened to crack the coating of the scarlet body paint she *must* be wearing—*Nothing else could be that tight!* being the universal, albeit unspoken, verdict of the watchers. *It looks like she stepped right out of that poster. That big one over on the far wall . . .*

"Don't do that," Tiger said in a sugar-sprinkling voice, as she snatched a cell-phone camera from one young man's hand. "I don't like having my picture taken with all these clothes on." Without looking back, she flung the phone over her shoulder at Princess, who deftly caught it in one hand and closed his fist around it. The crunching sound that emerged didn't frighten any of the gamers—this *had* to be some kind of illusion, right?

When Princess opened his hand, the shattered remains of the phone drifted to the floor. By then, none of the gamers were watching their consoles, not even those who had been utilizing the slide-out panels on either side of the individual seats for "private play." All eyes were on Tiger as the Amazon hip-switched her way to the counter.

"Who's the boss?" she purred, leaning on the counter. Her scarlet-soled, black spike heels combined with her natural height to make it appear as if she were bending over extravagantly. The tables were filled with youngish males whose minds were too overwhelmed even to *think* the string of "OMG!!!"s that would otherwise be filling the micro-keyboards they all carried.

"We . . . we three are," a long-haired male with a wispy mustache said. "I mean, we divide—"

"Sssshhh, baby," Tiger said, so softly that he had to lean forward to be certain he could hear her. Tiger's body perfume wafted toward him, as if released by pressing her elbows together. Fortunately for his equilibrium, he was down to mouth-breathing by then. "I'm just . . . curious, about this place. Is that okay?"

"Sure! I mean . . ."

"Oh, stop teasing! I just want to show you a picture. A photograph, that's not much to ask, is it?"

As the other two partners moved closer to the man between them, Tiger reached down to her gorgeously sculpted thigh and pulled one of the twin daggers strapped around it. Her hand flashed; the dagger spiked into the wood counter. It stayed there, vibrating, as a photograph that had been tightly wrapped around the handle unrolled itself loose.

The dagger was back in its holster before any of the three could look at the photo. But when they did, they were silent.

"Come on, now," Tiger whispered. "You don't want to make me beg, do you? That would be a shame—the last man who tried to make me do that won't be back anytime soon. Unless those zombies you're always watching in your movies are real. Maybe they are, for all I know. But here's what I know for sure: *I'm* real. And so is my friend back there. And that darling little puppy."

"If we let you—" one of them said, stopping when he caught a look from the others.

"Oh, I know he's not back there *now*. But this place, it's got some more depth to it, doesn't it?"

"Uh . . ."

"I understand. If all those boys watching me see me go behind that nice blue velvet rope and disappear, they'll stay until you close up, waiting for me to come out. That wouldn't be good. You've got another way for people—certain people—to get back there, yes? Sure, you do. And they pay real money to do that. You want to know *how* I know?"

None of the partners spoke.

"Never mind. I know, that's all. But I still have to see it for myself," Tiger said, not asking permission. "I'll just disappear behind those two staggered mini-walls you flash stuff against . . . like those tarot cards that are being dealt right now. It's *so* clever, the way you have it set up."

"There's no one in—"

"Oh, that doesn't matter. The way we'll work it is, I'll just walk back there and *disappear*. See this cute little glass ball?

When I drop it—*Poof!*—a lot of pretty scarlet smoke. By the time it clears, I'll be gone. Cool, huh?

"Now listen, after tonight, you'll be able to double your prices. 'Cause I'm going to walk out of there the same way people walk *in*. You follow me? Ah, never mind, here comes the really cool part. In a couple of minutes, I'm going to walk in the *front*. And drag my friend back out with me. By the time anyone blinks, we'll be gone.

"They'll all have different stories to tell, but they *will* tell them, am I right?"

The man in the center risked leaning forward again. "There's someone back there now. Only one person at a time. If he—"

"When *I* leave a room, every man in that room follows me, believe that. When we've cleared out—just the way I told you we would—that room will be empty. I promise," she said, licking her lips as if to make certain her lipstick was going to stay painted on.

WHEN THE scarlet mist cleared, Tiger was gone.

As she silently entered the inky back room, she could make out an indistinct form hunched over a holographic keyboard projected onto the black surface of a small table in front of him. Another soundless step and she could see the images on the sixty-four-inch 3-D monitor that transfixed the viewer, pulling him virtually inside the screen.

The viewer pushed back his monk's cowl, lightly tapped a key, and an audio icon blinked. That's when Tiger noticed he was wearing an elaborate set of earphones. She quickly glanced at the screen. *He's scoped onto the kill-spot!* filled her mind. *Just like there is on an alligator. Only alligators don't have any choice about what they are. . . .*

The Amazon came back from wherever she'd gone. Looked through the red mist as it wisped away from her vision. The man was nice-looking; well dressed, nothing extreme except maybe that oversized wristwatch. One of Tiger's daggers protruded from his spine, a surgically bloodless strike between the C1 and C2 vertebrae.

Deliberately looking away from the screen images, she ran her forefinger down the dead man's back, found a belt—*alligator*, she thought grimly, her thumb against its grain. Hoisting him like a golf bag in one hand, she used a blue LED flash to guide her out the door of the private cave.

Kicking a heavy black rubber wedge under the door, she stepped into the night air, drawing a deep breath in through her nose. The Shark Car was where she'd expected it to be, trunk already slowly opening on its own. She tossed the dead man inside, knowing the trunk would be lined with a triple-thick black plastic wrap.

The Shark Car waited, as silent as its namesake.

As Rhino entered the now empty back room, Tiger walked around the corner and entered the gaming parlor.

Heads swiveled. Tiger waited until the owners were looking directly at her, pointed at the back of the room, shook her head with a clear message: "No." Turning to Princess, she whispered, "Let's go, sweetheart."

They were inside the car in seconds. It was gone in less.

"ROLL NOW, Buddha," Cross said. "I've got to pick up a car in the Badlands, and then come back for Rhino."

"I could—"

"Take her back to our spot," Cross said, cutting him off. Turning to include Princess, the gang leader said, "Getting rid of that outfit isn't going to make you invisible, Tiger. And, Princess, you go with her, make sure nobody—"

"Nobody's going to be a problem." Tiger stopped Cross's instructions with the pad of a talon pressed against his lips. "I've been over at *my* place for hours. Princess has always been after me to take him along, so . . . tonight was the night."

"Me and—"

"Oh, honey, *please*! Didn't I promise you? All the girls are going to love Sweetie, I guarantee it. Fair enough?"

"Sure! You hear that?" Princess crooned to the beast. "The ladies won't be as beautiful as Tiger; that's 'cause they *couldn't* be. But they'll all be nice to you."

THE SHARK CAR ripped past the abandoned semi that marked the entrance to the Badlands and spun into a J-turn.

It blasted away while Cross was still rolling on the pavement.

A pale-yellow Scion xB, its flanks generically flamed in blue peel-offs, was waiting less than twenty yards away. The car was running, its undersized engine virtually silent. A young man, with the bowed spine that had given him his name and a bright-blue Mohawk that could be gelled down flat, stood next to the opened doors.

Condor was watched by the pack of runaways who had made a home on top of what the city called a toxic waste dump. As their leader, he had the honor of personally handling the instructions Cross had barked into a cell phone on the way over.

Secretly basking in his reaffirmed status, he listened intently for the gang leader's next words:

"Get behind the wheel. I'll be in the back. We want Uptown and we want it *quick*. I'll give you the street-by-street once we get over the border."

"Me?"

"You got a number two already named?"

"Sure. Just like you said—"

"Then whoever it is will know what to do until you get back. We get stopped, the cops are gonna *expect* someone who looks like you to be behind the wheel."

"I don't have—"

"If you mean 'time,' we don't, either," Cross snapped, tossing a rubber-band-wrapped wad of paper into the front seat. "License, registration, insurance. Your name is Johnny Lee James, got it?"

The Scion was already in motion.

"You live on Wilson," Cross continued. "The address is good. You were born here. Chicago, I mean. But that hillbilly name, that was from your parents. Kentucky. They're deceased. You work at the Tomahawk Chop Car Wash. And you're just out for a ride tonight, got it?"

"Got it," the young man said, an Appalachian twang already at the edges of his voice.

"We got one pickup to make. You probably won't get stopped. If you are, just be polite, you got that?"

"Yes, *sir,* officer."

"Cop wants to look in the back, fine with you, understand? We'll bail before anyone checks."

"You and—?"

"—sure. If things get stupid, you're not going to outrun anyone in this crate. That happens, just cooperate, okay? Car's not stolen, papers're good. Worse they can do is toss you into County on some flake charge. Don't say anything. To anybody. A lawyer will be there to spring you in the morning, when they call the new line down to court."

"I'll handle it."

"SLOW IT now. Next left. Sit there and wait. We'll be out soon enough."

"I'll be here."

"Don't play hero on us, Condor. You're not carrying . . . ?"

"Just my blade."

"Toss it back here."

A rustle of movement, a glove-muffled sound. Then Cross said, "Kid, I thought you knew better. This thing, it's way over regulation."

"I thought, if—"

"Being a *leader,* that takes more than just heart, Condor. You've already been on the run for, what, years? And nobody's looking for you. But if you get popped, your prints are gonna fall. We can deal with that, like I told you. But a new charge? That'd be dumb."

"I . . . I know."

"Forget it. It never happened. Now, slide in right ahead of that white Crown Vic, and—"

"That's an undercover car."

"That's an *empty* car. Understand?"

Without waiting for a response, Cross pushed open the still-wedged back door of the No-Chance Gaming Parlor.

CONDOR SETTLED down to wait, using the panoramic mirror he held in one hand to eye-sweep the block in all directions.

It wasn't long before the back doors of the Scion opened, then closed soundlessly.

"Go," Cross said, pulling another phone from the coveralls he wore. "Nice and smooth."

"THERE CAN'T be a *trace* of this thing left," Condor told his crew as he climbed out of the Scion. "But no boom and no fire. Take it apart, then—"

"We got this," a tall, muscle-and-bone young man said.

"Counting on you, M.Z.," Condor said. "On *all* of you."

"Did they really take you with?"

"Don't know what you're talking about, 'Zeus. And *you* don't, neither."

"Just sayin'. I mean, you came back alone. . . ."

"I never left," Condor spoke over his shoulder as he walked off into the deeper darkness.

"WHERE'S JOHNNY EYES?" Condor asked, pointing at two of his crew with forked fingers.

"Crow's Nest," answered a girl with two tears tattooed under her left eye, using her hands to speak.

Condor gestured "Send him down." And then made a "sit down" motion, which he knew would be interpreted as "Take his place until he gets back."

The girl left without a sound. This wasn't some kind of submissive gesture—Q.T. had been left profoundly deaf from the last beating her mother's boyfriend had dished out, before calling the police. His story was he had kicked her out for "whoring to buy drugs" but she'd broken back in—"with that big knife, the one right on the floor there—probably to kill both of us."

The police had taken the girl's silent response to their questioning as defiance, ignoring the blood already flowing down the side of her face. Unceremoniously dumped into a holding facility, she was eventually transferred to an institution for "juvenile incorrigibles," where she earned her second tear by pressing her thumb so deeply into the eyeball of a "heavyweight" that she would have faced an attempted-murder charge if she hadn't gone over the concertina wire that same night, following a crudely drawn diagram to the Badlands one of the other girls had given her.

This is the last time, Condor promised himself. *It's like Cross is always saying: if you want to be the boss, you can't use your people; you have to make sure they get what* they *can use. I don't know if Maria could possibly take another one in, but, first thing tomorrow . . .*

"NOTHING DOING, chief." Johnny Eyes interrupted Condor's reverie. "Not since that rolling boxcar came back in."

"Bounce this over to them: 'Boxcar back in the house, full empty.'"

"On my way," Johnny Eyes said, making it clear he knew who "them" was, and what he had to do.

As Q.T. came down the steel ladder, Condor was already handing out more assignments:

"We got anyone working outside tonight?"

"Donnie and the new guy," an Asian kid said, consulting a tablet.

"You can get word to them?"

The Asian kid worked hard to keep a "Du-uh!" expression off his face and nodded once.

"I need a looks-like-them-all ride. Keyed correct. By tomorrow, sunrise."

The Asian kid was already tapping at his tablet.

"THIS IS it," Condor said, pulling to the curb of a two-story cottage with a good-sized yard and two-car garage, letting that action substitute for the words the girl in the seat next to him couldn't hear.

She followed him to the back door of the house, where they waited patiently. A handsome young man opened the door. He looked calmly competent—not crazy-fearless, like some of the boys in Condor's crew. But Q.T. could tell that getting past him could take some doing.

Condor slid back the hoodie just enough for the young man to recognize him. The response was immediate: "You know where to sit. I'll get Maria," the young man said, leaving the two of them alone.

"What *now*?" said a strong-boned blonde woman with a still-beautiful face despite soft blue eyes that had seen too much, too many times. She wasn't as annoyed as her words should have sounded.

"I've got—"

"Condor," she said, playfully pushing his Mohawk against the grain, "no sales pitch today. Just give me what I need."

"This girl," Condor said, making certain that she was included in the conversation, his gestures making it clear that she wasn't some package he was dropping off, "she's with us. You already know how that happens. Only, she—we call her Q.T., because one of the newbies called her 'Cutie,' and grabbed her . . . you know. We had to pull her off before she blinded him, but the name kind of stuck. She can't hear. And she can't speak. Wasn't *born* that way. You know the rest. You know what those tears mean. She's wanted. Not for the usual runaway stuff—looking at serious time downstate. Only she had no choice."

"You want me to take her in?"

"I know it's a lot to ask—"

"Don't work me, young man. But you tell that 'friend' of yours I can't risk giving up nine other kids just for her. So I need prints to disappear. And—"

"I'll get it all for you," Condor said, chastened. "Give me a few days. Just keep her inside. If I can't get it done, I'll take her back with us."

"All right, you *do* that. She'll be here when you come back, either way."

She bent down and kissed Condor on the cheek, ignoring his flaming face. Then she held out her hand to the girl—half invitation, half command. The two of them walked out of the room, together.

"YOU KNOW what you're asking?" the cheap-suited man with thick wrists and a prizefighter's face said.

"I know what I've *been* asked," Cross said quietly, leaning into the front window of McNamara's white Crown Vic. "And I don't recall ever passing."

"All I can get is the codes," said the ex-cop, whom the department had allowed to keep the white unmarked as a retirement present. "After that . . ."

"Ghost in, ghost out," Cross said, and walked off into the darkness.

"WHERE WE dropped you. Ten minutes."

Cross popped the SIM card, then used two pairs of pliers to crack it into tiny pieces, all dropped into a handkerchief spread across his lap. He tossed various bits and pieces out the passenger-side window of the Shark Car as it motored toward that private back room of the No-Chance.

Buddha rolled into the space recently vacated by the white unmarked as Rhino stepped out the door, a canvas bag in each hand. The back door hissed open. The mammoth climbed in.

"Wait till we all get back," Cross said.

The Shark Car passed a solid-front building, marked only by a narrow strip of inset neon spelling out . . .

O
R
C
H
I
D
‡
B
L
U
E

. . . and continued on to the first alley opening. Cross was already tapping a numbered keypad.

Tiger and Princess strolled out the back door, the black-masked Akita now unleashed and walking between them. Tiger got in front, Princess and his dog in the back.

"Well? What did you—?"

"When we get back," Cross interrupted the Amazon. "There's something we've got to do first."

AS THEY entered the back of Red 71, Cross saw a tiny blue light, blinking on one of the sawhorse struts that held his desk.

"Message out front," he said, parting the ball-bearing curtain and stepping into the poolroom.

The tables were about three-quarters occupied, but nobody glanced at the unremarkable-looking man walking to the front desk.

"Cop left this for you," the old man in the ancient green eyeshade said, handing over a baseball-sized wad of paper, tightly wrapped in black duct tape.

"Cop?"

"Not a blue boy."

"Say anything?"

"Not even that he *was* a cop. Just rolled it across to me and walked back out the way he came in."

Cross completed the round trip as invisibly as he had the first half.

Entering the back, he tossed the wrapped ball to Tracker, saying, "Rhino will need whatever's inside. Probably alphanumerics."

Rhino, hearing this, began assembling his cyber-B&E materials.

Tracker was already at work with a piece of flexible razor steel, carefully working it under the outermost roll of duct tape.

Cross went back behind his desk, lit a cigarette.

A few minutes passed in silence.

"Ready?" Tracker finally asked.

"Go," Rhino said.

As Tracker read each line, Rhino touched his immense

laptop's keyboard, checked the black-and-white screen, and repeated, "Go."

Within a minute of Tracker's saying, "Thirty," Rhino announced, "I'm in."

Cross recited from memory all the information Condor had taken from Q.T.

Another minute passed.

"No record," Rhino said. "No wants, no warrants. No prints."

"None *now*?"

"Yes. Erasing footprints, just a . . . There!"

"She was never arrested?"

"Erased," Rhino answered again. "And nobody ever glanced at whatever record *used* to be there."

"Mac's good as gold," Buddha said.

"He's better," Cross responded. "Price of gold fluctuates, right?"

"Got it, boss."

"*Now* can we—?"

"Reloading now," Rhino said. "Another couple of minutes."

"IT'S JUST one station back there," Rhino said.

"One keyboard, one screen," he continued. "On that screen, it's something out of a movie set. Tower stack, empty slots. Probably each person who uses it has his own—the slots are the wrong size for anything I know about, too big for any USB key, and they're shaped more like a triangle than a rectangle.

"The cable isn't co-ax. As thick as—I'm guessing now—six, seven inches. I didn't know how much time I had, so I just took measurements as best I could. But storage went off my scale, and I could tell there was plenty more left. Tetrabytes by a factor of . . . maybe a few hundred. Connected underground, private feed. My tach topped out, too . . . and it covers all the way to speeds that aren't supposed to exist. So at *least* fifteen hundred megs. Nobody can type that fast, so it has to be for streaming at an insane rate—much more than you'd need for any movie."

"Back-channel?" Cross asked.

"Deeper than that. There's layers and layers in there. Getting *to* the channel isn't the deal. That would only let you watch, not . . . participate."

"Pay to play?"

"Must be. It's too complex for gaming, even with thousands of players on at the same time. There's really no way to tell, not without going in . . . and I didn't want to try that. Probably self-destructs without an access card."

"That room's too small for more than one at a time. Two at most, and only one at the keyboard," Tiger said.

"They must make appointments," Tracker added. "With plenty of space between them, so they never eyeball each other."

"*That's* why there's two ways in!" Tiger burst out.

"It's blackmail waiting to happen," Buddha said. "They gotta have cameras—"

"They used to," Rhino squeaked.

"So Long was right," Buddha said, unable to keep pride from his voice.

"She was on the money," Cross conceded, letting the

double meaning of that compliment hang in the air. "Too bad you had to make that Lao dead, huh?"

"I—" Buddha began, before a look from Cross silenced him.

"She's at your house, now?"

"Yeah . . ."

"Okay. You need to talk to her. Not on the phone. Does anyone know Pekelo's gone? Can she find out where he lived? If the cops have already visited, no point in us taking a look. But it hasn't been *that* long. . . ."

Buddha was already exiting.

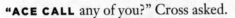

"ACE CALL any of you?" Cross asked.

Silence was his answer.

"Okay, this much we know, then: He's looking for Percy. If Percy's looking for Blondie and Wanda, okay. But if he's *guarding* them, Ace is all done."

"How can you say that?" Rhino demanded. "Ace is as good as—"

"If Ace took them out, he would have gotten word to us. If he's still looking, he wouldn't call. The way things stand, that last, it's the best we can hope for."

"For Percy, it would be a job," Tracker said. "Whatever he is told to do, that *is* his job. The mission is defined. He had nothing but contempt for those two, but if he was told to protect them, he would do that. All of this is true. But I know they—Percy and Ace—they have made a decision to hunt together."

"How could you know that?"

"I was . . . present when they discussed things."

If the gang boss was surprised at Tracker's quiet announcement, he didn't change expression. "Percy's job was to make those two disappear, he'd do that job," Cross said. "So we won't know until we hear from Ace. The G has its cyber-slingers on full go—Wanda wouldn't open any channel that could be traced."

"I can think of a channel I'd like to open," Tiger added.

No one responded; it wasn't a statement that invited questions.

Cross closed his eyes and lit a cigarette.

Don't push it! his mind admonished him. *You can't get to wherever it is. But if you wait, it might come to you.*

Time passed as the urban mercenary let his mind drift.

"What else am I gonna do?"

"You can still go anyway you want once you're free," Cross told his only friend. "Me, all I can do is get over that Wall. And keep moving."

"Yeah, you so special? I got a parole coming; sure, I know that. But what then? Go to night school, get a GED, just for some slave job? The only trade I know is the one I learned in here. Be yourself, brother."

"I had to—"

"What? Try? I called you 'brother,' right? Not 'Pops' or any of that stuff. I didn't have no father. And my momma didn't have no judgment. I'll be by myself."

"Not once I figure out a way to—"

"Oh, you'll do that. You been doing it since you

was a little kid, the way the guards tell it. So . . . you're saying we keep on working together? Sure. Why not? Ain't neither of us coming back Inside, I'm telling that true?"

"Yeah. Yeah, you are. But if we're gonna work, we might as well ramp it up—pass on all the small scores. You know I read all the time, right? Well, you know what I've been reading lately?"

"No."

"Lies. 'Money can't buy happiness'—how many times you heard that? But here's the thing: Happiness is . . . what? For me, it's not coming back. For you, too, now. And that's something money *can* buy."

"Like lawyers and—?"

"Sure. But even that's not the whole thing. As crooked as this town is, name something money can't buy. But you remember what that rhyming guy is always saying? About money?"

"You flash the cash, people be looking for your stash?"

"On the nose. But I don't want a fancy car, or jewelry, or even nice clothes. I want to be safe. They'll be looking for me until they get tired, or . . ."

"Or what?"

"Or until I stop being me."

"Man, talk sense."

"All I am is a name. In here, not even that—I'm a number. But I can lose my name. And I won't have a number on the other side of that wall."

"Yeah? What about your prints? I didn't get in any kind of trouble until I landed here. But they took my prints, same as they did yours."

"There's only one way they get to use those prints, brother."

"Not mine, not yours, not ever," Vernon Lewis said to Marlon Cain, holding out his fist. The other boy touched that fist with his own, sealing the pact.

CROSS OPENED his eyes.

"I don't need any damn messages from space to tell me what I already know," he said aloud. "Ace is still here. I don't know where he is, but I don't have to. I know he wouldn't leave without me." The hackles on the back of the Akita's neck rose, but the dog made no sound.

"Someone's coming," Princess said. "Sweetie always knows before I do."

Soon enough, Buddha proved the truth of Sweetie's sensory powers.

"I got the address, boss. But . . ."

"Buddha, there's no time for this. *What?*"

"So Long, she's out there. In the car. Said it would save time if she could call while I was rolling, and I know we're short on—"

"Tracker, you got a ride around?"

"You can use my—"

"Thanks, Princess, but we might have to carry some stuff out, and your bike doesn't have a lot of storage," Cross said, not mentioning that a Pepto-pink Harley with open pipes wouldn't promote a silent approach . . . or an unnoticed departure.

"I'm driving," Buddha said. "But I have to leave So Long here. That okay?"

"I'll keep her company," Tiger said, as innocent as a felonious schoolgirl.

"You—"

"She's playing, Buddha. Let it go."

"Boss, I . . ."

"Let it go, or take your woman back home. Just leave us that address."

"DAMN! THAT is one fine-looking tower," Buddha said. His eyes flicked upward, measuring. "Twenty-one-B, that has to be top floor."

"Yeah. Probably *half* the floor, too."

"Doorman," Tracker said.

"No time to scam our way in," Cross said, pulling a small aerosol can from inside his jacket and tugging his watch cap down into a ski mask. "Buddha, that uniform better fit you."

"DOORMAN WON'T wake up for thirty minutes, minimum," Cross whispered to Tracker. "And he won't remember anything when he does. You already fuzzed the lobby cameras. Ready?"

Without waiting for an answer, Cross started up the stairs. If there were any more cameras along the way, they'd record only two shadowy figures, climbing.

"It *is* half the floor. But no yellow tape. Now, if Rhino's code reader works . . ."

The door was zebrawood, with a heavy block of cut crystal set into its center. The lock popped silently.

The two men entered and found themselves facing a solid wall of glass.

"Divides down the middle," Tracker said quietly, moving to his left.

They each scanned carefully, using blue-light LEDs aimed at the floor.

Cross heard Tracker's tongue-click signal. Followed it back down the hall and over to the left side of the apartment.

"It can't be *that* easy," the Indian said, pencil-beaming his light over a dull-silver desk. The light tracked a closed laptop, so color-matched to the desk surface that it visually merged into it. Then to a back panel of the same material, constructed of what looked like pullout drawers without knobs, an oval cut into the top of each serving that purpose.

"Arrogance" was all Cross said, stepping to one side and pulling the drawers out, one by one, starting at the bottom.

Tracker followed his lead.

Most of the drawers were empty.

"Here!" Cross hissed.

Tracker pulled open the Velcroed pocket of his field jacket, city-camoed to match the Shark Car's skin. Cross dumped a single handful of triangulated disks into it.

Less than three minutes later, they were in the lobby.

"Not a soul, boss," Buddha said at the door. "Should we—?"

"Leave him in the trunk for now. The plastic wrap went out when we dumped that body Tiger dropped in before. We'll leave this one under that viaduct we saw coming in. He'll be coming around soon. Should be safe enough—easy to see he isn't carrying anything worth stealing. Keep that uniform on, brother; we'll take care of it when we get back home."

"THAT'S THEM!" Tiger said excitedly. "The same ones I saw in that—"

"Rhino?"

"Give me a minute," the giant said, turning the strangely shaped disks so he could examine one from all directions.

The minute stretched into a half-hour before Rhino spoke again. "I had to risk opening one up, to be sure. But Tiger's instincts were true—these are nothing but key cards. When you pull them apart, they turn into rows of connector plugs. There's no data on them at all. What they're for is to open that access port."

"Why would he have more than one?" Cross asked. "Are they just backups?"

"I don't think so. There's no way to tell for sure, but my best guess is that each one is for a different channel. That would fit—no one key could actually get into wherever the material is kept, only a tiny slice of it. Storm-proof clouded, for sure."

"Just like he told us," Buddha said, as if to defend killing the Lao before he could tell them anything more.

"It's almost four in the morning," Cross said. None of the crew questioned how a man who never wore a wristwatch was always right about the time. "Might as well finish this part of it."

"Boss, can So Long stay—"

"I can speak for myself, husband. And I do not wish to stay," she said, with a quick glance at her Amazon companion.

"Nobody would even *think* about coming back here," Buddha assured her. "And with Princess and Rhino . . ."

"I must see it for myself," his wife said.

"LOOKS EMPTY," Cross said, speaking from the backseat. "But if there's a basement, they might have it fixed up like an apartment."

"You want me to take a—?"

"No," Cross told Tiger. "Next time we come around the block, we finish this. If the maggots running this darknet operation are in that room, they're not coming out. And if they're not, they're never coming back."

"How can you be so—?"

"Not now," he said to silence Tiger. To Buddha he said, "Stop right across from that back door. We know it's steel, but it's not built for what we got. Once it's drilled, a smooth, slow roll to the corner, turn right, and *keep* moving—breaking glass isn't a big trick."

The Shark Car glided to a stop just past the side door. The back window zipped down. Cross jumped out, dropped to one knee, shouldered a long tube of black metal, and squeezed off a single round. The rocket-launched explosive vaporized the steel door.

So Long watched, without interest.

Cross threw the tube into the backseat and followed right behind. By the time Buddha had taken the corner, the explosion was already reverberating, shattering glass in nearby storefronts. Cross jumped out, another launcher in each hand. He landed lightly, put two more rockets through the now aptly named No-Chance, and caught the Shark Car on foot within fifty yards.

Buddha picked up speed almost imperceptibly and began to float through alleys.

Sirens shrieked, tearing the fabric of the night, sending 911 operators into instant overload. Chicago PD's Command Central ignored the incessant stream of orders from Homeland Security to stand down.

Would-be reporters were running cell-phone videos straight to CNN. Some as-yet-unidentified individual on a small motorcycle with a tiny video cam strapped securely to his helmet was shot so many times by so many weapons that his DNA splattered the sides of buildings up to the third floor. Chicago PD could ignore Homeland Security's stand-down orders, but keeping them away was impossible. As would be questioning the motorcyclist.

Bloggers dueled for bandwidth; cables were torn from beneath the concrete by a blanket of cover fire laid down to protect the SWAT teams trying to enter what was left of the structure as the Fire Department's full range—chemical foam to high-pressure hoses—worked on containment.

Somewhere in a basement at Quantico, FBI profilers were

screaming, "More data!" as if summoning a genie from a lamp.

Bullhorns competed with human screams, neither winning.

INSIDE WHAT looked like a derelict gas station in the Badlands, Buddha pulled a tab, releasing torrents of air under the skin of the Shark Car.

Cross and Tiger each took a side and pulled off the city-camo, revealing a midnight-blue body that now resembled a limousine. Buddha stripped off the doorman's uniform and dropped it into an empty hazmat container before he re-donned his own clothes.

"Go!" Cross told Buddha, pointing both index fingers straight ahead.

Turning to Tiger, he said, "Come on."

"How am I supposed to walk in—?"

"It isn't far."

"What does—?" Tiger started to say, just as Condor dropped from his perch.

"Anything?" Cross asked.

"Nothing," the young man answered, meaning no vehicle had attempted to enter the area after the Shark Car. "But a panel truck came a while back. They dropped off this motor-cycle. I mean, one of them did—the other one never got out."

"Can you get the bike back here?"

"Sure. But we'd have to ride it."

"How else . . . ?"

"The guy who dropped it off, he *carried* it!"

"You've seen him before."

"Sure. But that thing has to weigh—"

"It doesn't matter. Just bring it down the road, we'll grab it there."

Condor stepped off into the darkness, already speaking into the old Army-issue field phone he carried on a sling.

"It's about a hundred yards," Cross told Tiger. "Keep your damn shoes on; I can carry you that far."

"Wow! You must be *so* strong!"

Cross dropped to the same firing position he had used earlier, scooped Tiger over one shoulder, and began to slog forward in a fireman's carry.

"You say something?" she demanded.

"Just a prayer."

"Are you trying to say—?"

"Can *you* try shutting up for a minute?" he said, smacking her rump with his left hand.

"Oh! That *hurt*!"

"Sure," Cross said, sourly, his palm still tingling. "What I was praying for was that Princess didn't drop off *his* damn scooter."

CROSS WOULD be hard-pressed to distinguish one motor-cycle from another, but he relaxed as soon as he saw it wasn't the Pepto-pink Harley.

Red 71 could be reached through the Badlands, but only if you knew how to navigate past a series of sensors before deliberately passing through a final strobing light to deactivate an open-on-contact twenty-foot drop to a pile of hacked-up I-beams.

Cross piloted the bike carefully, but Tiger held on as if they were about to go airborne any second. When they reached the back perimeter, Cross pulled in the clutch and cut the motor, letting the bike drift until it came to a natural stop. Few knew Red 71 could be accessed from that direction at all—those who did knew that no car could possibly traverse the torn iron maze. And that any first step would open a screen inside, with infrared cameras tracking movement of anything larger than a small dog.

"We'll leave it here," Cross said. "Nobody's gonna steal it."

"It's got to be another quarter-mile," Tiger answered. "And I know you're not planning to carry—"

"Not me. But somebody will be out here soon enough. Probably Princess and that dog. And you know he'd carry you up Sears Tower if you asked him."

"Oh, that's all right." She flashed a grin. "I may not have been Girl Scout material, but I'm always prepared."

Cross stood silently as the Amazon reached into a side pouch on her jumpsuit and pulled out a pair of thin-soled slippers. "The soles are some kind of plastic Rhino made—they flex, but you couldn't drive a nail through them."

Cross had taken some serious risks in his life, but he wasn't about to ask the Amazon why she hadn't bothered to mention those substitute shoes earlier.

"THEY PROBABLY got the coordinates wrong," Percy said to Ace. "Wouldn't be the first time for those desk warriors."

"Meaning, Blondie and that girl, they're somewhere around here, just not in the place they pointed you to?"

"Yeah."

"Got a car?"

"No. I don't know my way around here—it'd just weigh me down."

"You took the damn CTA dressed like that?"

"Night drop," Percy explained. "Black parachute. Not my first. Just picked a flat roof, and . . ."

"Yeah, I got it. But we can't do no house-to-house here. Sooner or later, some little gangstah will crank off a few just to be doing it."

"I thought you wouldn't have no problems." The warmachine's version of sarcasm.

"Man, it ain't *me* that looks all RoboCop. You out of some seriously dumb movie, son."

"You want me to, what, wait here? That's not what I—"

"Yeah, I know. You all kinds of bad. But unless you got some magic net to drop over that whole spot, they'll be gone before we get close."

"I'm not—"

"Rest easy," Ace said. "I just gotta make a call."

Percy watched as the slim black man shook a sleeve of his long leather duster, deftly caught the cell phone as it slid across his open palm, popped it open with his thumb, and tapped a single key with a long, slim finger, all in the same motion.

"I need a posse car," Ace spoke into the mic. "Four doors,

two men in front, backseat empty. How long till you get it over to . . . ?"

A CANDY-ORANGE Cadillac Escalade with ridiculously oversized wheels slid to the curb.

Percy hit the backseat first, Ace close behind. As the car pulled away, the war machine looked over at his for-now partner.

"This your idea of camouflage?"

"You ever been on the West Side? This one looks the way it's *supposed* to look. And nobody *be* looking at it twice."

Before Percy could reply, Ace said, "Good call," to the driver. Turning to Percy, he said, "Run it down. I don't know what they look like, except what I got off tape. You was locked up with the two of them for—what?—weeks?"

"White male, blond and blue, just under six feet, scrawny, small birthmark on his left hand, right near the web. Asian female, cream-in-coffee, dark eyes. Maybe five two, max. Smells like cocoa butter; gets her nails done every day, it looks like. She'll have to be near someplace where she can plug her computer into the Internet."

The front-seat passenger looked over his left shoulder. One quick glance was enough to convince him he didn't want another one.

"You working with partners, now, Ace?"

"I ask *you* any questions, boy?"

"I was just—"

"Shut up, fool," the driver said, trying to derail a conversation he knew had no possibility of ending well. But he'd reacted too late.

"I don't know you," Ace said, very softly. "I wanted to call you by your name, how could I do that?"

"I was just saying—"

"Don't be 'just saying' things. I couldn't call your name 'cause I don't *know* your name. You can't add that up? The man who sent you, you and the man behind the wheel—you know, the one who knows how to act—that man who sent you, *he* knows me. What *you* know is you gonna get paid for doing what I tell you. That's true?"

"Yeah."

"That's getting paid for *doing*, not for *saying*, we clear?"

"Yeah."

"Our two, they won't be walking," the assassin said to Percy. "Gotta hope they get to one of the Main Originals and pay rent before they get rolled on. Either one of them a shooter?"

"THEY NOT gonna *be* on the street," Ace told the driver. "So we play it like they already found a spot. Got me?"

"Only ones who could let them—"

"Sure. So, first step, we find one of the shot-callers."

"Alone? That's not—"

"Hey! You a driver, not some private eye. They still got that spot in Englewood?"

"The Green Lantern?"

"That's the one."

"Sure. But it's never empty."

"Not supposed to be. That spotlight above the door, the green one? It sweeps, right? And they got a couple of their boys in front, either side of the door?"

"Yep. Same as always."

"Okay, how it plays is like this: you pull up like you carrying a couple of men who gonna party."

"Can't park—"

"You not *gonna* park. You the driver, right? So you pull up, and the people in the back, they get out. That's your job."

"I got a job, too?" the front-seat passenger asked.

"Oh, you got a job, all right," Ace assured him. "An *acting* job. Like this is a movie, okay? Far as those doorposts know, whoever's in the back of this thing, they're major players. We pull up, *your* window goes down, so they can see you. You're the bodyguard—that's why you wearing that nice suit your boss had made for you.

"All heavyweight players, they got drivers, bodyguards, fancy rides. So you get out, open the back door toward you, and *stay* where it takes you. That's *behind* that door. Remember, you make sure you never take your eyes off the boys below that spotlight. That'll keep their eyes on *you*."

"Okay, so we drop you off, and . . ."

"And *take* off," Ace told the driver. "You got that pager your boss gave you? Okay. You take off, but you don't go far. You hear the beep, you get back *quick*. Soon as we load back in, you get us over the border. You stop; we jump off; you go back and pick up your money."

The driver made a leisurely left turn and headed west.

"You got something that don't make noise?" Ace asked Percy, his tone making it more of a statement than a question.

"Step two?" was the war machine's only response.

"You take out the door guards. We walk in. It's a small joint. Most of the people there, they just people, understand? Soon as they catch on, they're booking for the exit. The ones *we* want, they'll all be in this one spot on the far right, a couple of steps up from the floor. Got a brass rail all around it, little chain across the opening. Probably a man just standing there, holds up the chain if any of the Main Originals give him the word. You know, let some girl come up there and sit with them. Now, the second any of *them* see me, they gonna be plunging for steel—they know I don't party. Thing is, we need one of them alive."

"You move left," Percy said, as he affixed a flash suppressor to the front of a heavy-barreled pistol, working by touch. "I'll put down a spray to the right, then switch to three-beats. Inside, it'll be panic. You herd them out the door. Then get over to that brass rail. Ask whoever's alive whatever you want, but be fast—not gonna be quiet once I start sweeping."

"That works," Ace said, implicitly transferring authority to Percy. Cross had told him Percy could be expected to improvise as situations developed. He wouldn't make ego-moves, but he'd see Ace as a means to the end of his mission, so getting in his way wouldn't occur to him.

"You carrying anything besides that scattergun?"

"No," Ace lied. "I never dial long-distance."

"You want . . . ?"

"I'm good with this, bro. You the one doin' all the heavy lifting."

THE ESCALADE stopped outside the club.

The driver's-side window zipped down. As the two men standing on either side of the green double doors swiveled their heads into a practiced stare-down, the front-seat passenger exited, then opened the back door ostentatiously, as if presenting a royal gift. That move shielded Percy long enough to get off two hardball rounds, each hitting a guard just above the bridge of the nose. Both were dead before they hit pavement.

The war machine shoulder-rolled and came up with a heavy pistol in his right hand. Ace was already at the door, stepping inside the club just ahead of Percy, his sawed-off wordlessly sending a "Don't move!" message to the small crowd.

The first blast from Percy's full-auto was enough to change that message to "Run!" Ace used his scattergun the way a teenager would use her forefinger to sweep through stacked-up messages on her iPhone, herding the terrified cattle into their escape chute. No role players reached for anything except better position in the herd—Ace's black Zorro hat and matching leather duster were a message on their own.

The assassin whirled and quick-stepped to the right side of the club, which now resembled a Jackson Pollock canvas. Percy had already reloaded, but only two men were still alive, and no reinforcements had entered the slaughterhouse. Both of the living were sprawled on the green plush fabric of the horseshoe sofa, bleeding but breathing.

Ace put his face very close to one of them, said, "Where are they?"

"Huh? Who? Man, I—"

Ace used one barrel to interrupt by blowing the man's face off. He whipped the weapon around to face the lone survivor. "You gonna pull that stutter act, too?"

"Upstairs," the man gasped. "We didn't know nothing. They paid for—"

Ace ended the man's desperate plea with the second barrel, snapped open the weapon, and popped out the spent shells. He grasped two fresh loads between the fingers of one hand, re-chambered, and flicked the scattergun closed as he sprinted for the circular staircase.

Percy swept the entire room in one long burst, then followed right behind.

Three doors. Percy wrenched one open, Ace another. Both empty.

The third door was locked. Percy kicked it open, spinning onto the floor in the same movement. *No prisoners!* blasted through his brain as Ace moved past him, his mind screaming, *Hate them all!*

"Gone," the dark assassin said, pointing at an open window. "Can't be far."

"Blondie would have a plan," Percy said, grunting. "They ain't running down no blind alley. Got to be a—"

Ace spotted a pair of tablets and stuffed them inside his duster as Percy disappeared out the window. *Fool thinks I'm gonna hold the door for him?* he thought, working the beeper. When the man whose name made professional life-takers shiver stepped out the club's front door, the Escalade was just pulling in.

Seconds later, the Cadillac rolled off, its driver as unper-

turbed by the sound of approaching sirens as people on the
next corner had been by the sounds of what they assumed was
just another gunfight.

"WHERE THE hell is—?" the man in the passenger seat
started to say.

"We did what we got paid to do, right?" the driver interrupted. "We got him over the damn border, *right*? Don't
be asking questions, bro—we don't get paid extra for being
stupid."

Even as he spoke, a man in a different part of town
answered a cell phone with "Go."

"Job's done." Ace's voice came over the phone Cross was
holding. "But not *finished*. Clear?"

"Clear. Car coming."

"Which car?"

"Same snake, new skin. You know where. Go!"

"AND THAT'S where I left it," Ace told the crew, later.

"Maybe Percy was successful?" Tracker wondered out
loud.

"The man has serious skills," Ace conceded. "Not afraid
of nothing, and don't mind who he got to kill to prove it. But
when it comes to those two, he's a freight train with no track
to run on. No way some little girl just jumps out a second-
story window—Blondie and her, they had a plan in place.
Plenty of time after they heard the first shots downstairs."

"Blondie, I don't think he's much," Tiger said. "But that Wanda . . . she wouldn't operate without a Plan B."

"So it was all for—?"

"Not so sure about that," Ace said to Cross. "I got these."

"Tablets?" Rhino squeaked, excitedly.

"Yeah. That don't mean they're—"

"You didn't turn them on or anything?"

"Man, I wouldn't *touch* those things."

"Good," the double-wide man who'd once been a tortured child said. *I'll come back for you, brother,* echoed in his mind, as he calmly said, "I'll need the robot room."

THE CREW watched through the long viewing slit of triple-layered ballistic glass as Rhino's shovel-sized hands delicately worked a pair of joysticks with the precision of a surgeon implanting a pacemaker.

The first tablet opened silently. And the second.

"No triggers there," Buddha said, quietly.

"There wouldn't be," Tracker said. "Not if Wanda set them up. If they're nothing but shaped charges, she'd want them to take out anyone who tried to access data."

Another tap of the robot's padded tip, and the first of the tablets came alive, its screen filling with icons.

Rhino fired up the second one. That one showed an out-of-focus haze.

"Camera-feed," Cross said. "They were probably watching everything downstairs. Gave 'em plenty of time."

Rhino ignored the speculations, gliding the robot's point

over the icons on the screen of the other tablet. Minutes passed, until a row of vertical boxes, white on a black background, came into view.

"Passworded," the mammoth said. "Eight slots. It'll be an alphanumeric. I'll have to put a generator in there and let it hunt. Could take hours, even days."

"But you can get in?" Cross asked.

"I think so. But I don't know how far. It probably is set up like a beehive—resistance at every level before we get to the queen."

"Yeah, that'd be Wanda," the gang leader said. "But we got nothing else, brother. And if Percy finds them first, he's not taking prisoners."

BACK AT Red 71, Princess said, "Did you take anything else, Ace? From that room, I mean."

"Nothing else there. Lucky that beastmaster didn't look back," the assassin said, grimly. "Percy saw me do it, I'd probably still *be* in that damn room."

"Ace's right," Cross said. "He'd know how the G feels about 'specimens.' If he wasn't in such a rush, he'd have searched the place, too."

"For what?" Buddha sneered. "So they prove something in court? It's not like they got secret identities or anything."

"They probably do," Tiger said, thoughtfully. "They have to be holed up *somewhere*. There's plenty of legit places they could rent, and just as many off the books, too. But they'd have to *look* different. Blondie would just need a decent dye job and a padded jacket. Wanda could put her hair in pigtails, throw a couple of colored streaks into the other part, slam on some makeup, and turn herself into a college girl."

"How would that help us? It's like those dumbass 'profiles' you read about every time a serial killer's on the loose. Give you everything you want to know about him—white male, lives in his mother's basement, blah-blah—except where you can *find* him. You see the news reports? 'Gang-related,' of course. Only thing they know for sure is that all ten of the killers were black."

Feeling Tiger's nails on the side of his neck, Cross realized Princess might be feeling ignored. "Why'd you ask?" the gang leader said.

"Sweetie!" the armor-muscled child blurted out. "If we had something they touched, like a tissue or something, Sweetie could probably sniff them out."

Buddha rolled his eyes, but the flash from Cross's left palm stopped him from speaking.

"That might work," Cross said, as if considering a proposition. "But there's no way for us to try it. If we went back, the cops might try and grab Sweetie."

Mollified, Princess lapsed into silence.

"I don't like doing nothing," Tiger said, stomping her foot like a defiant child.

"We *are* doing something," Tracker said.

"I'm with Tiger," Buddha piped up again.

"No, you're not," the Amazon replied.

HOURS PASSED.

"You and Tracker, you spent the most time with them,"

Cross said to Tiger. "Maybe we're going at this all wrong. If Percy's chasing them, they got no friends, not anymore. So why come back to Chicago? Taking us out—even *all* of us—that wouldn't square them with the G."

"Boss, maybe they can see it, too?"

"You mean—?" Cross suddenly stopped speaking as the tiny blue symbol burned harshly.

"They cannot," Tracker said, his tone clearly indicating that he was simply stating a fact.

"What makes you such an expert?" Tiger snapped at him. "My tribe existed long before yours was formed. If anyone would know—"

"I am not stating tribal knowledge," Tracker said, patiently. "This is deduction only. I *feel* the truth of deduction, but logic isn't spiritual."

"Hey! How about the both of you speak English, okay?"

Tracker and Tiger both shifted position to look directly at Buddha. They internally reconfirmed their ongoing agreement not to waste insults on a man immune to such.

"If those who originally hired us to collect a specimen—not the blond one and the Asian; the agency who paid their salaries—if that agency had *any* indication that Cross could be . . . touched by what they sought, they would have acted upon that information by now," Tracker said. "He didn't *have* that . . . mark, or brand, or whatever you call it; he didn't get it until . . . well, we don't know, exactly. But it was *after* that thing they all trapped down in that prison basement escaped."

"And you think, because we all can see it, a surveillance camera could as well?" Tiger asked.

"Why not?" Buddha demanded. "*We* didn't all get to see it at the same time. I mean, it wasn't visible right away."

"Not to you," Tiger said, disdainfully.

"Fine." Buddha shrugged off her scorn. "And so what? If it came to some of us slower than others, why couldn't it reach the G, eventually?"

"They have not abandoned surveillance," Tracker said.

"There's a better reason," Cross spoke. "We know for sure from what Ace just told us. Percy's hunting Blondie and Wanda, not me. The G's made up its mind: either this . . . thing doesn't exist at all, or they're gonna need another ten years to come up with a new plan.

"Probably the first—we're about to have an election, remember? Even if they keep most of that agency, whatever it is, even if they keep on the same personnel, you think they want to report that something from . . . who knows where . . . has been watching *them*?"

"Percy?" Tiger snapped. "He's a thug, not a thinker. Whatever they tell him to do, it's no different from pushing a speed-dial button."

"Okay," Cross agreed. "And that means there's nothing personal in what he's doing. Hunting those two, that's an assignment. But none of this explains why Hemp gave that order in the first place."

"That Lao told us."

"Sure he did, Buddha. But he was *playing* the game—he didn't invent it. If the G wanted us dead, they'd just send in the troops. Percy's not the only asset they have."

"Boss, look—"

"Shut up," Tiger hissed at him. "It's *blinking* now. Can you feel it?" she asked Cross.

"No. Not like before. Look, we can't read whatever their messages are supposed to be. Mural Girl, she might know something, but even if she does, she's not gonna tell us anything more than she already has. We got a ton of information, but it's like a bunch of dots on a wall. We can take guesses, but it's just more dots—nothing connects."

"It does now," Rhino squeaked, stepping inside the room, one of the tablets almost completely covered by his closed hand.

"THIS ISN'T what you'd expect," Rhino said, the squeak barely present in his voice. "It was set up like an old-school video game. *Donkey Kong*," the mammoth said, shaking his head in wonderment.

"I don't like that one," Princess said. "It's no fun. That big gorilla on top, he'd never want to be friends."

"You know, there's some people like that, too," Rhino said gently. "But this wasn't a puzzle. More of a . . . taunt, I guess. Every little node held a coding test. If you passed the test—I don't mean if you knew some password, more like a skills test—if you got through one node, there'd be another. It didn't get . . . trickier as you went along. It was more like—"

"*Ninja Warrior!*" Princess interrupted. "That's not a game; it's real. But the players, they don't fight each other. Like one of those . . . obstacle courses, right?"

"Exactly like that," Rhino said, giving Princess a look that told the hyper-muscled man that it was time to stay quiet. "No antagonism involved. No 'Hah! You lose!' kind of pop-ups. But there was some kind of perverted sense of humor in the whole thing. If you could work your way past . . . past every obstacle, just like Princess said, you 'qualified' for that *Donkey Kong* game."

"This is difficult to follow," Tracker said. "Are you saying what is on that tablet is some qualifying test?"

"Yes."

"As in the military, then? You have to prove many things about yourself besides the ability to shoot before you would be admitted to their sniper training?"

"Maybe. I don't know what kind of mind would build this," Rhino said, gesturing with the tablet held between thumb and forefinger of his left hand. "But it might have a message of its own."

"That this is all some game?" Tiger said. "That would be *exactly* like that Wanda bitch. For her, it probably *is* a game."

"You're saying she *doesn't* want us all dead?" Cross asked, firing another cigarette as he spoke.

"The blond man, he is a coyote," Tracker said. "Not a transporter," he added quickly, as he saw Buddha start to interrupt, "a trickster. But he has many more layers than any shape-shifter. He is as cold-blooded as a Gila monster, but his venom is not for hunting. Or even for self-defense. It is as if both merged inside him. His blood *is* venom. There is no shortage of places where this quality would make him valuable. And with that woman to help, they could have departed for such places long ago."

"He's hanging around just for revenge?"

"He would not understand that concept," Tracker answered Cross. "He would not seek insight into his own motives. He would never question himself. But it would not be possible for him to . . . fail. Were he to fail . . . fail at anything he undertook . . . he would not be losing a game, or a contest. Or even a war. He would lose himself."

"You know this . . . ?"

"From watching. Listening. Breathing the same air. For a long time. I was there first. Before Tiger, I mean. And she is very sensitive. But, for Tiger, 'sensitive' is a double-edged blade. One with no handle."

Tiger took a breath. But this time, the breath was shallow. Cross watched her right hand. The slim pair of daggers strapped to her thigh *did* have handles. Tracker went very still.

Sweetie launched across the room, airborne from the first thrust of his hindquarters. And landed in Tiger's lap.

"He doesn't want you to get mad," Princess said, walking over to the Amazon. "Me, neither."

"I wasn't mad, honey."

"Yes, you were. Sweetie could tell."

"I give it off *that* much?" she asked Cross.

"Tracker hit one of your spots, that's all."

"My spots?"

"Tigers have *stripes*," Princess said, now standing between Tiger and the rest of the room.

"Princess, easy, okay? Tiger's not mad"—looking meaningfully at the warrior-woman, catching the slight nod of her head—"she just wants me to explain what I was talking about."

"That is *so* true, sweetheart," she said to Princess. "I'm not mad. Not at all. Nobody's going to hurt me. And I'm not going to hurt anyone. Okay?"

"I . . ."

"Princess, baby, you know I'd never lie to you."

"I know. I was just . . ."

"You and Sweetie, both. Sure. He's a *very* smart dog. Maybe the smartest dog in the whole world."

"You hear that?" Princess asked the Akita, scooping him up in both arms and carrying him away like the animal was a piece of spun glass. "I knew it! You're a . . . genius or something. Didn't I tell you, Rhino?"

"You did," the patient giant confirmed.

"I am still waiting—"

"Your spots," Cross cut her off. "I meant a trigger point. Everybody has them—some are just buried deeply, that's all."

"I trained for years before I ever—"

"It doesn't matter. You trained to fight. That's a test you've never failed. Tracker has it in him. How he got his name. That gift. He wouldn't need his eyes to follow a trail."

"I wouldn't need mine, either. So he picked up on me thinking Blondie is slime, so what? I could tell Tracker thought the same. That blond . . . thing, he had no respect for either of us—we were the hired help. Remember back in that rolling office the G had, when Tracker offered to share tobacco with you? You knew what that meant. Not Blondie. That wasn't something he'd understand. Or care about if he did."

"That's him, sure."

"But all I did was despise him, right? What good is that? Tracker, he was *studying* him. That's what you're really saying, isn't it?"

"No," Cross said.

Minutes passed. Tiger blinked first. "So what *are* you saying?"

"Tracker respected *your* gifts. Wanda was outside anything he'd ever encountered. But you were probing for a way into her. Tracker could . . . feel that. So he left you to your work and went about his. Okay *now*?"

Tiger looked over at Tracker, caught the Indian's confirmatory nod, and settled back inside herself, shifting her body to tell Rhino she wouldn't be interrupting him again.

"Your wife's analysis was correct," Rhino said, clearly referring to Buddha. The pudgy man with adjustable scopes behind his unblinking eyes said nothing, waiting for whatever else was to come. "I only brought back one of the tablets—the other one made a little snapping sound when I tried to get into it," Rhino went on. "Probably the bellows mechanism—it discharged a spurt of some yellowish gas. Anyone opening it without protection would gasp at the sound *or* the sight. Either way, it would be his *last* gasp."

"What's that got to do with—?"

"So Long connected all of this to that No-Chance Gaming Parlor. It was full of those who believe themselves capable of winning any online game, and telling them they had no chance of winning would only entice them to prove themselves. Every gambler is *sure* the next spin of the wheel will land on his number. But if the wrong tablet were to be opened—they are identical in appearance—the wheel would land on zero. There was, indeed, 'no chance.'

"So the first obstacle would be random. But even if the coded tablet were opened first, the second one would be opened at some point. Maybe in the belief that there would be some work-around to the first one stored on it. Or even a key to the coding. So, while it appears that the odds were fifty-fifty, they were actually nonexistent—any gamer would lose."

"That Wanda is one evil bitch," Buddha said.

"Amen, brother!" Ace echoed.

"We expected them *both* to be looking for revenge," Cross said. "But that was off—Blondie wouldn't care, and Wanda wouldn't come to us."

"That *is* her," Tiger agreed. "But if she gave us a way to find her . . ."

"She didn't," Rhino said. "This was her own version of Mural Girl's wall. A way to transmit messages. Messages only we could understand."

"You think she knew—?"

"Oh, *hell*, yes," Cross said, blowing twin jets of smoke from his nose as he spoke. "I don't know whatever she had going with Blondie. Maybe nothing. Maybe it was her own game, and only the G could get her access to all that equipment she wanted. Maybe Blondie was just part of a package she put up with. But it was a *camera* we used to pick up those playing-card messages from Mural Girl's wall, right? Not our own eyes, so there couldn't have been anything special you'd need to see them."

"A message to Wanda as well?" Tracker asked.

"I don't think so. Can't see where they'd do her any good even if she could read them. But she *had* to see them. How do I know?" said the man who led the most feared crew in a city of gangs. "Wanda wouldn't have been with Blondie in the first place unless she was convinced that the Simbas were more than a myth or a legend. For all we know, she was never with the G—could have been pure freelance. Even Blondie could have been. 'Private contractor' is the right label for him—he was too superior to take orders, but he'd take jobs. Especially ones that challenged him. No better way to up your quote."

"Not Percy," Tiger said.

"No way," Ace agreed. "You don't get that kind of . . . loyalty, I guess you'd call it—not from somebody who's there for the money."

"We work for money," Buddha said, very quietly. "We take money to do jobs. We don't fly a flag, we don't salute. But . . ."

"We're mercenaries," Cross finished. "But not the kind anyone's used to. We're not loyal to whoever pays us—we don't feel anything for them, and we'd turn on them in a second if we saw a better score that way. But the difference between us and other mercs *is* loyalty. That's loyalty to each other. No one's seen it before, so no one's ready for it when it shows."

"There's plenty of tight units," Buddha said. "Worked in a couple of them myself. Guys you could trust."

"So why did you quit?" Tiger said, archly.

"When we ran across So Long . . ."

"Somebody died," Tiger said, her tone clearly communicating that she wasn't speculating. "Maybe more than one. That 'tight unit' you were with, a couple of them had different ideas. Different from yours."

"They didn't turn on me," Buddha said, hollow-voiced. "I turned on them."

"They must've been bad people," Princess said, forcefully.

"So was I," Buddha said. "This whole 'loyalty' thing, how far do you think it goes?"

"It went far enough for you to put your body between gunfire and Princess," Rhino said, so gravely that the squeak disappeared from his voice. "When Muñoz kidnapped him to get us to—"

"That was . . ."

When nobody finished his sentence for him, Buddha passed up the opportunity to finish it himself.

THE BLACK-MASKED Akita had completed two full circles of the room, checking each individual like a bomb-detecting dog, before Cross spoke.

"Rhino, you got to the end of that game?"

"Yes. But even with getting past all the coding barriers, if I hadn't known who designed it, I wouldn't have."

"Meaning . . ."

"Meaning, this game, a little guy in a plumber's outfit is supposed to climb up this building structure. Actually, just the skeleton of one, like a kid's Erector Set. He's supposed to rescue this damsel-in-distress from a giant gorilla. For the actual game—*Donkey Kong*—there must be a way to win. . . . Otherwise, it wouldn't have lasted as long as it did. Like *Pac-Man*. It's difficult, but you *can* win.

"I couldn't envision Wanda going to all that trouble just to construct what any *gamer* could win. So, instead of trying to work my way across the grid to reach the top, I spun through the options first. Wanda had added one of her own. A cutting torch. If you picked *that* up, you could topple the whole thing."

"That wouldn't rescue the girl," Tiger said.

"The object wasn't to rescue the girl," Rhino told her. "Not the way Wanda put it together. The object was to bring it all down. When it crashed, the screen cleared, and there was a schematic displayed. You could follow every step. Step *by* step. It was the most complex branch-out I've ever seen."

"When would she have—?"

"There is no way to tell," Rhino answered Cross. "She could have been working on it for a long time, not activating it until she needed to."

"Activate what?" Buddha said, almost absently.

"The whole chain," the twice-normal-size man said. "She . . . she knows something about how it feels to be nothing. Like that man caged on the top floors of that house."

"She was in contact with *him*?"

"She was in love with him," Rhino said. "They were connected in a way only people like them could even understand."

"He was a psycho," Buddha said, as if that covered everything.

"They were *all* there. That thalidomide baby, Holtstraf and his two pals, Pekelo, Wanda . . ."

"So . . . the back-channel site?"

"Yes," Rhino answered Cross. "Wanda and that imprisoned man, they found each other there. They put the rape-tape plan together, from the very beginning. They didn't know Pekelo, but they knew *someone* would have enough information about you to try and win all that money."

"Pekelo did say it came from the Cloud. . . ."

"It wasn't So Long's fault," Rhino assured Buddha. "Pekelo won only because he was first. Sooner or later, another scrap of information would float up. Pekelo knew about Ace's house. Someone else might have followed Princess one night. Or maybe a woman from Orchid Blue . . .

"It doesn't matter. They—Wanda and that captured man—they knew, with that much money up for grabs, they couldn't lose. *They* weren't gambling. One way or the other, we would all die.

"There's no way to tell when that plan was hatched, but those two were communicating—online, I mean—they were communicating with each other for *years*. Remember that phone call? From Thalidomide Man to the two still left in that rape-tape thing? He couldn't possibly have believed there was any safe harbor for him anywhere in the world. What he wanted was for them to take him to someplace where Wanda would be waiting. *That* was always the plan, for them to be together.

"But Wanda was already on the run when we . . . finished that thalidomide man. That's not your fault, either, Buddha. We could have questioned those two you shot for years—they couldn't tell us what they never knew. Maybe they—Wanda and the man in that house, I'm saying—maybe they had some kind of emergency signal. . . ."

"So there never *was* any damn AI program?" Cross cut in. "When Wanda reached out and he wasn't there, *she* checked the camera-feed he had installed. After that, it was Wanda running things. We'd killed her demented dream—her and Thalidomide Man, together for real. So what's left for her except revenge?"

"Yes," Rhino said gravely. "If those two rapists had managed to pick up the man in that house, he would have directed them to where Wanda was hiding. After that, it would be just the two of them left. But *we* took the man she was waiting for . . . and by then she knew Percy was after her, too. Her and the blond man. They only stayed together because—"

"Because Blondie had some skills Wanda didn't," Cross concluded. "If she'd managed to get together with that psycho who set this up *with* her, Blondie'd be on his own. Only question was when they'd remove him. And however they did it, he'd never see it coming.

"But now, with her . . . I don't know what to call whatever Wanda and Thalidomide Man had between them . . . she's down to her last card," Cross said.

"Boss . . ."

"What?"

"Maybe she doesn't *have* a last card. For all we know, Percy took them both out. Her and Blondie, I mean. We'd never know, would we? I mean, it's not like he's gonna report to *us*, right?"

"Percy could not take Wanda," Tracker said.

Everyone went quiet until Rhino tuned to Tracker's frequency. "You watched her. For a long time, at close quarters. The blond man wouldn't have watched *you*. Nothing to do with trust. You were just as you said: A hired hand. A long-distance killer. Wanda was inside all her computers. Even Tiger couldn't fully . . . distract her.

"But this seems to be a circle, with each open end moving toward intersection. I believe you must be right about Wanda. No matter what, she would not place all her chips at risk. So, even if Percy were to find her—"

"Damn!" Cross interrupted. "*There's* that AI program we thought was running. It'd still work, just like we thought it could. But Thalidomide Man didn't create it, *Wanda* did. So, if she doesn't check in when she's supposed to, the program's going to activate again. The only question is, what will it do?"

"I DON'T *know*, man." The voice coming through the speaker of Ace's relay belonged to the head of one of the West Side's most feared gangs.

"Easy, my brother. Just be calm. Tell me what happened; I'll take it from there."

"We're slow-walking to our ride. Just representing. Showing the flag, you know?"

Ace said nothing—the equivalent of "Get on with it!"

"This man—this *white* man—he steps out of the car. Looks like something out of one of those movies, you know, like a little group of white men drop into some African country, rescue the pretty bitch—a couple of hundred niggers have to die to make that happen, so what?

"Anyway, before we get over, like, how this mofo get inside *our* car?—ain't nobody crazy enough to do that, not with all the security we got around the spot—before we even *see* all the bodies scattered around, this guy, he says, 'I got a message for Ace.' Just like that. 'I got a message for Ace. I only need *one* man to deliver it.'

"We all got *that* message. All except for that fool Heavy. You know who I—?"

"Just talk," Ace said.

"Heavy goes for his piece. The white man's gun—I never seen one like it before—it makes this little noise, and Heavy's double-dead. 'You still got five left,' this white man says, but we don't say nothing. Then he says, 'Tell Ace she's still out there. *Just* her.' And then he gets back in our car. *Our* car, man. He gets in and just drives away.

"Nobody gonna bother *that* car. And we don't even think about chasing it. You got *white* men on your payroll now? Look, whatever it's all about, not our business, okay? We did what the man said to do, and—"

Ace tapped a button and the connection went dead. He tapped another button; the hissing sound told him it would stay that way.

"FIRE-TEAM positions," Cross snapped over his shoulder, as the Shark Car rolled past the barricaded entrance to the Badlands and swirled to a full stop.

"No spike, diamond. Buddha and Tiger triangle behind me. Tracker holds drag."

Cross headed for what he knew would be an opening in the tangle of barbed wire, chain link, rusting pieces of girders, and sharpened-edge rebar. He was first through, followed by Tiger to his right and Buddha to his left. Tracker was already roosting on top of the de-wheeled semi, his night scope scanning. Buddha's pistol was out, but, like Tiger's dagger, it was held loosely at his side.

"How bad is it?" Condor's voice, most of the teenage reediness gone; he was stepping into his new role.

"We don't know," Cross said. "There's only one hostile still in the field, but we don't know what *she* knows. They knew where I lived—where I used to live—so they could have been mapping this place, too."

"*She?*" Condor said. A quick glance at Tiger instantly told him he was asking a stupid question.

"Rhino and Princess are cyber-tracking," Cross said. "Ace is working another field. If she hits this place, it won't be the kind of assault you can stop with firepower. So, until this is over, you know what to do."

"Why didn't you just—?"

"I'm not saying this again," the unremarkable-looking man said, no tonal change in his voice. "We don't know what she knows. Remember when that . . . other stuff was going on, a while back? The G was collecting info on us, on all of us, before they made their move. None of that matters, not now. We don't know what info she may have been trusted with. So we're not using the airwaves—no phones, you got that?—not until this is over. She won't be short of money, so, if she knows this place, she could pay some professionals to—"

"Not in Chicago, she couldn't. Nobody comes in here, not without you flashing us the green light."

"Condor, she wouldn't be paying locals. Which is why we're pretty sure we have some time. The way we came, it's the only way an assault force could come without you spotting them. That's why Tracker's on top of the truck.

"But this is an all-in game now. So you're going to ground. You *lead* them down to that tunnel, and make sure they keep moving until they get to the first intersection. Just as if I told you there was going to be a flight of drones dropping heavy-weight bang-stuff all over, understand? They wouldn't need daylight to do that."

"Why can't we all go to—?"

"Red 71's closed. So is the— So are a bunch of other

places. You take your people where I said—not beyond that point. You can last an easy three, four weeks down there, you have to. If nothing lights up on the wall by then, send *one* of your people out to look around. If it looks okay to him—if he comes back and *tells* you that—it's safe. For *you*, it's safe, I'm saying. You might not see any of us again. But it'll be over. You got that?"

"Can't I—?"

"No. You have to be the *boss* now, Condor. You're responsible for your whole crew, so you have to be *sure*. Test is: If you can't be counted *on*, you can't be counted *in*. If you have to keep checking behind you, then you can't move fast enough."

"Sure. Like you always say. But this—"

"This is a new game, kid. It may last a couple of days; it may be over for us . . . but *not* for your crew. There's a half-million in cash down there. All in used twenties, fifties, and hundreds. Not funny money—real thing, no risk using it.

"Okay, when you're ready, have one of your people lead all the others down the left branch. Tell 'em something *may* be coming. That happens, you want to surprise them. Take this: it's one of Buddha's own pieces, better than perfect. A .357 mag. It'll buck on you, so be careful if you use the heaviest stuff. Four fifty-round tins—two are .38s, two of that heavy stuff. . . . This piece, it'll take either kind."

"I don't need no—"

"Yeah, you do," Cross said, the words coming out like rusted-from-exposure steel. "Not to shoot anyone—but to make sure everyone in your crew knows you *can*.

"Now, listen: When you're alone, use the keypad. Tap

each key the number of times that's *on* the key, understand? Tap the '7' key seven times, like that. Then step back, quick. A big chunk of rock will roll out. The money's in knap- sacks. Just use what you need. But if you have to go on the move, remember you'll need a few people to carry it all out. After that, you do what you have to do. Your people, they'll follow you. Anyone you're not *sure* of, you don't take them into the tunnel. If it turns out you made a mistake, you *leave* your mistakes there, understand?

"Remember, you never have to move the crew—*your* crew—out of this territory. It's yours for as long as you can hold it. Just like we did. If we're not around when you check, if you don't hear from any of us, doesn't mean we're gone for good. But *never* look for us—you'll run into some bad people that way. Same rules: they won't come here; you don't go there."

"I'll handle it."

"I know," Cross said.

Ten minutes later, there was no trace of the Cross crew anywhere in the Badlands.

TIGER STRUTTED spectacularly into the suite of rooms set up in the back of Orchid Blue.

The rooms were windowless; air exchangers hummed too quietly for anyone to hear from the outside. The brick façade was backed by foam-filled cinder block.

"That's a lot of boys for this place," the brunette at the entranceway said, half-smiling with her mouth and half- questioning with her eyes.

"My entourage," Tiger said. "I thought I'd get them all familiar with my place. You know, just in case."

The brunette *didn't* know, but the sight of Rhino and Princess was enough to make her lose any interest. She caught Sweetie's eye, heard the faintest of warning growls, and came to the only decision possible. "I'll just leave you all alone," she said, as she got to her feet and walked out.

"Don't even," Tiger warned Cross. "Yes, girls gossip. Tempo, she won't say a word. She's the bookkeeper. Sometimes I keep her back here. You follow me?"

Cross nodded. Rhino took that for his cue and immediately began plugging in the hundred pounds of equipment Princess was handing over to him, piece by piece.

THREE HOURS later, Cross took the third drag of his cigarette and ground it out in a heavy stoneware bowl.

"We're not gonna find her," he said. "Not this way. And it's only her that's left. Percy is one bad bulldog, but he's no bloodhound. Probably ask his bosses where to look—good damn luck with *that*. Ace has got his finger on the pulse and he's gonna stay put . . . but no way she's going back into the Wild West. Buddha's slow-rolling, and we can call him in if there's something for him to do—that's why Tracker's riding along.

"Patience is a good weapon; we all know that. But, this time, we can't wait. If Wanda's got stuff ready to launch, it could hit anywhere. Wouldn't get all of us, no matter what . . . but body counts aren't the way to locate the enemy, not in *this* jungle."

"I'm not giving up," Rhino squeaked. "Like you always say, Cross: *being* smart doesn't mean you're going to *act* smart."

"I know what makes people act stupid," Tiger said. "No joke. There's one sure way."

"I know! I know!" Princess thundered, raising his hand like a geeky kid in a classroom.

Tiger put her hands on her hips. "You tell them, honey. Tell them what I taught you."

"Love!" Princess said, his voice jumping up a register. "If you're in love, you don't think about nothing else, right? Right?"

"Yes, baby," Tiger said. "But Wanda—"

"Wait!" Cross cut her off. "Rhino, on that tablet you cracked, it was there all the time. We just didn't pay enough attention to it. We were all sure Wanda knew me . . . and wanted me dead. But what we forgot was that she knew Tracker was *with* me when we hit that house."

"What difference—?"

"Rhino, stop looking for her. It's not going to happen; she's not going anywhere close to that back channel again. But there's something on that tablet. *Maybe* something. If it's there, it's time for voodoo."

"What in the name of Sappho are you taking about?"

"I had to do something once, Tiger—it doesn't matter what—but I learned something I thought I'd never have a use for. All voodoo has the same root. . . . Maybe that's why they *use* roots; I've heard Sharyn talk about them a few times. For healing or for hurting . . ."

"That's just a Gypsy hustle," Tiger said. "For all we know, they passed it along to people on one of those islands a couple of hundred years ago."

"The *root*," Cross continued as if Tiger hadn't spoken, "the root of all voodoo is that the dead can walk."

Sweetie made a noise nobody could interpret. Even Princess—he'd never heard it before.

"Rhino, *scour* that thing. Somewhere in there, we could find his special e-mail, the one he made just for her."

"Thalidomide Man?" Tiger said, trying to keep the skepticism from her voice and not quite succeeding. "You going to make *him* walk?"

"Not me," Cross replied. "I couldn't do it. I couldn't . . . feel him enough to even try. But Rhino . . ."

"IS HE okay?" Princess asked anxiously.

Cross and Tiger looked over to where Rhino had been sitting on the floor, filling the entire corner with his enormous bulk, the custom-sized laptop resting on the thighs of his gray jumpsuit. The huge man's eyes were closed, and his breathing came in a measured cadence. He had not moved for almost three hours.

"He's fine, baby," Tiger assured Princess. "He's trying to solve a problem in his head, that's all."

"But he hasn't even—"

"Princess, you know Rhino would never leave you. He found you, he brought you back . . . right?"

"*Sí,*" said the child who had been turned into a cage fighter by narco-guerrillas and given to their boss as a special prize, unconsciously lapsing into the first language he'd learned.

"So . . . ?"

"What if he's . . . getting hurt? I wouldn't let anyone—"

"Sweetheart, Rhino knows that. We all know that. There's nothing you can do, not now."

"Later?"

"Maybe," the Amazon said, very gently. "We won't know until he comes back from . . . from wherever he's gone to. But you have to stop fussing, okay? If Rhino thought *you* were in trouble, what would he do?"

"He'd never let anyone—"

"See?" Tiger said, softly. "If you get too anxious, you could make him stop before he gets where he needs to go. Look at Sweetie. He's getting all restless, just like you are. But he's getting that way *because* of you. He feels what's inside you. He wants to protect you, but he doesn't know how. That's not fair, is it? To make your dog all upset just because he loves you?"

Princess never hesitated. He pulled the Akita to him, patted his head, stroked his fur. "Easy, Sweetie. Nothing's going to happen to me. I know you want to help, but I'm fine. Okay?"

The dog settled at Princess's feet, thoughtfully nibbling at the wide strip of dried pork the huge child dropped.

If Rhino had been watching, the parallel would not have escaped him. He had never been called by the name on his birth certificate—he never would be. His search was painful. Deliberately putting himself in a state of near-suspended animation, traveling back to when his life was at the bottom of a deep lake. Always looking up, never seeing light. Going back to a time when he was sustained only by a faith that light would appear. A faith he could not have explained; a faith no religion could have produced.

He was back to when that dot of light had first proved true . . . whispered words in the ear of an always medicated monster kept chained to a wheelchair, whispered by a prison-hardened youth whose own name had come from what others had been saying about him for years: *That guy over there, the one you just said don't look like much? Trust me on this, bro— that is one kid you do not want to cross.*

And then he felt about in the darkness until he found that thread that connected him to Thalidomide Man—an accident of nature the world would never acknowledge.

But, just as Rhino's IQ had been grossly underestimated by his captors, Thalidomide Man had a mind that was far more powerful than his body—a mind unknown to those who kept him in the most luxurious of surroundings but allowed him no human contact.

"I can do it," the giant said, opening his eyes. "At least I think I can. And I've got to try. I owe it to—"

"No," Tiger said, stopping him. "You didn't do anything to him. Or to her. How they connected, we'll never know. Or even what Wanda must have gone through to . . . get like she is. He's gone. And she can't go where he's gone to. All that's left for her is revenge. She blames us for what happened. The whole thing. Either we stop her, or she stops us. I'm . . . sorry for . . . for both of them, I guess. But *we're* your people, not them."

"Yes," Rhino said, nodding his head as if reinforcing her words.

"Sweetie was worried," Princess said.

"Wanda doesn't even know about—"

"He was worried about *you*," the armor-muscled man said, sneaking a glance at Cross.

"I understand," Rhino said. "Tiger, is there a place to take a shower here? I want to get on this, but I need—"

"Everything you want," the Amazon assured him.

"RHINO, HE'LL be fine," Cross told her, as Princess and Sweetie departed. "Blondie's gone. The G wants Wanda gone, too. I don't think Percy could find her, but Ace isn't so sure of that—he says the guy's full-bore crazy. And not squeamish about wasting anyone that gets in his way.

"One thing we all know, both sides: Percy isn't going to stop, and Wanda knows that. Knows it *now*, for damn sure."

"BEFORE YOU try, can I tell you something, brother?"

Rhino gave Cross a quizzical look, the *When did you ever need to ask permission?* unspoken but clearly transmitted.

"I don't know what people believe. Or even why they do. I don't know how those two connected, and it doesn't matter anymore. But let's say Wanda knew what Thalidomide Man did—maybe she was even part of it. If she thinks there's any kind of . . . hereafter, or whatever . . . that's the key. There's only one way she can be sure to be with him in the same place. She wouldn't be looking for a hiding place—she'd be looking for a Suicide Bridge. One they can jump off together, holding hands."

"I understand," Rhino said.

Without another word, he started attacking the keyboard. An hour later, he looked up. "I've put the packets everywhere I can think of. But it has to work twice over. Wanda has to believe he's been looking for her. And that it's actually him that's looking. If she makes contact, even if its only to ask questions–just making sure it's not a trap—this thing will start beeping and flashing. Just like his would, if he was still here."

"Just don't *think* anymore, brother," Cross said. "No more logic. For this to work, you have to *be* him."

"IS HE sleeping?" Tiger whispered to Cross.

"The way a computer sleeps, yeah. Goes inert, takes some kind of action to wake it up. Rhino already said a signal would start beeping and flashing. Until then, we have to be quiet."

"Isn't your smoking . . . ?"

"No. Some part of him knows I'm here. He's like me—I don't understand some of the things I know, I just know them."

"And trust them."

"Yes."

"So you've tested them and—?"

"It's not like that. I'm no scientist. More like they test *me*, if that makes any sense."

"It . . . Oh! That's it. That has to be it."

"Tiger . . ."

"Those other computers, not that grand piano Rhino uses, the other ones over there, are we using them for anything?"

"No. They're just for—"

"Mural Girl," Tiger interrupted, keeping her voice below

a whisper. "We can't talk to her any more than we already did. But the camera-feed, it's loaded on one of those computers?"

"Far as I know, on all of them."

The warrior-woman pointed at her eyes with both index fingers, then moved one of those fingers so it was pointed at Cross, raising her eyebrows in a question.

MURAL GIRL was working with a series of black pens, creating an architectural image that was three-dimensional to the eye.

"What's that?"

"She's almost done," Cross said. "Just putting the finishing touches on the cash-out room."

"A casino? But the other things look like . . . little houses, schools, the Projects, a library with only a few books, a . . . I don't know what that is," she said, pointing at what Cross instantly recognized as a generic "training school" for juvenile delinquents.

Before he could explain, Tiger scratched one of her talons across the back of his right hand, as if drawing a "No" diagonal symbol across the bull's-eye tattoo. " 'Cash-out room,' that's an execution chamber, right? That gurney . . . it almost looks like a Christian cross, only laid down flat."

Cross didn't say anything.

They watched in silence, Tiger's hand slipping into Cross's.

"It's the path," the gang leader finally said. "Look over to the far right. That's a graveyard. You get it now?"

"No."

"Any gang boy would. 'The jailhouse or the graveyard.' They grow up to that soundtrack. None of them expect to see twenty-one without going one place or the other. Some of the OGs, they outlive the deal by doing time. They live longer because they're in prison. Shot-callers. They can reach out to the street anytime. But there's one thing they can't do. They can't walk away. That's what that lethal-injection chamber means."

Tiger leaned slightly forward, turned her head. "It's flashing. Can you feel it?"

"Yeah. But it's not . . . burning. More like when an infection starts throbbing. Like it has its own pulse."

"Then . . . Oh, look!"

Cross shifted position so he could see the complex architectural renderings hold their starkly black-and-white position as they became the background for two playing cards: king and queen of spades. Within seconds, two more cards popped up on either side, each one the ace of hearts.

Bracketed by . . . what, love? ran through his thoughts, just as a final card fluttered slowly down, spinning so that it was impossible to make out the face side of its checkerboard-patterned back.

When it finally came to rest, Cross and Tiger saw a card lying across the others. A translucent pale blue, with a large, hollow "3" in its center.

What the . . . ? joined their thoughts as the see-through blue background turned darker and darker and . . .

"It's the same!" Tiger whispered urgently.

"What's the same?"

"That blue color. It's the exact same color as the . . . brand they left on your face."

"Are we supposed to know what it—?"

Whatever Cross had been about to say stuck in his throat as they watched the hollow "3" fill with colors, flickering from one to another so quickly that it was impossible to register any single one.

Finally, the "3" became the same color as the background, a solid rectangle in that same blue that had branded Cross just below his right eye ever since that . . . whatever it was had butchered its way through the prison's abandoned basement.

It held that position, as if to be sure even the slowest pupil in the classroom had time to memorize it.

Then everything disappeared. The wall had returned to pristine white. And Mural Girl was gone.

CROSS HELD his finger over Tiger's lips.

At any other time, she might have playfully nipped it, but she took it for the signal it was and let Cross move her head so she was facing Rhino's big-screen computer monitor.

It was silently flashing an image of a knotted rope.

A beep sounded.

Rhino's eyes opened.

His cigar-sized fingers hovered over the keyboard.

"It's him," the once-chained man said. "*I'm* him. She's there now, too. Wait . . ."

```
>say name

<Joe Hill

>clever. never died. where, then?
```

<below house. prepared for years. steel tube,
Teflon-lined. U know my shoulders just slightly
wider than my head, raise hands, slide down.
equipment first.

>how long?

<until U come 4 me.

>how shelter/food/clothing?

<air exchangers, dried food, tap into water
line, storage batteries. house gone, only
foundation left, cracked many places. siblings
gone, their children grown. in France, paying
taxes on land, house not on market.

>how survive shot?

<forehead. U know: shelf over eyes. bullet
still in there. like walls of shock absorbers/
baffles. knew that was where they would shoot.

>police?

<long gone. theories, no facts, no motive.
nobody here when explosion, house under-
insured, no motive.

>but *they* know?

<no. "nobody here" = now truth to them.

>never truth to me.

<will never understand that. U have seen: Me =
hideous freak. U = beautiful. Perfect.

>mind/body = ☯

<does not compute. U genius, not need more
mind.

>trapped, both us.

<Yes. I waited. give you time.

>2?

<Decide.

>No. us, together, decided long ago. me
running. alive, always B *un*wanted.

<I *never* wanted alive.

>C?

<Not right.

>No. but we can be together.

<no way 4 me 2 leave.

>I know. but I come, B w U until . . .

<no no no. you can still get away. I have $$$
I can get $$$ 2 U, easy.

>no place for me except 1. with U. *we* decide
when 2 go. and we go TOGETHER.

>Wanda

. . .

<R U still there?

```
>yes. 4ever.

<*together* forever.

>we will not die apart?

<no! we took . . . we *exchanged* vows. how
can I get there?

>foundation has surface cracks. most weather,
but one I made. SW corner, you will see two
<<2>> cracks intersect. insert 4-foot fiber-
optic probe. flash 3x, then stand back. my
robot will pull cracks apart, hydraulic power
still working. U come in until past hips, then
hands above head & drop. robot can close crack
behind you.

<soon. very soon.

>I have waited all my life. just be careful.

<I have been careful all my life. U + 2 = Us.
1 + 1 = 3
```

"That's all," Rhino said, laboriously squeezing out each word. "They won't make contact again until . . ."

"We'll be there, brother."

"You know . . . she's right, Cross. What they did to him, *that* wasn't right."

"It wasn't. I know. . . . I think I know. . . ."

"They must have done something like that to her."

"Rhino . . ."

"She's pretty; she's smart; she could have been anything

she wanted. But something happened to her when she was . . . small. I know it."

"They've probably been . . . together for years," Tiger said. "She couldn't tell anyone about him, so maybe she was hoping, if they ever got that 'specimen' the government wanted, she could tell the G what a mind he had, and they'd step in and pull him out.

"Maybe he was doing all kinds of evil things, but not to *be* evil. You saw what you just wrote, being him. It was like he was stashing money all over the place for *her.* So she could run, like he knew she'd have to, one day. It's insane, but . . . it's a love story, Rhino—it doesn't have to make sense to anyone but them."

"Could you . . . both of you . . . just take a drive somewhere? Please? I want to be by myself for a little while."

"We'll go inside the club, honey," Tiger said. "I've got my phone. Just call when you want us to come back, okay?"

"Thank you," the behemoth said. And closed his eyes.

"YOU DON'T think—?"

"Not a chance," Cross assured her. "Rhino's heart hurts. But he's never gonna leave Princess on his own. You just sit there in that dark little spot you like. I'll have a couple of smokes. It won't be long.

"How do you—?"

"I know *him*," Cross cut her off. "I've known him since before he was . . . a person. He may not know why he snatched Princess out of that jungle, but I do."

"Hey!" a hard-faced woman in a tuxedo suddenly said to Cross. "I think you're in the wrong place, pal."

"No, he's not, Bella," Tiger said, leaning forward out of the darkness to face the woman. "Anyone who's with me, how could they be in the wrong place?"

"Oh!" the woman said, startled at the Amazon's appearance. "I didn't see—"

"Ah, that's what we say about *them*, isn't it, girl?"

Bella's face was instantly transformed by her smile. She turned and walked away without another word.

"WHAT'RE YOU doing here?"

"Saving your life, fool."

"I don't need nobody's help."

"Look, bro: you one seriously mean motorscooter, I give you that. But slick ain't your speed. You left a trail Ray Charles could follow."

"Not your problem," Percy assured Ace.

"Yeah, it kinda is. You follow orders, right? Me, I follow obligations. And I got one owed to you. Those two you was chasing down, I wanted them more than you did, trust me on that."

"Why should I—?"

"Oh, man—that's an expression, not some spy-crap. But try this one on: Those two, Blondie and Wanda, I never met them. But they were the ones who set it up for my wife and my children to die. Just to smoke me out. Smoke out *any* of us.

"So I'm going to make them dead. Or at least *see* them dead. Not about revenge, like you probably thinking. But with you after them, they know you never gonna quit. So until I see bodies, my family can't come back home. To *their* home. Understand? Killing them, it don't mean no more than shoveling the walk and throwing down the rock salt, so my family can get to the door without slipping on the ice."

"Blondie's done."

"Heard that. Heard that happen, I'm saying. That fancy machine gun of yours don't make a lot of noise, but down an alley, buildings on both sides, I figured *one* of them was finished."

"How could you tell which—?"

"—Blondie's probably faster than that bitch. Probably carries, too. But she's smarter. Man like you, you'd always take the harder shot first."

"Didn't *look* harder. That blond punk took her wrist and spun her into the wall. I'm no sprinter. Figured she'd still be there. But she wasn't."

"Don't surprise me none. Blondie might hate . . . some of us, sure. But Wanda, that foul bitch wanted us *all*. Don't know why. Don't care. And once I saw that it was *you* who was moving after them, I knew they couldn't run to the G."

"So, yeah, we teamed up good," the indigo-black assassin finished. "But that partnership's over now."

"I didn't ask—"

"Look, chump, you in *way* too deep. Wanda ain't any-where close to this side of town. It was a smooth trick, but it's already been played. Only thing left to do now is get you the hell out of here. What you think? The G's gonna do some kind of liftoff for you? Or drop in some more ammo for your last stand?"

"I have to—"

"I know," Ace told Percy, with something almost like sympathy in his deceptively soft brown eyes. "But, like I said, I'm a man who pays his debts. You come with me; I'll get you across. Not just some damn border in this town, get you to O'Hare, okay? You tap your phone, you get a ticket to . . . wherever, right?"

"I'm not—"

"Man, rest it! You tell the G the job is *done*. We got Wanda hooked, hooked *deep*. All we gotta do is reel her in. Not gonna be long—probably before you even land wherever you're going. But you got to *go*, understand?"

"Wanda—"

"If you gonna say she'd sell everything she knows to the highest bidder, you right. She's not gonna get that chance. I give you my word."

Percy was as still as a statue for thirty seconds. Then he extended his hand, sealing the last bargain the two men would ever make.

"YOU PROMISED," Rhino said.

"Cross wouldn't lie to you," Princess said, absolutely sure of his own words.

"We got the idea to watch, same way we watch Mural Girl's wall," Cross said quietly. "Tracker's got an infrared planted. Not as close, but it's got a little zoom to it. We'll see her coming. She'll get down to wherever she thinks that thalidomide man is, and—"

"He's got a *name*," Rhino interrupted.

"Not one he ever knew," Cross said. "You want me to call him something else, I will, but it won't make any difference to *him*. Wanda, she has to die. What she wants is not to die *alone*. That's the promise. The promise they made to each other. The promise that's gonna get kept. Once Wanda gets underground, it'll be what *he* wanted. She won't get that far, but she'll get to him. I can't say where, but they'll be together, okay?"

The behemoth nodded.

THE CREW slept in shifts—never less than two on the monitor at any time.

It was nearing seventy-two hours when Tiger whispered, "Got her!"

Everyone was instantly alert.

"How can you be so—?"

"Because she's a tiny thing wrapped in a quilted jacket with a hood pulled up. Who else would be *walking* this time of night?"

"You think she walked all the way from—?"

"Buddha, my daggers against your .177?"

The pudgy man lapsed into silence, as the walking figure never hesitated, never picked up speed . . . just proceeded directly to the cracked foundation, where she pulled a thin tube from inside her long jacket.

They all watched as a small woman emerged from the jacket, raised her hands high above her head, the palms touching . . .

"I wonder how long . . . ?" Rhino started a sentence that was never finished.

A geyser of fire erupted from underneath the foundation, climbing so high into the dark sky that the camera couldn't follow it.

"Damn!" Cross said, vehemently.

"What?" Tiger asked.

"The . . . brand. Their mark. It's burning, now. On fire! Burning like all hell. . . ."

"Amen," Ace said, solemnly.